ADAM'S REIGN

Mom + Dad
2020

THE HIDDEN KINGDOM :
BOOK 1

BY
JONATHAN MACNAB

Adam's Reign

ISBN 978-1-7320417-0-7 (Paperback Edition)

Library of Congress Control Number 2018902764

Printed in the United States of America

First Printing, 2018

Fiction Reborn Publishing
P.O. Box 7312
Monroe, LA 71211

www.fictionreborn.com

This title is also available as an e-book at most online retailers.

I write in the name of My Father, Yahweh God, who made all that there is, and rules over it with love and justice. His Kingdom is the one I hope to show you, because only under His rule can we find the freedom and life we were meant to have. He loved me enough to rescue me from the prison of my own selfishness and adopt me in as a firstborn son.

Now, I live a new life in His name as an heir of His Kingdom!

This book is dedicated to my beautiful wife Laura.
She is my forever partner in life and supports me with her whole heart.
I would not be who I am without her, because her selfless love has helped Jesus shape me into His image.
Every truth in these pages is able to touch the world in large part because of the work of God in her soul. She has listened to the Creator of the world, and helped us to see who we are in Him. We are God's children, and this is our story.

Now this is eternal life: that they know you, the only true God, and Jesus Christ, whom you have sent.

John 17:3

TABLE OF CONTENTS

Chapter 1 - A Meeting with Majesty   1

Chapter 2 - Prophecy at Work   12

Chapter 3 - Reach for the Carrot   27

Chapter 4 - Three is Company   39

Chapter 5 - Grave Tidings   52

Chapter 6 - Communion and Confirmation   64

Chapter 7 - Unholy Alliance   79

Chapter 8 - An Uninvited Guest   94

Chapter 9 - It Takes Two   109

Chapter 10 - Casting Stones   129

Chapter 11 - A Heavenly Calling   146

Chapter 12 - On the Road Again   163

Chapter 13 - Dragons, Demi-gods, and Demons - Oh My!   174

Chapter 14 - A Joyful Occasion   187

Chapter 15 - Is It Victory?   198

Chapter 16 - Friend or Foe?   211

Chapter 17 - It's Not About You   229

Chapter 18 - Prodigal Sons   247

Chapter 19 - Betrayal   259

Chapter 20 - Lord of Hosts   276

Chapter 21 - What Greater Love?   291

Chapter 22 - Taste and See   305

Preface

In the pages of this book, much like life, you will find truth amidst fabrication, silver covered in dross. You will find yourself caught up in an epic set in a very real time in human history, populated with real people who lived, loved, and lost. Yet, you will doubt the words even as you read them, because the truth, sometimes, is harder to believe than a lie.

Rest assured, however, this story is ours; it is part of us, though much of this era and the adventures of these people has been lost, and so, the details are highly imagined. It is a tale with all the shape of the truth, but lacking in its full substance. With that in mind, I invite you to dive in, considering that when you find yourself in the story, you may very well find this ageless story living inside of you.

Prologue

Man is not alone. As he has roamed the earth since ancient times, built cities, and studied the universe, he has been watched. He sleeps and rises, puts his hand to work and mind to create, searching for love and meaning, and all the while there are others laboring alongside him, beings that he cannot see or hear who take part in the world that he and his kind would call their own: beings who – if truth be told – have far more to do with his fate than any person he might chance to meet. Tucked just behind the veil of sense experience, wars rage and captives are taken as kingdoms collide and man is caught in the middle, a part of the struggle but unaware of his role.

In this place, there are principalities and powers, personalities whose thoughts and deeds would relegate the most notorious of tyrants to the sidelines of history. Refined by the passing of ages, their unholy plans are carried out daily by the ignorant and malicious alike. Man himself is both the end and the means.

Hidden with these foul creatures beyond the line of sight is another race, the same in myriad ways but nothing alike at the level of the soul. These beings could be called man's friends, if only he knew them. What might be more accurate to say is that they are his guardians, a ready aid in times of great need. They, unlike the former spirits discussed, do not follow their own way. Though they have a powerful will, they have chosen to subject it to another, one as much greater than their own as the sun's radiance surpasses that of a candle.

This One, this ruler of the powers beyond the veil, is a true force to be reckoned with - is, rather, the force that brings a reckoning to all, and He, in His might, is the one to whom mankind must give account. The battlefield and the victory belong to Him.

CHAPTER 1

A Meeting with Majesty

ANY MINUTE NOW, Micah was going to see God. He sped onward, flight fueled by his growing eagerness to be back in that good land once again, as with each mighty stroke of his ephemeral wings he drew nearer to heaven. Invisible in the skies, he streaked towards the stratosphere, quickly distancing himself from the mountaintops below. Beneath him, the sea glistened, reflecting the sun's rays, and he was reminded of how God had made him and his brethren to reflect the radiance of His great light. Though the humans worshiped it, the sun was nothing but a glowing coal at the end of the night in comparison with the One who spoke it into being. Micah knew; he'd been as close as any being dared be to either of them - and in moments he would be yet again.

Here, at the barrier between heaven and earth, where the clouds ended, the fun part of the journey began. Extending his wings for one final thrust, Micah opened his mouth wide in anticipation and crashed into a wall of water. The flood all at once refreshed and shocked him as his body was engulfed. Then, without batting an eye, he crossed over, stepping through the veil between worlds. Leaving the physical realm, he entered the spiritual like walking through a curtained doorway. He was there in the courts of the King.

Though moments ago the sky had been empty apart from Micah himself, here in the spirit kingdom the air teemed with life. Angels of every shape and size darted past him, eyes fixed ahead - always ahead - for angels are creatures of unwavering purpose. Give them a mission and they will not rest until its object is gained. Immortal, they had no need to eat or sleep, and they did not face death, which made them beyond bold and all the more certain to accomplish a task. This was how the King had made them, and they were His to command - entirely His - but not because they were forced. No, God was a good King, the only true good, and He ruled them with such kindness and justice that every angelic heart was eager to do His will. This willingness itself was a testament to the sort of King God was, because these creatures were quite powerful in their own right, made to withstand extreme conditions far beyond what any human could bear and able to wield weapons with such strength and skill that they could level an army in moments.

Though the angelic brethren took many forms, all were formidable. Some looked like beasts of the earth, while others resembled humans in some features. Most were some fantastical mix of a variety of earthly beings, and all shined like the stars in the sky, clothed with light. This, at least, was how they appeared to one another in the spirit realm, though they could take entirely different form when in the physical world. Each was its own unique thread in the vast tapestry of the Creator's imagination, an expression of His desire and love. And so, accordingly, they served Him – or, at least, most of them.

Some had drunk too deeply of the cup of their own glory and risen up in rebellion against God's rule. Led by Lucifer, the Shining One - perhaps one of the most beautiful of God's creations - a full one third of the host of heaven had dared to defy the Most High. That damned Lucifer, drunk with his own arrogance, had risen up in rebellion with a sizeable host won by his silver-tongued artifice. Together, they had attempted to storm the mountain of God. Their defeat was swift, and they were thrown down from that holy mountain, out of God's immediate presence to await condemnation at a later time. Until that day, the one called Satan and his demons waged war on the only thing they could influence – mankind. These enemies of the kingdom of heaven knew full well what judgment awaited them at the end of all things, yet they pressed on for vengeance with dogged determination, their souls beset with an unquenchable lust to steal something – anything - from the hand of their enemy whose magnificence alone far eclipsed their own. And it was precisely such magnificence that Micah was about to witness.

A moment passed, and Micah was in the throne room, for such was spirit travel. Instantly, his consciousness was drowned in a flood of sound. Unearthly thunder reverberated through the room, rumbling into every corner and shaking even the spirit. Striking in tandem with each thunderclap, lightning danced all about the titanic throne in the center of the temple, as though performing for the monarch upon its seat. Truly, Micah's heart and soul came alive together to join in concert with that light show, lifting up in praise to its Maker, as did all creation when it encountered Him. The throne itself appeared to be crafted entirely of the purest sapphire, wreathed in flame and born upon wheels of fire. It sat upon an endless shimmering sea of crystal, transparent and inundated with shining images reflecting the otherworldly scene that played out above.

There, behind the throne were the seraphim, his brethren, like him in substance but unique in form and duty. These four mighty angels guarded the throne (an honorary position to be sure, for God needed no protection) and what an honor it was! Each of them had distinctly different bodies, one much like a man, but with six massive wings, and the other three a trio of very contrasting beasts, though each majestic in its own way: an ox, a lion, and an eagle. As one, they shielded their feet from view, as though these things which had trodden one earthly soil had no right to God's presence. Their faces, too, they veiled with yet two other wings, hiding what could only be a hopelessly lesser image than the One they beheld with their eyes. Of these, there were many. Eyes carpeted every inch of the creatures like a living garment, viewing from every angle, so as to experience at all times in every way the beauty that so enraptured them that it drove them to song. And sing they did – lifting angelic voices in unison to praise the one seated on the throne:

"Holy, holy, holy is the Lord Almighty, the whole earth is full of His glory!"

Again and again they sang it, never tiring nor losing full vigor, content to spend themselves forever in serenading their good and gracious King. He was holy, set apart from all things, because there was nothing and no one who even began to be like Him, and having made all things, He deserved the honor, the glory, and anything His creation could offer. They owed Him all, for He was the Giver of life. So, suspended in continual chorus, the seraphim hovered above the throne sustaining their ethereal melody for eternity. And they were not alone! A thousand thousands served Him, and ten thousand ten thousands stood before Him sounding out a transcendent aria of praise.

Though all these things assaulted the senses when Micah entered the throne room, there was no room in his thoughts to perceive them. His heart, soul, and mind were utterly captivated by the One he had come to see, his eyes fixed unwaveringly upon the image of the Ancient of Days. In that moment, Micah was sure he would be destroyed instantly, annihilated by the ferocity of His presence, for God was a consuming fire. Certainly, everything around him was a moment from extinction if only God stopped upholding it all by the word of His power. This was what it was like to be a creature before the Creator, feeling that any second he could be extinguished by the sheer force of a Being that much greater than himself.

Enshrouded in a living rainbow, the Lord of the earth sat, Himself blazing with purest light, the Light of the World. A robe as white as moonlit snow hung on His shoulders, spilling over the fiery sides of the throne unsinged and filling the entire room. His figure itself was colossal beyond belief, radiating heat like gleaming, molten metal, like burnished bronze encasing flame. As Micah's eyes drifted upwards to God's face, he saw that there were bright, luminous orbs in the Lord's hand that he thought could be stars, and the hair falling down the back of the robe was white as finest wool. Stranger and more spectacular still was the massive sword proceeding from God's mouth, the sword of the word. It was living, active, and pierced even to the dividing of soul and spirit, of joints and marrow, discerning the thoughts and intentions of the heart, for He knew all.

From here, Micah tried to look at the visage of the King, shining like the sun in full strength, and it felt like he was trying to gaze into the depths of the sun, if not for the fact that the sun itself would wilt in God's presence. And His eyes... His eyes were a living flame, burning into the soul, buckling the knees in worshipful obedience, and both urging the onlooker to flee from His presence and inviting them to bask in it all at once. In those eyes Micah felt the all-encompassing call of the indomitable will that brought forth existence, and he surrendered to it. He would go wherever the Almighty sent him and obey his orders without question.

As Micah looked on the Lord, he let his thoughts drift back to the first day, when time began. God, the Father, Son, and Spirit, had always been: one being enjoying perfect, unbroken communion for eternity past. In that joy, they shared a longing to create. As anyone experiencing genuine joy would testify, it is greatest when shared – made complete by sharing, even. This truth came to life in the Trinity in that time before time, as God loosed His treasure trove of intimacy in a fit of creativity. He was making a people in His image, His children, with whom He would share His endless life and the wealth of His kingdom.

For them, He would do anything, and so He set to work building a world for their pleasure birthed from His infinite imagination. He spoke, and his words wrought life! As natural as exhaling, light issued forth from Him first, illuminating the void of nothingness for the scene that was about to play out. Then, immediately the heavens began to form, shrouded in water above and below, as measureless blue sky stretched out like a blanket to clothe the naked Earth. Fathomless, clear water filled the orb of the earth with no end in sight, unblemished - until the Lord began again.

Now, He was crafting a place for His creatures to dwell, a vast, multifaceted work of art that they could explore and care for. At God's call, all the waters of the earth swarmed together, revealing mighty mountains soaring to the newborn sky amidst miles and miles of untainted soil ripe for new life. As it appeared, the land roiled and rocked, shifting into wide valleys and rolling hills, broad plains and beaches white with unsoiled sand.

Evening passed towards morning and suddenly the plains lit up with life! In that moment green commanded the scene as the Great Artist went wild with every shade in His pallet. Holly bushes and hydrangeas rose up next to towering redwoods, creeping cypress trees, and stately oaks, all bursting with splashes of purple, pink, and blue, a festival of fauna for the inauguration of the world. In the midst of it all, reams of grass carpeted the land, spreading as quickly as dye though water, softer than satin with not a thorn or bramble in sight. Such things had no place in God's earth, as He only gave good gifts to His children.

Like all created things, though, the plants needed a source of life, and the Creator was quick to act. From his fingers He flung forth the stars, moon, and sun, this last with such force that it pulled the galaxy into its sway, dragging into its orbit every planet in the midst of its forming. An everlasting message, the sun stood to remind all things that existence revolved around something greater, as the trees all over the earth reached out their limbs toward it grasping at their source of life. Yet, the sun in its vastness and the galaxy itself were a drop in the bucket of the near infinite cosmos that was then born, in much the same way that mankind would forever pale in relation to the unsearchable depths of God.

At last, the Earth was prepared for living, breathing creatures. On this, the fifth day of history, the first King of all created the first subjects of the first kingdom. It was at this point that Micah remembered God's words taking on a near feverish pitch as His concert moved toward its climax. Even the angels were awestruck at the sheer variety of creatures He had imagined and the meticulously crafted complexity of their structures. From parakeets to ostriches and porcupines to grizzly bears every part of every beast had meaning and purpose, chiefly to showcase its maker's glory.

Cattle crawled out from the feet of mountains to roam the plains and flocks of seagulls streamed over the coastal sands. Below the gleaming waves, the water began to teem with life as rainbow trout grew scales and manta rays learned to swim. Coral grew instantaneously into intricate formations of bright blues, greens and golds, in a moment transformed into aquatic villages as populations exploded.

Everything was unique, everything a delight, and it was all for the Father's children.

Now it was ready. God's great gift was wrapped and waiting.

At this moment He stopped, His Spirit moving down to meet the dust, and He lovingly crafted the first man, Adam, and His wife Eve – she from Adam's own substance so that they were in every way one. God breathed into their beings the life that flowed from His own being, and in that way, became a part of them. They all would share one spirit, and nothing was kept hidden.

As Adam and Eve rose from the dust and met the eyes of their Maker, around them was springing up the most spectacular garden the world would ever see, the Garden of Eden. Every imaginable tree was there, all bearing delicious, succulent fruit with a plethora of flavors. Through the garden ran a river, sparkling in the sun like a field of diamonds, and it watered every living thing in the garden.

God turned the eyes of the two newborns to their wedding present, letting them take it all in, and said, "It's all yours, every inch of it, yours to enjoy and work and keep. You can explore the world I've made and make of it what you will. I give it to you to rule over, as king and queen of the world, regents under my rule. Go forth and fill it! Have children and raise them in the land I have made for you! All I ask is that you do not eat of the tree in the midst of the garden, the tree of the knowledge of good and evil. If you eat the fruit, you will die."

Next to the tree in the center of the garden God had made another tree, the tree of life, and His desire was that rather than death, they would choose life, eating forever from that blessed tree.

It was precisely this element of God's handiwork that Micah and the angels understood the least – His trusting these creatures with all that He had labored to create, and the capacity to ruin it. Micah would never have done such a thing! And yet, God's wisdom was far beyond his own; this he acknowledged fully and without hesitation.

Though provided the perfect start, Adam and Eve did not long reign in Eden before calamity struck. Allowing the enemy to deceive them, they trusted a lie instead of the truth, and they took of the tree the Lord had commanded them to leave alone. Eating it, they brought evil into the world, beginning in their own hearts. From there it spread like a plague through every corner of the world they ruled. Earth was under their authority, and so it obeyed their corrupt will to turn against its Maker. Mankind had left their source of life, choosing to go their own way, and so death was their reward.

Even so, God had mercy, giving them many, many years on the earth before they would perish from the choice they had made, but removing them from the presence of the tree of life so they would not live forever as cursed creatures. So it was that man was divorced from God and the ancient war was set in motion, with demons fighting to destroy mankind to spite God and angels serving as protectors and messengers to them in God's divine plan.

Into these thoughts came what felt and sounded like the cacophonous rush of the Great Falls, and Micah stood at attention. God was speaking from the throne.

"Micah".

"Yes, Lord," he stammered.

"I want you to go to my servant. You know which one." Each syllable slammed into Micah's spirit, resounding through him. "Tell him the time is close, and he must begin."

At this, Micah thought he saw tears running down God's gleaming visage. "Protect him."

Chapter 2

Prophecy at Work

CURLS OF WOOD TUMBLED OFF THE TABLE, shorn from its surface by the freshly sharpened iron planer. Gnarled hands guided the tool with practiced skill, worn, yes, but strong and sure as sunrise. Methuselah was nearly finished. He'd been working on this particular project off and on for nearly six months. But what's a few months when a man has plied his trade for five hundred years? Excellence takes time. He'd always stood by that; anything worth doing was worth doing well – and slowly. After all, the Creator could make things with a word and it still took Him a week to make the earth! That was proof enough Methuselah was right, and he didn't care who knew it.

In fact, he had half a mind to go and tell that son of his just that; the boy was always pushing him to finish a job. Rising up from his work-piece, the master carpenter cast his eyes over the table. It was going to need a good sanding and a touch of oil and that would be that. He grabbed his sander, which was simply a bit of leather embedded with crushed rock, and set to work rubbing down the piece. It wasn't long before a light haze of dust drifted through the air, filling his nostrils with the familiar scent of pine.

He'd enjoyed the smell of fresh cut wood for as long as he could remember – and that was a very long time – because it reminded him of his father. They had whiled away many an afternoon cutting wood together in the grove near where his father had built their first home. All the while he would teach Methuselah about the trees, speaking as though each was a priceless work of art over which he had long brooded.

Methuselah was willing to wager he would have lived in a tree if it wasn't for his mother's fear of heights. His father was sure it would work; all they needed was an average sized tree of nearly any sort as long as it had broad branches for a foundation. He had often joked that an apple tree would do best – they could grow as much as ninety feet tall – and what's more, when you walked outside in the morning you'd have a plump and juicy breakfast waiting. But that was not to be.

So, they'd built together, father and son, a lovely little home safe down on the ground. Methuselah had lived in that home for the first one hundred years of his life, and he missed it just now, it and his family. They were long gone. His father was Enoch, the one whose legend was shared by children's bedsides all over the known world. Enoch was the only man who never died. It was said by some that an angel had met him one day on the road and whisked him away. Others scoffed, claiming wild animals had eaten him, leaving no trace of death. Clearly, these latter were foolish young folk, as animals in those days didn't harm people, not even the dragons.

No, Methuselah knew the truth, because he'd seen it with his own eyes. God had taken Enoch personally. On the day Enoch turned 365, a year of years, he had been strolling under the willows by the lake after an evening of festivities, regaling his son with observations about the eternal beauty of the stars – God's handiwork. Before long, he had begun to sing, rejoicing in the good life he had been given. We were made to praise, he used to say. But in the midst of his song, without notice, he had just disappeared. In a moment, just like that, he was gone, his song still ringing on the breeze.

Methuselah knew that God had taken him away, but he still didn't understand why. His father had always been so close to God's heart... perhaps God just hadn't wanted him to have to see what the world would become. Since that day it had felt like the world had taken a step off a precipice, and it wouldn't stop until it reached rock bottom with a sickening crunch. He wished Enoch was still here.

"Metushlah!" A voice called out from the front of the shop, mushing the syllables of his name together so as to make it nearly unintelligible. He knew who this was – no one else sounded like that.

"Metushlah! Where ya be?" The gravelly voice was drawing much closer. Methuselah just kept sanding. The old farmer would find him soon enough. If he wasn't so short they'd have met eyes already.

Methuselah would make it a bit easier on him. "You're getting warmer!" he shouted.

As if on cue, a pair of tattered moccasins stepped out from behind a tall shelf followed by the squat figure of Dane, a local wheat farmer whom he knew very well. Immediately the stench of manure mingled with sweat and strong drink assaulted Methuselah's senses as the man moved to greet him.

"Why there ya are Metushlah; was beginnin' to wonder if you was asleep or summat."

"No, not quite old friend; these things don't build themselves," he said, gesturing toward the pine table. "I do believe it was you that I found snoozing in the hay on my last visit to the farm." He laughed, giving Dane a wink. The man was somewhere in the range of 700 years old – a fair number, yes, but nothing to Methuselah, and he slept more than he worked.

"Y'er funny, you are. Say, hows about you make me another o' them wheelbarrows to carry my crops an' all? That last was a fine 'un."

"Yes, it was that. What I can't help but wonder is what you did to it? When you brought it back to me it looked as though a giant had sat on it." The carpenter had his own thoughts on how that mess had come about. It had split right down the center and the wheel had come clean off, appearing as though something very large had stepped straight through it, likely during one of Dane's cat naps. At this point he imagined slaves did most of the farming out there anyway – the man grew fatter by the day and appeared to drink far too much, if the slight slur told him anything. This world really was in decline, and Dane was proof.

"Aww, you know, things just happ'n." came the stumbling reply. Dane wasn't even going to try to blame Methuselah's handiwork. No one made a better product anywhere.

"Right, well, let's get you a new one then. And you can just give me another few bushels of potatoes." He spared the farmer further embarrassment and moved things along. He had work to do. "It'll be about three days, but I'll bring it to you when it's done." He began moving towards the exit. Before he could usher the man out, however, the solid oak door flew open, revealing a young boy with dirty blonde hair and even dirtier skin, covered in stray bits of straw and smelling much like Dane minus the hint of wine.

"Sabba! Sabba!" He was gesticulating wildly, yelling something about snakes and evil spirits intermingled with repeated shouts of the word for grandfather.

Dane was ambling over far too slowly while telling the boy to pipe down, so Methuselah touched his shoulder to calm him. "Josiah, slow down and tell us what's the matter."

The boy was breathing heavily, as if he'd just run a good distance far too quickly. Methuselah could feel the boy's heart beating into his hand. "It - it was terrible, just terrible." He struggled to begin. "Joseph and I saw Satan! He went home to tell his dad."

Though most people would have dismissed such a notion without a second thought, the wide-eyed look of panic on Josiah's face told Methuselah that there was more at work here than imagination.

"Shut y'er trap boy and let's be goin'!" Dane growled. "Metushlah ain't interested in such idle nonsense!"

"But, sir..." He tugged at Methuselah's tunic sleeve while looking at his great great grandfather, "Methuselah taught me that Satan is real, and I saw him!"

Before the old farmer could blow his stack, Methuselah chimed in, "Josiah, I told you the stories about Satan passed down from our fathers, but no one has seen him in a very long time." He knew that even this might be too much for Dane, but he wasn't going to lie to the boy – the world was doing far too much of that already.

"But you also told me that Satan can take the form of an animal like he did in Eden!"

"This is true, but..."

"And I saw a snake today in the forest! It sure looked evil, crawling around on its belly in the dust, tongue flicking in and out, and it had scary eyes! It even jumped at us!"

Now, that was odd, to be sure. Snakes were rarely seen, and if so, only for a moment. They weren't known to be violent either. "Josiah are you sure it attacked you?" He asked, looking at the boy intently.

Dane stepped back into the conversation at this point. It seemed he'd had enough. "Of course it didn't, and so what if it had? Boy should've just killed it like I taught him and got it over with. No use screamin' 'bout it."

Methuselah didn't appreciate the influence Dane had over young Josiah, so he took a moment to set some things straight. "Now, Dane, I don't tell Josiah to go looking for evil spirits under every tree, but you can't act as though these things don't happen. You know what our fathers told us, how Satan deceived our first parents by speaking deceit through the serpent's lips." His voice was growing more confident with each word, "And evil spirits still roam the land, looking for whom they can destroy through their lies. They are not above attacking little ones." He cast a glance at Josiah. "And besides, you know it isn't normal to see a violent animal at all."

Dane looked disconcerted talking about things of such depth, so he made a quick exit. "Right, well, we'll be going now." He grabbed the boy by the arm, looking back, "I'll have that wheel barrow as soon as you can get it." And they were gone.

Grabbing a container of linseed oil off of a shelf on his way back, the carpenter made his way to the table to apply the finish. He didn't like the sound of this episode with the snake. Of course, it was always possible that the boys were telling tales, but Methuselah had learned over the course of his long life that most tales had a touch of truth to them. Animals didn't just attack people, for one; they only ate plants. And Josiah, while imaginative, wasn't known to lie. Methuselah knew that there were spirits roaming the land, heartless beings whose only desire was to destroy everything God had made. He'd run into a few in his time, and they were masters of disguise and artists of deceit. One might appear as a creature of astonishing beauty or as a simple beast of the field hiding in plain sight among the shepherd's flock. With their vile whisperings they could lead a man to murder his neighbor in the night and convince him it was his own idea. If he hung himself afterwards from guilt, all the better to these wretched fiends. And you could see their work: wickedness running rampant in every village and nearly every family, especially cities. It seemed that the more people congregated the more corrupt they became.

This was why Methuselah had chosen to live in a rural area like Kadish. Here, at least, he'd hoped that the havoc would be limited to family quarrels and the occasional stolen sheep, but even in Kadish there were beginning to be more and more strange deaths like he'd seen when he spent time in Arnon, one of the great cities. People were such selfish fools! He knew the truth and he had told everyone he could that this way of life serving oneself and taking from others without thought was not God's way. There were very real enemies to face, and they were not of flesh and bone!

But none had listened, and he'd been forced to leave that cursed city with his children before the darkness took them as well. People were too drunk with pleasure and the pursuit of power and wealth to believe it was all a lie, that there was another way, that the stories from of old were true. There was a God in heaven and He could be trusted; His way of life was the only one that did not lead to destruction.

His dedication to the truth had cost him dearly, as the enemy did not like anyone stealing his prey. Methuselah's wife, Selah, had been killed, murdered in the night by a man who had disagreed with Methuselah on the price of a project. The man had crept in through a window and, after quietly ransacking the family's store of coinage, saw fit to complete the revenge by stabbing what he must have thought was the carpenter's sleeping form. Methuselah woke when he felt the jolt, and in confusion leaped upon the man. They had grappled for control of the dagger for a few moments, his wife gasping for air but clearly fading, and he did the only thing he could think to do. Yanking up a clay pot from a side table, he slammed it into the man's head with all his might, and the man crumpled to the floor. Though this only took a matter of moments, he could see as he turned that his wife's spirit had already gone, her body a lifeless husk on the bed. That day, a part of his soul had died, he was sure.

The next morning he had taken the children and made for the country, certain he'd never return, and what a melancholy caravan they had made - weeping and wailing as they walked. It was all a blur, the entire three days of travel. He still didn't know how they'd made it all the way to his cousin's in Kadish. But then, He did: God's grace. He was, forever, their shield and help in times of trouble. Here in Kadish God had built the family a new, safer life, and for that, Methuselah owed Him everything.

But now, perhaps even Kadish was changing. The enemy never stopped advancing; his appetite for devouring lives was never satiated. The carpenter supposed it was only a matter of time before there wasn't a safe place left on earth.

This was why he clung to God, why he'd grabbed ahold of his father Enoch's stories and taught them to his children. It was said that there would be a savior one day, from Adam's seed, and that he would crush the head of that great serpent, defeating him for good. Without that, the world would have no hope. In a world of lies truth was his comfort. He'd made friends with history, becoming what he figured might be one of the world's first historians. People needed to know the truth.

However, he was beginning to wonder how long it would last. He was getting old, and the world was getting dark. Not many people were left that even wanted to hear the truth. Their itching ears yearned for meaningless platitudes and shut the instant that even the hint of something uncomfortable came to mind. Folks in Kadish were generally no exception.

Then there was Josiah. He was different, not yet tainted by the world's deceptive charms. He would listen to Methuselah's stories with awe, receiving them as truth. There weren't many like him, even among the children.

"Hullo!" a voice called out from the shop front. This too came from aged lips, to be sure, but it differed from Dane's in its timbre. It was strong, confident.

"I'm here, Abba, we need to get moving." That was his son alright, perennially preoccupied with the passing of time. One would think that after nearly seven hundred years of life the man would grow some patience. The worst part was that Boaz wasn't even moving towards him – he was that eager to leave.

He would set that straight easily enough, "Boaz, the chairs are back here with me, and I didn't ask you here to move them myself." Footsteps followed, and Methuselah could almost hear the sigh that most assuredly accompanied them. He'd only heard it some five thousand times or so. Boaz was hoping that if he had stayed by the door his father would make a quick exit for once.

As Boaz stepped into the room, he was forced to pass through the remnants of sawdust haze left over from the table-sanding, and he couldn't hide his displeasure. He sneezed, "I don't know how you've lived this long, working in these conditions."

"And how else do you do woodwork, son? Have you found a way to do it without sawdust?" the old man quipped.

"You can do it outside," he said dryly.

"Right, and then my equipment would be inside, and I'd have to lug it back and forth, wasting precious time, that most invaluable of commodities." He knew that would get his goat.

Boaz's reply was immediate, "Good point. So where are the chairs?"

"Over there," the carpenter pointed vaguely to the left over his shoulder. "But you'll have to wait until this table shines. I've only got about three hours of work left." He was kidding, but his boy didn't know that.

"Three hours! Just leave it 'till later, it's only been a year since you started this thing anyway, what's one more day? Besides, I've got to be at Noah's for dinner before long." He sounded nearly frantic.

"If you weren't so serious, people might like you more, Boaz. It was a joke." His lips cracked into a wry grin. "And it's only been six months since I started the project. So, dinner and I'm not invited?"

"Of course you are, but I had hoped to tell you *on* the road, so we could avoid precisely what we're doing right now – wasting time. Let's go!" Striding towards the chairs he hefted a couple in each hand and made his way out of the shop to load the wagon they'd made together. He didn't tell his father that neither of them were technically *invited* to dinner, at least not in any sense beyond that in which all relatives are perpetually invited to meals on a permanent basis.

"That boy, I swear..." The older man muttered to himself, meandering towards the stack of hand-crafted chairs. They were beautiful, if a little different from any he'd made prior. This tavern owner was a unique sort and had peculiar tastes.

When Boaz came back inside for a second trip Methuselah touched his shoulder, saying, "You know I love you, right? I appreciate your help."

Boaz smiled, a rare occurrence, but it was genuine. Everything about him was, and his father was proud of that, even if he was a bit difficult at times. Together, they made short work of the score of chairs and were soon headed to the tavern in the ox-drawn wagon.

Rolling down the well-worn path through the center of the village, the wagon was making good progress. Was that a faint rattle Methuselah could hear or just the clack of chairs over the occasional bump? His wagons didn't rattle, he thought, but, then, he had been using this one fifty years. Decay – it was the way of things. Even his own bones were beginning to creak uncomfortably now and then.

He looked about at the scattered collection of dwellings that made up the mountain village of Kadish, broken up by the odd craftsman's shop here and there. It was a simple place with simple people, but it had its own natural beauty. Most of the homes were made of trees from the forest that surrounded them, sometimes even underneath the root systems of the largest ones. The potter Elkanah's house was cradled in the lower boughs of a towering cedar, its limbs interwoven into the roof supports like a piece of living artwork. How Methuselah loved the man's artistic spirit; man was created to create. Still other homes like Dane's were out in the fields where other farmers and shepherds lived, and those who stayed closest to the mountains sometimes used caves as their fortresses. The whole of Kadish was in the foothills.

Everything was so close together in the village that it didn't take long to see the tavern's pointed roof peeking above the housetops. The strong scent of roasted vegetables and ale was beginning to waft over the wagon, as they heard what sounded like quite a ruckus in the building ahead. When they arrived, they could see that it was already crowded, even at this time of day. Why so many folks would be drinking this early in the afternoon the two weren't sure, but then, Sheba also served some excellent food, and the tavern doubled as an inn for weary travelers.

Fighting through the press of people, father and son parked the wagon near the front, with Boaz resolving to stay with the cargo and protect it from unsavory folk. He'd been that way for as long as Methuselah could remember. He didn't trust the world, and who could blame him? Methuselah made his way inside, passing merchants and day laborers who hadn't found work that morning, along with the smug faces of the village doctor and dentist at whom he nodded. He was looking for either Sheba or Saul, the tavern owners, as they'd ordered the score of chairs. Yet, looking at this lot, he wasn't sure even those would be enough by evening.

Then he heard a man boom across the tavern, "Hoy there! Good to see you old man!"

That would be Saul, larger than life. The people all called him some variety of old, so he wasn't insulted, but Saul and his wife he found to be a tad brazen. Perhaps one had to be in order to bandy words with this lot on a regular basis.

"Right, Saul, where do you want the chairs?" Methuselah gave a warm handshake and smile but was feeling like his son for a moment, eager to be finished.

"Just fill in the empty spots 'round the tables. They're holding up well by the way." The big man winked. "Then join us for a drink on the house." And he was off – busy again.

Heading back to the wagon, Methuselah passed a few haggard looking fellows speaking in gruff, hushed tones. He couldn't catch what they were saying, but he knew one word that he caught for sure – gold. So they were gold-diggers. He'd seen their type before here in the mountains, and, certainly, there was gold somewhere, but why they were so far from Havilah, the land of gold, was anyone's guess. He now knew where he planned to put the first chairs.

He passed through the doors and signaled to Boaz. "Let's get in there. He wants them put inside." They hopped to it, with Methuselah setting up just behind the gold-digger table, straining to hear what he could.

"...It's not the same anymore, you can't hardly go anywhere without meeting soldiers..." said a weaselly looking man in a dirty sheepskin coat.

"That's why I made my way South," said another. "Havilah was crawling with them." Aha! So that was it, thought Methuselah.

"Wars in the East. That's what I hear." A bearded man who was sitting further back from the others offered.

"Seems there's always a war somewhere these days," whined the first again.

A chill ran across the old carpenter's back at this. Between this revelation and the episode from this morning with Josiah, Methuselah's spirit was alert. Perhaps God was warning him, and the man was right – something was coming.

When they'd finished and set off to see Noah, Methuselah prodded his son, "Did you see that rough bunch?"

"The gold-diggers?"

Methuselah wasn't surprised; he was observant, that one. "Yes, they mentioned wars in the East. Have you heard of this?"

"Only whisperings," his son answered. "But they're becoming more frequent. What does it mean?"

"I think it means its time." The older man grew solemn, his voice grim, "You remember why my father named me the way he did. Maybe he knew something. Either way, I think we will find out all too soon."

CHAPTER 3

Reach for the Carrot

TUBAL-CAIN DOZED FITFULLY IN HIS CHAMBERS. He was the lord of what was fast becoming a nation of its own, and so usually slept the pampered sleep of kings, but not tonight. No, tonight he didn't even know where he was.

He was walking down a vast white marble corridor, its stark appearance interrupted only by long, thin fingers of gray. The walls were lined with brilliantly crafted tapestries depicting a series of battles, all victorious, led by a king that bore a striking resemblance to himself. What was this? He was no king, though he had more land by this point than some he had met. Every day more of the Assyrian people sought his favor over their land.

Could this be a vision of the future? If so, he certainly didn't mind. Ambition had long ago become a close friend.

At the end of the hall, a pair of tremendous wrought-iron doors barred the path. In all his days as a metalworker, he had never seen their like: bordered with tempered iron curved to look like ocean waves, fine inlaid silver curved sinuously across the face of the door like a gleaming snake, forming what looked like a crest of some sort that he did not know. It was nothing like his own, the crossed pickaxe and hammer, but it was beyond beautiful.

He reached for the iron handle but stopped, grimacing, when he realized how close he'd been to impaling his hand on carefully concealed spikes. How clever! This ruler would not have unannounced visitors enter his presence, or they'd pay the price. Before he could knock, he heard a commanding voice call out "Enter!" and the heavy doors swung easily open, seemingly of their own accord.

Entering a colossal throne room, his eyes met a scene so astonishing that he forgot to breathe for a few moments. Everywhere, covering every surface, lining every wall, gilding every piece of furniture, was gold – so much gold it would take a year in a gold mine for a thousand men to collect it, much more craft it into such exquisite forms as filled this room. It wasn't just any gold either, not the crude, contaminated sort found occasionally in his mines; this was a pure gold, refined in a furnace time and again until not the slightest blemish of dross remained. And it shined! The entire room was aglow with an almost otherworldly light far brighter than any flame he'd seen. The mysterious part was that he could not see a source for it.

It took a moment for Tubal-cain's eyes to adjust, but when they did his attention was arrested by the throne in the center of the room. Black as moon-less night, it stood in stark contrast to the near-blinding décor, but rather than seeming out of place, it served to highlight with glaring emphasis the figure upon its seat. It declared: look here, only here, and feast your eyes on glory.

"Do you like it?" said the same voice that had bade him enter.

Now that he could see the man that belonged to the voice, Tubal-cain understood the air of confidence. Before him was a powerful man. Robed in royal purple from head to toe, this prince sat at ease, cheeks creased into the smug grin of a man accustomed to having his will carried out. He was nearly taller than Tubal-cain sitting down, and, though comfortable, wore his custom gold-inlaid armor with a battle-hardened readiness that said he was no stranger to conflict. Bright eyes stared boldly at him from an ageless face, accented by a meticulously managed beard that framed a strong jaw. Who was he?

"Do you like it? I said," the mystery monarch repeated, patting the throne arm. "It's yours you know."

His?... "Who are you?" was all Tubal-cain could muster, floundering for words.

"Of course, how boorish of me – My name is Lucifer, the morning star." The man stood, and, with a flourish of his arms, bowed low, though his eyes never went to the floor. "But that's not important – it's you I want to talk about."

Shocked all the more by this latest development, Tubal-cain struggled to gather himself; he didn't want to betray his status by appearing unaccustomed to such surroundings. "My name is Tubal-Cain – "

"Yes, the lord of the Eastern lands! There is no one in all the world who can wield a hammer with such strength and skill. The quality of your people's craftsmanship is legendary!" Lucifer leapt up and crossed the space between them in one swift movement, gripping his hand warmly and pulling him into a strong embrace after the tradition of his people. The cloying fragrance of pure nard accosted his senses. The man even smelled wealthy!

"I am honored that you have heard of me and my people." Tubal-cain was gathering some courage, emboldened slightly by the praise. "We do make the finest farm implements in the land."

"And weapons I hear."

"Yes, our blades are unmatched. Yet, I find myself impressed by the grand workmanship in this room. Who made those doors?

"Why, you did, my friend," Lucifer responded, a twinkle in his eyes. "In fact, you did it all. Everything you see is yours."

Dumbstruck, Tubal-cain began to wonder what this man was playing at, but between what he saw and the overt flattery, greed was beginning to cloud his mind like a dense fog.

"How is that?" he asked after a moment.

"Well, you see, it's yours sure enough, but you have to take it. I serve as a sort of temporary caretaker - a steward, if you will - of all that is coming to you. These riches are rightfully yours. You deserve them! It is your destiny to rule."

Tubal-cain's curiosity was peaked. He agreed. He had worked hard, for many, many years. No one had been as instrumental as he in the development of the modern world. This was his due. "How might I achieve this destiny?" the metalworker asked, eyes gleaming.

"Follow me, and I shall show you." Lucifer wrapped an arm around the back of his shoulders, grinning as if this was a rare treat. He snapped his fingers in command, and the golden chamber dissolved before their eyes. When their feet met solid ground again, the two leaders stood atop the palace parapet at the highest point, looking down at an enormous mountain kingdom hundreds of feet below. It looked like a military compound, as the eye didn't travel far without meeting squads of armed men marching, and the air resounded with the clank of shield and buckler accompanied by the tramp of countless boots.

"You must build a great army to take what is yours. The world will not simply give it to you," began the robed prince, "but already you have what you need. The entire land of Assyria is loyal to you, for your tools have given them bread, and your weapons are their only protection. If you call upon them, they will follow you."

Tubal-cain was intrigued. Truly, the people were in his pocket. "And what of the kings of the west and south?"

The other man chuckled knowingly, "They do not have the skill or the means to make weapons such as your men will have, and on top of that, they love gold. Men can be bought."

This was true enough, Tubal-cain thought, though it seemed to escape his notice that he was in the process of being bought himself. He was warming to the plan.

"Did you see your throne? The onyx beauty upon which I sat when you arrived? And the room of gold? You will take Havilah, the land of gold and onyx stone. It is as certain as tomorrow coming. When you do, you will have all that you need to see the known world bow to you." This last sentiment he expressed with such intense satisfaction that one would swear he was the beneficiary of this venture.

Pointing a bejeweled finger, Tubal-cain's guide directed his gaze out towards the winding path of the River Hiddekel, and instantly the men were transported to a mountaintop in the midlands where the four rivers met. Here, a mass of troops that stretched for miles and spilled out of two cities was sprawled across the hilly landscape. Within view to the northwest was the land of gold itself, encircled by the frigid River Pishon.

"This is the day you will conquer, and the known world from the east to west will belong to your people, even to the end of the Gihon River by the sea." The clever prince had been playing this game a long time, and he knew when the fish had taken the bait.

Tubal-cain cast his eyes to the south, and Lucifer finished, "One day, even the great city of Arnon will be under your feet, and its glory will be yours." Time to drive it home. "The house of Tubal-cain will be honored from sea to sea, and the people will tell tales of your fame from generation to generation."

Then a cock crowed.

Tubal-cain sat straight up in bed, adrenaline pumping fiercely at both the sudden wakeup call and the prospect of great opportunity that had already taken firm hold of his mind and heart. It had been a dream? The old man scratched his beard pensively. It had felt so very real, having none of the random senselessness of dreams, and he had felt quite clearly the firmness of the castle under his feet; he'd swear the acrid smell of war still clung to his clothes – all sweat and smoke.

If not a dream, then perhaps a vision of the future: a prophecy given from on high... Throughout Assyria and in other kingdoms people worshipped many gods, and each had what they called prophets or priests that swore they spoke of the future. He'd never sworn himself to any such "god", and didn't plan to, but perhaps if such beings were out there then they realized that he deserved such a kingdom – or, perhaps, needed him to shape the world, because of his great influence. Or maybe it was simple inspiration, his own mind crafting a brilliant plan in the deep mystery of slumber. Either way, he liked the plan, and he did have all that he needed to achieve it as the dream figure had said. He also had time, and he decided that such things were best left until after breakfast.

Throwing off his sheets, Tubal-cain sprung up from bed feeling spry despite his years and began to ready himself for the day. Ordinarily, he only sought the assistance of servants when he was busy and required something menial accomplished that was not worth his time to do. After all, he'd long earned his living by his own hand and could certainly dress himself, but today, he felt like a king. So, grabbing an iron goblet, he rapped it against the large bronze gong his sons had made for him last year, unconcerned when the remnants of last night's wine sloshed to the floor. Two servants rushed in, looking slightly alarmed as though expecting a fire, only to see Tubal-cain standing in his robe with a smug look on his face.

"Dress me for battle. Today is a day for warriors!" He issued the command excitedly.

The pair exchanged bewildered glances, stammering, "...Ah, yes my lord," and one hurried off to the armory while the other inquired about his sleep that night.

"Fantastic! Couldn't have been better, my dear. Fetch me some breakfast, please." This last he chided himself for. He'd have to get used to being more kingly if there was any chance of his vision coming to pass, and kings didn't make requests; they issued orders.

The servant girl Rhoda set to work preparing a table for him and darted outside to grab breakfast, clearly nervous at the unexpected mood. Within moments, the ruler could smell the tantalizing scent of roast sausage, and the two servants reappeared together through the doors, one clanking away and the other looking relieved at having made it back without incident. Meat...a guilty pleasure to be sure, but one that he was glad he had taken the liberty of adopting. Many of the common folk still ate only the fruit of the land for fear of disobeying the God who made it. His own parents had spoken of the tales of the first man and woman, and how God bade them eat only what grew, but his people were not fond of this God, if He was even out there, so Tubal-cain saw no reason to heed His word. No, Tubal-cain would have what he wanted, when he wanted it – and what a delight it was!

Shortly, he was warm and well-fed, ironclad in full battle regalia, a remnant from his early days making a name for himself in the metal trade. He'd started out as a young, inquisitive lad in the mountains, exploring and digging away, always searching for something, though he knew not what. That was until one day, he found a rock that was different, that felt strong, useable. As if by inspiration, the thought came to him that he should make it into something, as he'd done during childhood with clay, even discovering how it changed in properties when placed in the fire. He followed his instincts, and, though it took some time to find a way to get a fire hot enough, he discovered a way to heat and shape iron. Thus, metalwork was born.

Within days of making his first rudimentary spade, Tubal-cain's talent became known throughout all the village where he lived, and soon enough the whole region as men traded some of the tools he produced. Eventually, he taught many of the members of his family while simultaneously beginning to discover the wonders of other metals like tin and bronze and how they could be fashioned into attractive objects that were pleasing to the eye for people from every culture.

At first, the young man enjoyed the deep satisfaction that he found in what he felt was his life's calling, making things for the people that improved their lives and kept food on their tables. Then, however, he had sons. As his wealth grew along with his two boys, he began to live with a constant, growing fear of it all being snatched from him. Many out there in the world desired what he had, and would not hesitate, he believed, to take it. So, as he thought on this, he devised a way to protect his wife and children – the sword. Unfortunately, his actions, rather than bringing safety, attracted to his small city exactly the sort of folk that he feared.

Violent men greedy for gain traveled from all over the land - and even from afar - to buy his weapons, and though he had their temporary respect, he knew that would not last. And so, he had made a choice to enlist mercenaries to protect his family and to become what he had never intended to be: a ruler of the people, and, when it was required, a man of violence. He fashioned himself the most impressive set of armor he could muster and set about forming a small army - only enough to secure his lands.

To this day, Tubal-cain had not ever lifted a sword against another man, but now, standing again in the armor of his youth, musing on the future, he thought perhaps it was time to take up arms. Regardless, it was time to check on his would-be kingdom.

Striding out into the plain stone walls of his mountain fortress, he was reminded of the extravagance of that dream castle, and inner conflict began to brew. He had always chosen practicality over luxury, even as his family grew in wealth. All of his profits he sank into building forges and training men, and, eventually, digging for ore in the mountain depths. His greatest desire was to build something that would last when he was gone – a legacy - and he had instilled these values in his sons. What would they think of this grand plan to change course and become conquerors?

As if on cue, his two sons appeared in the courtyard as he stepped around the corner. It was a massive, sprawling array of forges and workers' ramshackle homes surrounding the stone fortress that his family called home, all of it running right up to the mines where he employed still more men. In the midst of it, other folks who belonged to neighboring villages had begun plying their trades and building homes and shops with his permission, so it had become a city in its own way, he supposed.

"Ho! The conquering king shows his face! Are we going to battle, father?" His oldest son Iram shouted to him, grinning wide. His younger son, Oshik, was lost in concentration, busy firing an arrow at an effigy of a deer for target practice, so he paid no mind to his father's arrival.

With a slight chuckle, Tubal-cain replied cryptically, "That remains to be seen..." but then, as if catching himself, quickly quipped, "A man can relive his glory days, can he not? I wanted to feel again the weight of the sword in my hand and see if these old arms can yet swing it."

Oshik turned at this, "Swords! Why, father, forget about swords; we have made something new!" He went and picked up something from the ground, a wooden instrument with an iron head shaped like a leaf with sharpened edges. "We call it a spear," he said enthusiastically, jabbing it towards Tubal-cain playfully. "We plan to use it hunting mountain lions on the morrow. You can fight with it at close range or hurl it great distances." He swung about at this and promptly skewered the target from ten cubits. Tubal-cain's chest swelled with pride at their constant progress in the trade. They were gifted, without doubt.

"Yes, father, we were going to surprise you, but now that you are ready for a fight, perhaps you should join us for once?" Iram entreated.

"Perhaps I will!" Tubal-cain exclaimed, clapping his sons on the shoulders. "But first, we have business to discuss about the future of our operation here."

At that, the eyes of both men lit up with intrigue. They knew their father was getting on in years, and they expected to take on the day to day operation of the compound at any time – more Iram than Oshik.

The older was the ambitious one, always living to please his father, while the younger was doubtless very talented but preferred to spend his father's money on good times rather than spend any time earning it.

As they were about to head inside, however, a group of what looked like weary travelers stumbled into the courtyard. There were about sixty of them: men, women, and a few children who looked hungry, all led by an older bearded man who stepped out in front wearing a long brown tunic with tattered edges. The man had a scar forming on the right side of his neck, and, after seeing this, Tubal-cain noticed that a few of the people had fresh wounds as well.

Running to the ruler's feet with what seemed the last of his energy, the man stammered something about a group of bandits in his town having pillaged and driven them out of their homes. Then, he looked up at he who had so much and asked, "Will you help us? You have weapons and men. Will you help us reclaim what is ours? If you do, we will serve you and be yours entirely. You will be as a king to us."

At this, something changed in Tubal-cain. He had planned to speak with his sons carefully, sounding out their thoughts on the idea of expansion before suggesting that they actually build an army. Yet, surely after the dream, this was all the confirmation he needed. His boys had better get ready. They were going to war.

CHAPTER 4

Three is Company

MICAH LEFT HEAVEN'S THRONE ROOM as reluctant as always to again be apart from the Lord, but eager still to please him as a good servant must. Armed with holy purpose, the angel streaked across what was now an evening sky tending towards dusk, his wings bathed in the subtle warmth of the setting sun. He had a love-hate relationship with the night; it reminded him of the time that darkness had smothered the light of Lucifer's once bright soul, just as the night was now draping its black cloak slowly over the glimmering orb of the sun. Still today all creation felt the effects of that fateful day. Yet, night was also the time when the stars came out of hiding, when all the world could see the mark of his angelic brethren in the sky.

The news Micah carried was grim, however, so tonight he would accept that darkness was no friend to him. He was headed to the midlands of Havilah to find Nathan, an angel that the Lord had stationed there some time ago. He was nearly always somewhere on earth, among the people. It was just how the Lord had made him. He was a gift to all who knew him, and Micah believed he would be invaluable for the mission at hand.

Just ahead, he spotted a small village nestled among the hills several miles from the mountains, its nighttime fires beginning to wink into life here and there as families settled down for the evening. Fathers would be heading in from working in the fields while mothers called the children in for supper. At least, that's what would happen for most children. Some would face the night in the cold, stomachs rumbling with hunger pangs as the cold descended upon them. These were the unfortunate product of selfish unions between the many travelers who came to the mountains seeking gold. Such people did not come to build families and dwell in the land, but to strike it rich, come what may. Beset with greed, these men and women would stop over in villages like this one while they traveled to and fro seeking fortune. Then, whenever riches or incident befell them, their children were left as orphans, with other residents too often overburdened by their own families' needs to offer them safe haven. Then, they'd grow up as best they could on the streets, thieving or begging, though the latter wasn't likely to work well in places where people could hardly feed their own children. It was among a group of such orphans that Micah found Nathan.

Micah spotted him within moments, his kind face smiling as he stood next to a ragtag band of teenage lads in tattered clothes all huddled around a makeshift fire. He held a pot of steaming hot soup that he must have prepared himself, and he would look at each young fellow's dirty cheeks with a twinkle in his eye and give them a squeeze on the shoulder or an encouraging word while ladling them some broth into a bowl. With each one, he was ever so careful to spread God's grace. With them all fatherless, he knew that the way they saw God would be formed by how he and other men treated them, whether for good or ill. Such was the way with all fathers, and such was the world's trouble that so few ever raised a child with love and discipline.

Micah knew that drawing Nathan away from the village might be difficult for him, given that he had grown relationships with many who lived there. Yet, the matter at hand was much bigger than all of them, and it demanded the assistance of his best angels. Nathan would understand the stakes. God first, self last – so was the angel's way.

Landing quietly a good distance away, Micah manifested into physical form, making sure to appear as unassuming and approachable as possible so as not to tip off the youths, though he was not used to taking such pains. Then, stepping into the open street he came face to face with a young woman of about sixteen. Clearly shocked to see a rather large man standing in front of her clothed all in white, she gasped, dropping a pot of water she had been carrying. This Micah promptly caught, inches from the ground, as his lightning fast reflexes kicked into gear.

He handed it back to her slowly, conjuring his best attempt at a smile, and introduced himself, "My name is Micah. I am glad to meet you." Then he added, "Sorry for the scare," hoping to diffuse the tension of the moment.

"My name is Ruth," she stuttered. Having not been attacked for a few moments must have bolstered her courage, because she then followed with, "I haven't seen you before? Who are you?"

The angel felt a bit sheepish. These human interactions could be so awkward for him at times, but he was the one who lived forever and should be leading such a conversation, not the girl who had been alive mere moments of his time. He blamed it on the surprise and began to take control of the situation, though he could feel God laughing in his spirit.

"Right, yes, well I am here to see my good friend Nathan and request his assistance in a matter of great importance."

"Oh, you mean that guy?" she said pointing back towards the fire. She seemed slightly more at ease since the mention of the connection, but still wary, so Micah supposed she knew Nathan somehow. The hesitance was understandable. He imagined that run-ins with strange men at night weren't a great experience for any young woman, particularly here.

"Yes, do you know him?" Micah asked, attempting to endear himself to her further.

"Not exactly," she replied slowly. "I just see him around town now and then. It's funny...he seems to just appear. I know that sounds foolish, but it's as if he's always there when someone needs him, then he's just gone all of a sudden. I've wondered if he was a ghost a time or two." She laughed nervously. "Anyway, if you want him, there he is. I suppose I should go over there as well. It looks like I might can get a free meal." Her stomach growled, clearly empty. The angel realized this might be the only food she would get for quite some time. "Let's walk together then." He said, going first so that she didn't feel like he was following her.

Micah did look back after a moment to see if she was really coming with him; she was, though at a safe distance, her simple dress billowing in the breeze that brought with it the enticing aroma of roasted vegetables and spices. Though angels did not need to eat, his sense of smell was all too present when he had a physical body. He thought at this moment that perhaps he understood why Nathan spent so much time among the humans.

Then Nathan appeared, full of life in plain, brown woolen clothes that belied the inner vitality of his spirit. He greeted Micah warmly, drawing his fellow into a tight embrace, as though it had been a very long time since they'd been together. It truly had been, Micah supposed, as a hundred years must have gone by for the humans since their last cooperative assignment, but for him it all ran together in an eternal blur. Nathan must have been getting used to the human way of life.

"Hello old friend! What a sight! Truly God has smiled on me today." Nathan beamed.

Micah responded in kind, "It has been a few moments, yes, and I've missed your company on the adventures the Lord has given me. In fact, that is why I am here..." he said, glancing around at the young people, who, by this point, were all gawking at him wondering who on earth this new sojourner was. "Perhaps we should speak alone," he finished. Micah knew that Nathan was in the midst of duties that required his full attention, but the humans had no place overhearing what he had to say next.

The other angel winked knowingly and signaled to the young lady that had finally made her way over to the fire. "Ruth, why don't you come help yourself to what's left of this soup here." He handed her the pot, grinning at her confused but thankful expression followed by the groans of consternation from fellows who felt they hadn't gotten near as much. Then, he waved goodnight to the young men - a few grunts of thanks were all he got back - and stepped away.

When the two angels were alone some distance away, Micah got right to the point. "It's time, Nathan," he said quietly but forcefully. "The Lord has called, and we have to answer." Then, looking towards the camp, he added "Everything for all of them is about to change. The time we have long feared has come."

"Yes, I know." This answer surprised Micah, but, then, it shouldn't have. God always prepared the path for His work.

"So, you are ready then? We must leave tonight."

At this, the kind angel winced visibly, but his reply was calm and sure, "I live to obey the voice of the Lord. So be it. Everywhere I go, people will be in need."

"Yes, yes, they will, and I have a feeling there will be more than enough for you to do in the days ahead." Micah replied.

Nathan did trust his King, whatever his eyes might see. To know Him left no doubts about His faithfulness.

"I'll meet you outside the city," Nathan said as he walked towards town. I have something left that I must do before I leave.

The other understood.

He was not as fond of the humans as perhaps he should be. They just seemed so very ignorant of the importance of the role God had given them. The earth and all that filled it belonged to them. It was their gift, and yet they spurned their Maker and their responsibilities, choosing time and again to waste what He gave them on worthless pursuits. Nothing mattered more to Micah than God's honor. It was His due, and it was His creations' place to give it to Him for having made them.

So, though he had a surface understanding of Nathan's affections for the people of the town, his own spirit was not yet deeply touched for them. He did sense God's great love for them, however, and he knew that he wanted to care along with His King. Right now, though, honoring God meant delivering His message, and nothing else clouded Micah's vision.

Before long, the angels were in flight, each lost in thought as they sped towards entirely new surroundings. They were going to the land of Eden. There, they hoped to find the third member of their band. Where this mission was leading them, they'd need the help, and it was an unwritten proverb that a trinity was the strongest formation, just as God Himself was Father, Son, and Spirit.

As the sun began to peek over the horizon, the duo's view burst with green. Ahead, every imaginable form of plant life stretched towards the sky, some of the trees nearly reaching as high as the angels could fly. Here, like no other place on earth, life had the ability to truly thrive. Here, God had placed His full hand of blessing over the land and had never removed it. Now, however, it was overgrown and haphazard, because there was no one to tend it, but it was still beautiful.

The garden of Eden had once been paradise on earth, the jewel of the East, a haven for all living things. Truly, there had never once been death within its borders. That had come later. The humans betrayed the Lord and became corrupt, earning for themselves eternal banishment from their heavenly home. He could not allow them to remain within reach of the tree of life and live forever, so they were exiled, and the garden was left to ruin.

Now, a flaming sword guarded the entrance to the garden in the midst of two cherubim, guardian angels who had served in God's presence. Even today some humans still tried their luck seeking the fabled fruit of life, but none were allowed to come even within view of the entrance. That was the job of their angelic friend they'd come to collect.

Gurion, angel of judgment, was appointed by the Lord of Hosts to wage eternal warfare against the demon hordes under Satan's command. His current post was the garden's outer perimeter and his mission to secure it against any and all intruders. The enemies of God had as much interest in the life-giving fruit as the humans themselves, as they'd set it as their permanent goal to thwart any of God's plans and steal whatever portion of His glory they could. This was perhaps why the reception awaiting Micah and Nathan was somewhat less than friendly at the Eden border.

"Stop!" A voice boomed like thunder from above them, arresting them in the air. They knew that voice. "Go no further, or you will face my blade."

Descending slowly into view came the massive, winged form of Gurion. He really was an intimidating sight, even for immortals. His torso was that of a man, albeit one larger than a giant, covered in gleaming bronze armor that was all the more blinding in the morning sun. Then, one saw that his legs were those of a lion, taut with power, and his head the same, eyes glaring with violent intent, framed by a glorious mane. Two enormous wings kept him aloft, themselves much like his armor but in the shape of eagle's wings.

Micah was impressed, but not frightened in the least, himself borne upon four magnificent wings resembling pure starlight, and his entire form that of a human warrior wreathed in flame. Neither of them was a being to be trifled with. But he'd had enough fun. "Gurion, my brother! I'm not sure if I should be insulted or proud at such a stern greeting. You stand before friends! Do you not recognize us?" Micah shouted with a smile.

In the lion's eyes there was a flicker of recognition, but the response was cold. "My enemies are not beyond masquerading as angels of light. They are masters of deceit; may their kind be cursed forever!" The warrior spat the last words.

Not a little taken aback, the other two angels reeled a bit, wondering what had been happening to warrant such caution, but not surprised by the fact that their demonic foes had stooped to such levels.

"You remember the times we've shared, Gurion, as do we. I still often think on the day that you tanned that demon lord Moloch's hide when God sent us to put a stop to his evil machinations in the western villages. They were sacrificing children in his name, and you gave him a beating for it that he'll remember until judgement day!" Nathan said to the warrior with a grin.

Gurion's sober countenance softened at this and the two were immediately swept up into a crushing embrace, the previous moment's tension entirely forgotten. That was Gurion, forever brimming with passion, for good or ill, and one simply hoped to stay on his good side.

"So..." began Micah cautiously, "something tells us we are not your first visitors in recent memory. What has the Enemy done this time?"

Gurion's countenance fell as he gave a reluctant answer, "A few moons ago, I was out in the night, doing my rounds, when I saw what appeared to me to be a disturbance at the southern edge of the garden, a movement among the trees. Now, normally not even animals are able to make it through the overgrown brush from the garden to the outside, the Lord has let it grow so thick. Yet that night there were clearly signs of life. Then, when I swooped down to check on the area, I met two men in white robes. I could tell they were not frightened, so I thought perhaps they might be brethren, as the humans usually cower when they see me. Sure enough, the two lit up like stars and assumed spirit form, greeting me warmly. At this point, I let my guard down, though I was still confused about their presence there, and I came close to question them. Without warning, the two lunged at me, one pinning my wings while the other pulled a light spear from beneath his robes, intent on skewering me..." The big angel paused here, letting the anticipation build, and finished, "Thankfully, my great strength came to my aid and I threw off the first attacker, cleanly dodging the would-be missile, and swung my mighty spirit-axe straight into the belly of the thrower. With him doubled over by the blow, I had time to turn and swiftly parry the blows of the other attacker before slicing into his shoulder. Both of them shrieked in pain and fled, having more than met their match!"

By this time, the angel's lion-face was beaming with pride. He added hurriedly, "Thanks be to the Lord, for He delivered me in my time of trouble!"

Though they had started out concerned, Nathan and Micah were now striving to hold back tears as they shook with laughter. Good old Gurion. Trust him to make a simple report of events into a dramatic tale of triumph and woe.

"And did you do all of this one-handed? With one wing tied behind your back?" Nathan asked with a wry grin.

A brief look of offense flashed across the warrior's face, then quickly changed to rumbling laughter as well when he realized his friend was right. He *had* been a complete braggart there.

Then, his countenance sobering, Gurion said, "It has been a long time since I have seen such a brazen attempt to access the garden, and longer still since I have been caught by surprise in such a way by an enemy." This was true enough; the others knew they could always count on Gurion's constant awareness of danger in any situation. "Since they find it impossible to enter from the air, they are having to attempt ground raids. The frequency of disturbances is increasing as well. They are getting desperate. I think they are planning something, as though they are running out of time."

At this, Micah chimed in, "Yes, brother, let me speak of why we have come. You know that we would not be here if the Lord did not send us. We have come with an urgent mission, more urgent than anything else at hand." He was preparing the big angel for what they knew would be a difficult moment – him leaving his post.

"You remember that God told us all many years ago, when man first corrupted the earth, that humans would not be allowed to live this way forever, destroying and being destroyed. He said a day would come when this age would have to end and give way to another." Gurion's eyes were wide by this point.

"That day is now upon us." The lead angel finished, face grim.

Gurion was reeling. "Truly? Have they gone so far as that?" He was speaking of the humans. The other two could tell he had not spent much time among people.

Nathan, fresh from the midst of the orphans' plight, replied, "Yes, my friend, and farther. They murder and pillage and corrupt what is good, planning evil as they rest on their beds. None stands for justice. None is righteous. They have together become worthless." Though he could have continued, he stopped here, eyes downcast.

"And we must go, all three of us." Micah brought the hammer down. "We need you, Gurion, to protect someone the Lord has chosen, an appointed servant who will be part of the next age that is to come. He, at least, God has counted as righteous, for his faith. He trusts the Lord His God."

"But there has been so many advances against us here! I never leave my post, especially not in the hour of greatest need!" Gurion was vehement.

"Unless the Commander says go. And so He has." Micah's words fell like stones through the air, heavy and sure. "You are not the only one who must make a sacrifice." He said, glancing at Nathan.

The lion angel struggled within himself a few moments more before doing just as Nathan had done, as they all must do – he submitted to the will of the King.

CHAPTER 5

Grave Tidings

IT WAS TIME! Noah rolled out of bed right onto his feet, shocking himself awake as was his custom. It always worked. Like he told his boys, you couldn't go back to sleep if you weren't in the bed. There was much to do, and it was his job to get it started. Tiptoeing around the house so as not to wake his still-slumbering wife Leah, he quickly dressed and headed out to the storehouse. He'd grab a bite of breakfast on the way.

Morning always came early for Noah, just before the sun bid good morning, but today was special because it marked the first day of seeding season. Today, he would begin again the process of sowing seeds for the coming year's harvest. He was a hardworking man who enjoyed his labor, and it was a special privilege to be able to provide for his family's future. This particular day always felt like a gift from the Lord, because Noah would go out and begin sowing these little seeds, the most insignificant of things, unable to see what would come from his labor, and then, months later, the most bountiful bloom of crops would fill the land, securing all that he and even his son's future families could ever need.

It was a wonder, because, though there was surely a significant amount of work involved in preparing the land, not a thing that Noah or his sons did could make a single plant grow. That work was the Lord's alone, and he was their true provider. So, every year, as if by magic, the land brought forth life.

Approaching the seed shed that he and his sons had built, Noah passed under a towering fig tree, probably sixty cubits tall, and in mid-stride promptly plucked a ripe, juicy fruit about the size of his fist. Now that was a good breakfast! The sugary sweet taste of fig filled his mouth and juice ran down his beard despite his best efforts, while a playful breeze tugged at his woolen tunic. He was reminded how much he loved this place, the land the Lord had given him. Here, he hoped to long enjoy the work of his hands and watch his sons marry and raise families of their own. He could imagine the hills echoing with the laughter of joyful children while he hammered away at some project intended for their pleasure – perhaps a seesaw or a slide.

Though his family farmed to feed themselves, they were woodworkers by trade, and had been since Methuselah his grandfather had passed the knowledge on to Noah's father, Lamech. His old man was still around, thank God, but was getting older and, somehow, wasn't quite as spry in his age as Methuselah who had surpassed him by nearly two hundred years. Noah hoped he would make it long enough to see his grandchildren, but that was in God's hands. Lamech was doing less and less of late, though he still tottered about the farm helping in whatever way he could. Often, this just meant watching everyone else work and telling them how they could do it better.

Reaching the seed shed door, Noah looked over at his sons' makeshift homes. They were hardly even ready to keep out the elements, but his sons were so excited to have places of their own that he really did believe they'd sleep through anything. In fact, they appeared to be sound asleep at that moment, as he heard no sound to disturb the still morning air. They usually would not rise until the cock crowed. Once they did awake, however, they'd get right to work helping him, and not one of them would stop until the day grew dim. Each was his own man, certainly, but they all valued the rewards that persistence would eventually bring.

So, easing open the infernally creaky pine door with care so as not to arouse his nearest slumbering son Japheth, Noah began his work, loading seeds of all sorts into woven baskets his wife had made. He grabbed lentils and tomatoes and sweet potatoes – oh, how he loved a good sweet potato! – and put each into a special compartment in the basket. Leah was so very creative: she'd seen him and the boys bumbling about spilling seeds into the plots of other plants year after year and had come up with a beautiful solution.

The baskets full, he headed outside to start sowing seeds before the morning dew finished watering the ground. This was why he rose so early on seeding day. His grandfather had told him that since Eden, God would send up a mist to water the plants early in the morning, and by it crops grew best. He stuck to the principle, and year after year the harvest was sublime.

The farmer now stepped into the pre-plowed field, prepared by his sons and the ox the days before, and began a tradition of consecrating the seeds to the God who made them. It was by God's grace that Noah expected them to grow, so he would set them aside to God in prayer, in his mind and spirit, asking for his King's blessing on the coming year, acknowledging that he and his family would wait, in faith, for the seeds to grow as God met their need. They would wait on what they could not see, because they had seen how faithful God could be.

In that moment, when, in his heart, he gave to God the coming year, he heard a voice break into his consciousness, as if in direct response to his words.

"Noah." It was just his name, but he felt a presence with him, and knew it was not his own thought.

Then, after a moment of silence, he wondered whether he was being foolish and got back to work.

"Noah." It came again, this time with a sense of peace, and it was that feeling that told him the Lord was speaking to him. The man had only ever felt such a deep sense of well-being when God was around him. It was like being wrapped as a child in a warm, protective blanket. He decided he had better respond. This was the King of the earth, after all.

"Yes, Lord, your servant hears you," he whispered aloud. Noah would never, for the rest of his days, forget what he heard next.

"I have determined to make an end of all living things, because the earth is filled with violence through mankind and their corruption. The entire earth and all that is in it is corrupted by their evil rule. Behold, I will destroy them with the earth." The voice, though still and small, spoke with abject authority, and Noah knew in his soul just how much power was behind those words. His mind flooded with a cacophony of thoughts and fears, but it was stilled nearly immediately as the voice continued.

"As for you, I will establish my covenant with you and your household. All of them, including your sons and their wives will be spared, because I have seen that you are righteous before me in the midst of a crooked and twisted generation. You trust me, so I count it to you as righteousness."

At these words, gratefulness washed over the farmer like a soothing stream after a hard day, but it was followed quickly thereafter by confusion. How would all this come about? When?

God was not finished. He continued, knowing Noah's thoughts. "I will bring a mighty flood of waters upon the earth to destroy every living thing under heaven. It will rain for forty days and forty nights, until all that is on the earth is blotted out. So, you must build an ark out of gopher wood to keep your family safe."

Then, as Noah's mind began to settle on this, a concrete step he could take to keep his family safe, the next words knocked the wind back out of him. "You must make it three hundred cubits long, fifty wide, and thirty high, with three decks. It will be filled with a male and female creature of every kind, and you must gather every type of food to feed yourself and them."

Three hundred cubits! A cubit was the length from fingertips to elbow, and that many would be the size of a large field. What's more, did God really mean *every* animal would be on the ship? How would they get to him? And all that food!

These and more thoughts bombarded him incessantly for several moments, leaving him standing dumbstruck in the still morning light that was now beginning to peek over the trees. Feeling its warmth, he realized that he no longer heard any voice, and hadn't for some time. He'd been so perplexed he had hardly noticed. He waited a moment in silence, gearing his mind back towards God, but there was nothing, at least nothing more than the usual sense that God was there and listening which he felt anytime he prayed. Well, either the Lord was done speaking or he'd had a wild hallucination. He did wonder. Certain berries were known to have such effects on the mind, but certainly not a fig?

Noah was not a man who took God lightly. He understood that this was the Creator, the one God whose voice governed existence, and he respected and feared Him as such. He would not ignore a direct command, whatever it entailed, but how could he be sure of such a wondrous thing as he had just heard? In any case, whether true or no, he had work to do. There was food to grow, and how much more if he was to believe those words.

Looking about, he could see that the sun was well on its way into the sky and his sons were stirring in their half-finished cabins. Their drowsy grunts and the occasional crash from one stumbling into something made that clear enough. Reality came rushing in, as time was getting on, so Noah set the flood thoughts aside, to be brooded upon later.

One by one, his oldest Japheth being first as usual, then Shem, and finally Ham the youngest, Noah's sons settled in alongside him in the fields. Ham always woke up first, funny enough, but he took his mornings easy, enjoying a slow breakfast and the sweet melody of larks warbling good morning. So, inevitably, he would be the straggler of the bunch.

Now, Japheth was first to work, because he opened his eyes with one thing on his mind – getting things done. Accomplishment was the driving force of his life. He made every choice with the finish line in mind. Indeed, if an ark *was* to be built, Japheth would likely be Noah's right hand. His only downfall was that he could sacrifice quality for progress. Left to himself, an ark would get finished in record time, but may not stay afloat for many of those forty days.

Shem, on the other hand, was the most balanced of the three, always trying his best both to get things moving and to do them well. Consistency was the word; he never stopped, and no setback could keep him from plodding steadily along. He was even middling in stature and coloring, as his skin seemed permanently bronzed, however much time he spent in or out of the sun, while Japheth was fairer and Ham near the color of soil. God really did have a sense of humor. What man on earth had such unique children?

Noah received a quick, "Good day, Father!" and a friendly jab at him having slept in (though he hadn't, of course, but they didn't know the half of it) from his sons. Besides that, the four men spoke hardly a word as they toiled through the morning up until noon, pausing briefly to lunch on yet more fruit and a few carrots left over from last harvest. Noah gnawed absentmindedly on one of these, avoiding the figs at all costs, just in case. As they ate, Ham actually offered him a fig because he had taken far too many for himself, and Noah swore God was having a laugh at him.

"So, Father, who do you think has the best chance of finding a wife first?" Shem asked playfully, grinning.

"Sure, who Father?" Japheth chimed in, attempting to remain nonchalant but sounding all too interested in the answer. "Not that it's a competition," he added hastily.

In a different mood, Noah wouldn't have hesitated to joke with the boys about such things, but today his mind filled with worries that perhaps they might not even find wives in time if this flood came. Caught in the midst of this dilemma, he grunted, "Ah, Ham, of course," with his best attempt at a smile, knowing that this answer would produce enough ruckus to keep them from prying at him further.

Sure enough, the youngest brother lit up with pride and proceeded to regale his older brothers with boasting of his many winsome qualities as they spluttered and stamped in protest. Noah bowed out during the fuss to get back to work, eager to be out from under the magnifying glass before anyone looked too closely.

Evening came quickly on the farm, and it wasn't long before the sun cast long shadows over their bent backs. In their toil, the men had built up a light sweat, but the weather was always temperate in ancient earth, a lasting gift from before the fall of Adam. Looking up from his labor, Noah gazed down the dirt path leading to Kadish, sure that he could hear someone drawing near. A moment later, the familiar sounds of his uncle and grandfather bantering drifted on the breeze. This was followed shortly by their two gray heads popping over the crest of the hill, and Noah's heart beat a little less wildly. If anyone could help him make sense of what he had experienced today, it was his grandfather Methuselah.

Tossing aside the hoe in his hand, Noah rose from work and ran out to meet the visitors. "Sabba! Uncle! Welcome, welcome, what an honor!" he shouted as he drew near.

"Good day, Nephew," Boaz called distractedly. It was obvious that he had been interrupted from a rather serious train of thought.

Methuselah, on the other hand, dropped whatever the two had been discussing without delay and opened his arms wide to receive his grandson. "Noah, my boy! It's so good to see you!" he said, wrapping him in a firm embrace. "Even a day is too long to be apart from family."

The farmer couldn't agree more, particularly as he wondered about the Lord's words. "Have you come to stay with us?" he asked hopefully as Shem, Ham, and Japheth crested the hill behind him.

"Yes, of course," Boaz chimed in, coming to himself. He could be a bit dry at times, but he did love them all very much. "I wouldn't miss your wife's rhubarb tart for the world. Besides, I need a break from this old geezer," he said, pointing an accusatory finger at Methuselah.

"Speaking of food," the older man interjected, "I do believe I smell something good in the wind. Leah must already be hard at work! Just as you all stand milling around like lay-abouts."

He was clearly joking, but Japheth looked near indignant at the notion that he wasn't spending his time well. Seeing this, Noah saved his son the embarrassment of explaining himself by moving the party towards dinner. "Right, well, we've done enough for the day boys, let's go 'lay about' inside and have some supper," he said with a nod towards his oldest son and a sly wink at his grandfather.

As the party headed towards the main house where Noah had raised his family, the tantalizing scents of roasted squash, fresh bread, and sweet baking things washed over them, quickly causing every stomach to growl if it had not felt the need to do so before.

Entering the wood home was like attending a crafts fair, as every wall and corner was adorned with some aged piece of handmade furniture or décor. Leah loved to make things beautiful, and Noah loved to make beautiful things for her. She would sometimes fashion beautiful tapestries of cloth that depicted things from Methuselah's stories, like the one in the common room above the mantle; it displayed in vivid color the day that Adam and Eve ate of the tree of the knowledge of good and evil. They were, for her and all in the house, an everlasting reminder that to reach for something God had not given could only bring misery, and that peace and joy were found under God's care and leadership alone. Both she and the boys' father wanted them to know where they had come from, who they were, and who their God was so that they didn't waste their lives trying to find an identity like the rest of the world.

The party halted suddenly as it passed by the kitchen, the men struggling to restrain themselves. At this, Leah promptly popped out brandishing a large wooden spoon, barring the doorway while declaring in no uncertain terms what would happen to any dirty fingers that found their way into the food. Then, seeing the two guests, her rosy cheeks lit up with joy, and she hurried to hug them, exclaiming all the while, "Why, I didn't know you were coming or I'd have prepared more food!" She prattled on about this for the next several minutes even though everyone knew that, for Leah, food volume was never an issue. Cooking was one of her joys, and she never failed to deliver.

Noah ushered everyone into a larger room that served as the main living area, and they proceeded to seat themselves on the thick woolen carpet around a low fir table. Eating had always been a family affair, and they were used to crowding in close to one another. Within moments, Leah appeared, a massive wooden tray in hand brimming with delights, and Noah thought how lovely she looked in her long cloth dress that touched her toes, dark tresses spilling over her shoulders. She was not a tall woman, but she had an inner strength that belied her stature, visible only in her hazel eyes. In these eyes he could always find solace, and today was a day he needed it.

She was followed by another, still more petite form carrying the loaf of bread they'd smelled earlier. That would be Tabitha, the only other lady in the household. Several years ago, Leah had found her when she was abandoned by her family. They, upon seeing Tabitha reach marrying age, attempted to force her hand to a wealthier family, but the suitor was no good man, and he treated her harshly. So, Tabitha had refused, and her family had fled to seek fortune in another city, blaming her for their troubles.

She had since become a part of the family at Noah's home, and he could see that she did not plan to leave anytime soon. In fact, he was nearly certain that she fancied Japheth. He cast a glance at his son as she entered the room, and he could see them lock eyes and smile. He was thankful; she would make a good wife to him, and that would just leave the other two to find love.

Now, it was time to eat!

CHAPTER 6

Communion and Confirmation

SUPPER WAS READY. The ladies set the table before them and eyes brightened all around at the lovely aroma, eager to dig in. So, clapping his hands together for attention, Noah as head of the household prepared to give thanks for the meal, as was his custom.

"Almighty God, Creator of heaven and earth, we come to you together to thank you for your goodness, that you've given us the relationships that we have with one another and the roof over our heads. We also thank you for this delightful spread that we know is going to taste divine, and we bless it in your name, joyful as we enjoy it with good company! Even this coming harvest that we planted today in hope is a hopeful thing only because of your faithfulness to us. All that we have is yours, Lord. Amen!"

At this, mouths watering in anticipation, everyone's hands shot towards the table, though there was grace even then, with each person waiting on the others as needed. In this home, dinner was a communal affair, with all partaking of the same massive dish of food, because they all shared the same source of life. This was symbolized through the shared breaking of bread, and it united them as a family as well. So, in a flurry of limbs, pleases, and thank-yous, the dishes were quickly dispatched. Merry talk flowed freely around the table, but most of it passed Noah by, a fact his grandfather noticed, though he waited patiently to address it. The dessert soon came out, and by golly if it wasn't a rhubarb tart! That Boaz – he had the nose of a hound.

At this point, Methuselah left the light conversation he'd been having with his son Lamech about the effects of old age in order to bring up matters of importance. Clearing his throat, he brought silence to the room; many of the family were expecting a story from him, no doubt. And a story they would have, though not a lighthearted one.

"As you all know," he began, "I often spend time with Dane's boy Josiah. You remember," he grinned, glancing around, "the one who likes my stories." As though *they* didn't! The old codger. "The boy takes me quite seriously, despite everything his old man teaches him to the contrary, and today, a rather unfortunate episode occurred which made him believe me all the more." His face turned grave. "The boy was attacked by a serpent outside the city." The old storyteller let that revelation hit them like a ton of bricks, watching their reactions as the men's eyes widened and the ladies' hands flew over their mouths. It was Noah in particular that he paid attention to, and he, though previously not paying attention, took interest at this point.

He continued, "Josiah is fine, thank God." Sighs of relief filled the room. "However, this is still a very serious situation. Never before has such a thing happened, not since the beginning when the first serpent deceived our first parents. All the animals have been subject to us. So, I fear that this happening marks a change in the world, a time in which the earth under our rule has been corrupted and changed by the violence it faces at our hands. You all know that every year we hear more and more stories of the evil doings in other lands, and though we, by God's grace, have escaped some of that by making our home here, you all know what sort of pain we have faced at the hands of selfish men." His old, warm eyes misted over at this as he remembered the passing of his wife. Everyone knew what he meant.

"And that is not all that has happened." He met eyes with Boaz. "When Boaz and I went to deliver an order to Saul at the town tavern, we heard a rather unsavory bunch mention wars in the East. Now, in my own memory, which is considerable I daresay, I cannot recall a time when I heard of all-out war as though it was average news. Every year there have been more stories of murders and kidnappings and people being mistreated, but not once has there been a force that sought to conquer other lands, at least not beyond small skirmishes between neighboring tribes and villages."

Boaz interrupted his father at this point, "Yes, father, but these may just be stories, the fanciful musings of drunken gold-diggers who want to sound knowledgeable." Methuselah could see that he wasn't confident of this assertion, just fearful of accepting the alternative.

"Perhaps." The older man replied evenly. "But I do not believe we should be surprised that hundreds of years of man sowing evil would eventually bring a day when the world must reap, perhaps through war, or some other means...." He paused, then pointed to his grandson. "I have a feeling Noah can shine some light on the subject. He has been rather quiet tonight, and for good reason, I think."

Noah was taken aback at this, but could not help but feel his grandfather was right. There was something momentous afoot, and it was no coincidence what he had experienced this very same day.

He swallowed and prepared himself mentally for what he was about to say. "I believe Sabba may be right. The world is reaching a point where it cannot continue to flourish under the unjust rule of mankind." He stopped, unsure of how to continue, of how much he should say when he was not confident himself of what had been given to him.

"I think God visited me today." A holy hush filled the room. Everyone knew Noah would not joke about such things. He continued, "When I was out early in the morning to get the seeds ready, I heard a voice call out to me. At first, I was sure it was my imagination, but then I heard it again, and that time I felt a presence with me. I knew it was God speaking to me, and I had to listen. So I told him I was listening." A look of panic flashed across his face, and he faltered. "But...I don't know how to say what came next...what he told me."

Methuselah spoke up, reassuring him, "If the Lord said it, then we need to hear it, son, because it is going to come to pass. His word always accomplishes what He sends it out to do. It doesn't matter what it is. He has never led us astray before."

Noah, visibly shaken, took courage at these words, and gave his grim news, "Our God told me that He has endured far too long the corruption of mankind on the earth. He said the world is filled with violence, that no one does good, that all the earth has been ruined by the unjust reign of the human race." Nods and words of agreement sounded out across the room. "And He said that He is going to send a flood to destroy it, to cleanse the earth of the evil that has plagued it since Adam's sin. He is going to wash it clean, and begin again." At this, jaws dropped, and everyone's face was changed. Some in the room just looked confused, like his wife, while his sons seemed nearly indignant.

"How could this be?" Leah said, overwhelmed. "We haven't even been married yet!" his sons shouted in unison. Methuselah was the only one who had stayed still and pensive during the moments following his announcement.

"I'm not finished." Noah said, as calmly as he could, though he could feel frustration bubbling up inside of him. "God said these things, but as I panicked, just like you, He gave us hope. He said that we would be spared, I and my descendants and their wives, so that we can begin again after God cleanses the world. He said that we will be spared because I have walked righteously before him, trusting in Him these many years. He also said we have to build an ark to keep us safe during the flood." At this point, Noah wasn't even going to mention the rest, about the animals and the size of this ark, because it all sounded ludicrous enough as it stood. He needed to sit on all of this and pray anyway. Why did his grandfather have to ask him what was on his mind? He had wanted to be absolutely sure before bringing any of these things to anyone.

Looking around, he saw scattered signs of relief mixed with equal portions of unbelief and fear. "Listen, I still don't believe some of this myself, so we need to just calm down. Maybe it wasn't God. Maybe I misunderstood. After all, why would he do this and leave just us? Then there wasn't even a mention of you, uncle, or you, father, or you Sabba," he said, gesturing to each of them, his grandfather last, because he didn't want to meet eyes with him. He didn't mention Tabitha, because he had a funny feeling that she was included as a future wife of his son.

Methuselah, eyes bright with understanding, interrupted him. "Noah, I don't want to alarm you, or any of the rest of you, but I don't believe this is a coincidence or misunderstanding. We have long known that a time of judgment was coming. This world, as we all agree, is evil, and you all know that my name means 'after he dies, the judgment'. It was given to me by my father for a reason, and he was close with the Lord. We may have chosen to forget this fact – I know I have for quite some time. No one wants to face heavy thoughts such as these. But I believe that all of this is coming together for a purpose. I believe God has spoken to Noah, and the world as we know it will soon be gone. God will begin again, and how blessed am I to have my children become a part of it!"

Lamech, Methuselah's son and Noah's father, finally spoke up, voice cracking with emotion. "I agree with my father. This time is upon us, and as for me, I am not long for this world. I know it well. God has begun to ease me into the time of my passing. It will come soon, and I am sure that this is why I was not mentioned in the prophecy. But we should take heart, knowing that while we will lose much through this time, we will be safe in the middle of the Lord's will. What must be, will be."

Stunned silence reigned for a few moments, and then Boaz thrust himself off of the floor and stormed out of the room into the night. He had not been mentioned as being protected from the judgment, and his father and brother had just accepted their impending doom. What was he supposed to think?

Noah also had had enough for the night, and he got up slowly, overcome with thoughts and feelings that he didn't understand. He spoke, "We need to get some rest. I need some rest. We can revisit this in the light of day after I have spent time with the Lord in the morning. Perhaps light will shine on the situation." He finished and began to take dishes into the kitchen for his wife who still looked dumbfounded. "We will leave these for tomorrow. Everyone just needs to spend some time in the quiet and take this in."

One by one, people left the dining area, nearly all of them headed to bed, but none to sleep. The thoughts of the evening weighed on them like a drenched cloak in a downpour: heavy, cold, and uncomfortable. All retired except Methuselah. He sat for hours in the same position in which he'd been left, musing on what tomorrow would bring and the days ahead. He had lived so very long that there was not much that could surprise him, and still less that could upset his outlook. Even this news of a coming flood, though unwelcome, was not entirely unexpected. He had known, deep in his soul, that a day would come near the end of his days when God would prepare to bring justice on the world. In Methuselah's mind, He had waited too long to unleash it already. Events such as what had happened to his wife were happening all around the world every day: people hating, thieving, murdering one another and worse. It was time for things to change.

The old historian was just glad that God had promised to spare his family. He had lived a good, long life on the earth, and if it was his time, then he could accept that, but he did understand the fears plaguing Noah and others. Walking with God was always a journey into the unknown, with many hidden challenges. There would be many grueling days ahead for them all – of that he was certain – but what he wanted everyone to understand was that not a single day would pass where God would not be there for them in the trials, through the fears. And if he had learned anything over his long life, it was that danger is not dangerous if God is in it. There was that one question nagging him though: If the judgment would come when he died, when would that be? How would that happen? What's more, he understood that in his current state, his son Lamech could also easily pass of age at any time, but what of Boaz? He seemed in the best of health.

Stepping out into the warm night air, Methuselah went to see his younger son. He found him slumped against a tree with his head in his hands, no doubt overwhelmed. The older man crept up behind him and joined his son at the foot of the almond tree, easing his creaking bones into a sitting position, unable to help the slight groan that escaped his lips as he did so. Looking at Boaz, he thought he saw a tear glistening in the moonlight.

"So, you're worried about what Noah said?" Methuselah asked softly.

Boaz was silent for several moments more, but his grandfather was a patient man, and he knew his grandson. The man needed the time to analyze what he was feeling and what he was going to say before he actually said anything. He was forever accurate, something he had inherited from Methuselah. Eventually he spoke, voice wavering slightly, and said, "Yes, and no. I'm not sure that I believe him, first of all. Would God really destroy the entire human race? That doesn't seem like the Lord we love so much and serve each day, who provides us with food and clothes and homes and blesses our families in the work of our hands." There was anger in his eyes as he said the words. He continued, "But then, I know Noah. I trust him. He has never been one given to flights of fancy. And I remember the stories you tell about your father Enoch: how close he was with the Lord. He definitely would have given you your name for a reason." He finished with a huge sigh, "So, I suppose I would say that I am confused."

"I see." Boaz's grandfather replied. "That is all completely understandable to feel, my son, and mostly true. Yet, I fear that you are forgetting something about our God that we said we accepted when we began to follow him, something that we even celebrated about him - his justice. He is a God who judges rightly and rules over the earth, giving to men their due reward for their deeds. This fact is part of why we trust that evil will be dealt with and that our own lives will be blessed as we do his will. If we accept this about him in the good times, we must accept it in the time of judgment. Perhaps this is that time."

His grandson sat for a moment, taking this in, and said, "I know. I do. I know that it is only right for God to judge corruption, but what of us who do not live corrupt lives? What of me?"

So here was the real issue. The man was afraid – afraid of his fate. To be fair, Methuselah himself was confused about why Boaz was not included in the words of the prophecy. So, he answered with what he knew. "Son, all I can say is that our God is good. If he has shown us anything by his actions over the years, it is that. That can only mean that whatever is coming in the days ahead is good as well, that somehow, despite all of the unknown, what He is bringing to pass is what *needs* to happen. His ways are higher than our ways, and his thoughts are far above our thoughts."

"But I need to know what is going to happen! How can I plan the future if I don't even know that there will be one?" Boaz said, nearly shouting in frustration.

"You can't. You, and all of us, are going to have to just accept that today is all you have been given, and you must trust the God that has proven Himself trustworthy. The future belongs to Him, not to us." With these grave words, the old man left his grandson to brood and went to find a place to rest. The weather was so temperate at that time that one could lay down in the grass nearly anywhere and sleep comfortably straight through the night. As he went, he glimpsed Japheth and Tabitha walking down the path together, and wondered what sort of thoughts were passing between them.

The young man was walking deliberately, careful not to step too quickly with his longer legs so that he could stay next to Tabitha. He had drawn her aside after dinner, asking her to take a stroll with him, and she had politely accepted his request. She was always that way, kind and submissive, willing to do whatever was needed for whomever. It wasn't that she was a doormat – far from it. She had come to their family precisely because she was unwilling to accept an unacceptable suitor. He hoped that perhaps she would think fondly of him, that he could be worthy of her, if God would allow it.

Afraid as he was to broach the subject, Japheth opened up the conversation to matters of importance. "So that was a surprise there at dinner, wasn't it? I did not see that coming." He laughed slightly, feeling awkward. She did not respond at first, and he worried that he had upset her. "Not that it's a laughing matter, I just don't know what else to do with something so absurd-sounding."

Tabitha gave him a slight smile, easing his fears. "I know what you meant. It is quite a lot to take in – isn't it?"

He felt a weight lift when she smiled. "My goodness – yes- it is! It's hard to believe, as well."

"Do you believe it? That God is going to judge the world and that only your family will be saved?" She sounded different when she said this. He thought he detected a note of worry, even fear.

He measured his words. "I cannot say. My father has always been an honest man, but who can receive such news as this? That would mean that everyone we know, everyone we care about, will be taken away from us." The young man truly was unsure about it all. There was no reason to doubt except for his own unbelief, but that was enough.

"Everyone you care about?" She asked in response, eyes shining in the night. He responded immediately, "No, not everyone, not you, of course – never you." His words were tumbling out almost faster than he could form them. "You must always be with me," he said abruptly. Tabitha stopped walking and turned away from him. "But how?" she whispered. "How can I be with you if this is true – if only your family will survive the judgment?"

Japheth felt a sudden surge of emotion, his heart brimming with desire and frustration and even what he thought was confidence or faith – he wasn't sure which. He suddenly knew what he was to do. Taking her hand in hers, he knelt next to her, looked up into her soft green eyes, and said, "Whether judgment comes or not, even if the world itself were to end, we could be together. Nothing need separate us for all of our days. I love you, and you mean more to me than anything on this earth. Will you be my wife?"

"Yes!" Tabitha squealed, overcome with a mixed wave of excitement and relief. She couldn't have asked for more.

Inside the house, Noah was having a far different evening. Though he had conducted himself with composure at the end of supper, upon reaching his room he had thrown himself on the bed and sobbed into his pillow. This was an impossible thing the Lord was asking of him. He could not bear it. Why did it have to be him? Why did he have to know such great and terrible things? He understood the need for justice, but surely, if it were destined to come, God could have just brought it suddenly upon the world and started again. Noah almost wished it were so, so that he could rest in peace, not having known what was coming.

Instead, he felt as though the weight of the world was on his shoulders, and the vast responsibility threatened to destroy him. He would be the one who would have to make choices for his family, to lead them into this future of which God had spoken. Yet, he was not even certain that God has spoken to him. Why should he fear so much? These thoughts and more came at him, but he knew, as soon as they did, that they were lies. He did know. It wasn't his imagination. God was there, and His plan was at work, and none of them could escape it. More importantly, none of them should seek to escape it. This was the God who had always been there for them, who had been faithful since before they were even born, since Adam and his righteous son Seth. This was the God who saw all, knew all, and who provided for their needs year after year.

Still, there were so many challenges if this were true! How would he care for his family if he were to spend all of his time building a massive ark the size of his entire property? How would his family bear the loss of everything and everyone that they knew? It seemed impossible. Drowning in these thoughts as though the flood had already come upon him, the head of the household drifted off into a much-needed sleep.

Morning came, bright and early, bringing with it some unexpected visitors. The cock crowed, waking up nearly everyone, but when Noah, Leah, and the others sleepily stumbled into the living area for breakfast, Methuselah and Lamech were already busy entertaining three strange men, all of whom turned to look at them as they came into the room. Noah was the first to speak.

"Hello friends! To what do I owe this unexpected pleasure?" Noah's people were forever hospitable, and though he was a tad flustered that these men were in his home without his knowledge, he was also thankful for the opportunity to bless them, as it was a gift from God to have that privilege.

One man, the average-sized one, stood up and moved to greet Noah, smiling, "Greetings to you as well! I am happy that you call us friends, for so we are, in more ways than you know. It is a delight to find you so hospitable - though I was led to expect no less." These words put Noah off somewhat, as it seemed like the man knew more about Noah than he did about the man. That must have been his father's doing.

"Can I ask who we have the privilege of entertaining today?" Noah asked, still uncertain.

"Of course, you would be wondering that, wouldn't you?" The man answered. "My name is Micah, and these two are Gurion and Nathan," he said, gesturing towards a man who looked very nearly like a giant and another who seemed on first glance to be barely more than a youth, but who had kindness in his eyes. "We are the Lord's messengers, and He has sent us to tell you His words."

No. Could it be? Noah was reeling. "He has heard your prayers, and He wishes to confirm to you that His word is sure. All that has been spoken to you shall surely come to pass."

Noah could have heard a feather fall - the room was so silent. God had sent angels to confirm His word. What a wonder! He didn't know whether to shout praises or to fall down and cry. So judgment *was* coming.

CHAPTER 7

Unholy Alliance

I
N THE MOMENTS AFTER MICAH GAVE Noah's family his
message, chaos ensued. Noah, stunned into silence for nearly thirty
minutes, eventually struck up earnest conversation with the angels,
realizing that he finally had a chance to have some of his questions
answered. His wife, on the other hand, became uncontrollably weepy as
the torrent of emotions hit her, but this was lessened slightly by the need
to entertain her holy guests. Tabitha joined her in the effort with
Japheth never far from her side, offering to assist her at every
opportunity. These two seemed considerably less upset than perhaps was
proper, but they had, after all, just been engaged. All that was left was to
announce glad news to the family.

The other sons were less than enthused, especially as they considered
the fact that there was now a deadline in some sense on them finding a
wife, but this had its perks as well. At least they knew they would have

one! In their hearts, though, no one in the house had fully come to grips with the depth of what those grave tidings would mean for them. How could they? No one had ever experienced what they were about to go through: becoming the last people on earth.

Last of all in processing these matters was Boaz, as he had stayed outside during breakfast when the message was given, still seeking solitude after the events of the night before. Lamech actually had to leave a rather stimulating conversation with Nathan about the nature of physical and spiritual bodies to go outside and break the news to his brother. He was not looking forward to the response he would receive.

The nearly decrepit old man hobbled outside, eyes peeled for a sign of his brother. It took a bit, but Lamech eventually found him out behind the seed shed, rocking back and forth in a chair he had fashioned from alder branches. In the considerable time it took for Lamech to walk out to him, Boaz never once looked his way, intent on whatever thoughts plagued his mind. His face was drawn, and his eyes were bloodshot from lack of sleep but as bright and aware as ever, completely focused on some invisible object.

"Good morning brother. I see you haven't slept," Lamech said smoothly, with a hint of a chuckle in his voice.

"Is it that obvious?" Boaz replied tiredly, finally looking his way. He wasn't uncaring, just self-absorbed at times. He really hadn't seen his brother walk his way.

"You tell me. You were pretty much staring a hole in that patch of grass over there. It seems foolish to ask in light of things, but I'm going to anyway - what's on your mind?"

The younger brother had spent the entire night contemplating the future, unable to sleep until he made sense of things. He knew God and followed him, but he had never been able to take life one day at a time. He was always planning the next venture, and he related to God primarily as the one who helped him make sense of his life, the one who made things *work*. So, when God Himself didn't seem to be making sense, Boaz just couldn't figure out what to do. However, in the still of the night, alone with only his thoughts and God, he had pondered his father's words about trusting in God's faithfulness, and those thoughts were beginning to sink in.

Eventually Boaz replied, carefully choosing his words. "I just need to know what to *do*." He paused here, seeing from his brother's raised eyebrows that this would not suffice, then continued, "I trust Noah, and I trust our father – mostly – and more importantly, I trust God. But none of this makes sense. I just can't see how God would drop this on us and not tell us what to do, so that makes me doubt whether he has spoken at all. I have always decided every step by what I expect to happen next. I pick a goal and I aim at it, making decisions based on the best way to reach the goal. Right now, though, I don't know my goal, and it scares me. What if God is finished with me...or...?"

Lamech clapped his brother on the back good naturedly, letting him know he understood, but he did not agree with his assessment of the situation. "Boaz, I understand you. You need a mission at all times, and when you don't have one, you don't know what you're here for. You have to remember though that there is a difference between not knowing your mission and not having one. God knows what's ahead. We *find out* in his timing. Now, as to whether God has spoken or our relatives are bonkers, there is no longer any doubt." He laughed, "We had angels for breakfast."

Boaz just stared at his brother, face blank. "What do you mean you had angels for breakfast? Is that something Leah is making now? Angel cakes? How does that help?" His frustration was evident.

Lamech's eyebrows narrowed, "Really? Sometimes I do wonder if I'm the smart one. No, we didn't eat angel cakes. God sent angelic messengers to visit us to confirm what Noah said! They're in the house right now. I've been having a scintillating conversation with one about what happens to our bodies when we die." He could tell now that Boaz was at least intrigued, as he had stopped rocking in his chair, but the cynic still didn't seem to believe him. So, Lamech motioned towards the house. "Let's go inside. You can meet them, and stop looking at me like that." The younger brother was still yet hesitant to move, so Lamech took him by the arm and yanked him upright as best he could. "Come on!"

Though it was slow going, the two ambled inside to discover that one of the men had disappeared from the table. Only the large one called Gurion and the one he'd been speaking with earlier remained. "Well, here we are my brother, sure as can be. Two angels straight from heaven," he said, waving a hand in their direction. "Introduce yourself."

Gurion spoke first, his deep baritone voice sounding out like a trumpet, "Hello friend! I see we have missed someone. How are you related to the family?"

Boaz looked awestruck by the size of the man as he stood up to greet them, but he still didn't think he was an angel. "Ah...yes, I am...ah...the uncle," he stuttered, pointing at Noah and the boys. "I am pleased to meet you. I apologize, I am just having a very odd day. Where have you traveled from? And my brother said there were three of you?"

Nathan could see that the man was confused, so he chimed in, "We are God's messengers, sent to confirm the word that Noah was given yesterday." Seeing Boaz's fearful look, he came close and touched the man's shoulder. "This is not a message of judgment towards this family. You do not need to fear us. I know your concerns, but you, like all of us, have a place in the will of God. He has a purpose for you, and you will not fail to fulfill it, whether you understand it now or not." He let the man sit on that for a moment. "And as for the third member of our company, your father Methuselah made known to us news of wars in the East, something of which we were not yet aware as we served the Lord at our posts prior to journeying here, and Micah has left to discern the matter more clearly. We may expect him to be a few days. He may learn something of import to us all."

Noah cleared his throat, "Permission to speak, sir?" The angel nodded, "Speak freely. You never need ask for permission from us. We ourselves are your servants for the sake of God's will."

"Thank you. I just wanted to bring before us the matter at hand. You say that we have been chosen by God for the task ahead, to save a remnant of humanity: to start anew. If I am to believe the word that I was given yesterday morning, this means more than we have so far discussed. I was told that we must build an ark roughly the size of my entire acreage, and collect animals and food of every kind to fill it. How do you suppose we do this?" The head of household was trying to remain composed, but this was a tall order, after all.

Nathan looked unsurprised. "That is right. Yes, it is God's will that this ark save your family and the animals needed to populate the cleansed earth. As to how it will be done –" he looked at Gurion, then flashed a smile to the group, "With help of course! Our help. And you are a family of carpenters, are you not?"

"God makes no mistakes." Gurion confirmed. "He chose you for this, and he has chosen us to protect you. Do not fear."

Boaz couldn't help himself at this point, and blurted out, "Protect us from what?" He didn't realize, of course, just how passionate Gurion would be on the subject.

The big angel grimaced, turning to him with fire in his eyes. "The most despicable vermin ever to set food on the earth: Satan and his demons. I pray earnestly for the day that the Almighty God will smite them in justice, obliterating their eternally corrupt ilk from the heavens for good, and I live in the hope that with each passing day I might be a part of bringing them closer to their fate."

Micah was on a mission. As soon as he heard the news from Methuselah about conflict rising in the East, he had felt his spirit surge with the sense that this was a matter of interest for the Lord and His plan for Noah's family. Micah was to go and see what they were dealing with, so as to be prepared when the conflict made its way towards them, as it undoubtedly would. Satan, their great adversary, was ever plotting to disrupt the Creator's plans and destroy His people. Once the enemy caught on to what was happening with Noah and the ark-building, he would likely have the whole world on their heels in short order. With this reality in mind and his purpose clear, Micah had slipped instantly into the spirit realm without much of a warning, disappearing from Noah's home. This he now regretted slightly, hearing God's whisper to him that the humans were fragile and didn't do well with sudden changes. Micah wasn't good at remembering such seemingly trivial details, but God was a good King, and He knew how to deal with His own people, so the angel was trying to learn.

He was following the Euphrates River due north, as Kadish had been located at the extreme southern point of the River where it fed into the sea. Settlements of every size dotted the countryside, and one after another passed below him in a blur, he was moving so fast. All angels could travel at a tremendous pace, covering in minutes what would take a full day of nonstop travel for humans. He was on his way to Tubal-cain's territory; it was a veritable weapons depot, since he had been the first to invent them, and Micah was willing to bet that if there were major conflicts in the region then there would be some connection to the master smithy. As the angel began to come to the intersection of the four rivers, he crossed into the eastern lands of Assyria, slowing down when he connected with the path of the Hiddekel River. All major settlements would be near the river where fresh water was abundant, so he knew that if there was conflict, he would find it here.

Several villages later, though, there was still no sign of anything even remotely resembling war. Micah had to remind himself that this was good news, certainly, but he couldn't help but feel as though there was much more to the situation than met the eye. The enemy was known for deceit.

Seeing no alternative, he flew down a little closer, unconcerned about the people below, as they could not see him unless he willed it. There, at the foothills of the mountains where Tubal-cain had built his mines, Micah saw soldiers patrolling the dirt roads, armed and ready. They didn't seem to have any particular mission or even any violent intentions. In fact, a group of about five of them was milling about chatting with the citizenry, some of whom seemed like they might be old friends! What in heaven was going on?

This was a reconnaissance mission after all, so he decided to descend, assuming human form as he did so. He would have to gather some intelligence personally. After a cursory glance at his body to make sure it wasn't glowing - *that* would certainly arouse suspicion - he stepped out from behind a thatched hut and ambled over to one soldier who seemed especially talkative.

"Hello sir!" he shouted in as friendly a tone as he could muster.

The soldier turned, eyes skimming over Micah as he did, no doubt trying to determine if he belonged to the village. That was a test that the angel most certainly would not pass judging by the soldier's familiarity with the populace. The man began cautiously, "Hello there. I don't believe I've seen you around these parts before. What business do you have here?" Though the man was being careful, Micah could tell that he lacked the confident assurance of someone accustomed to functioning with authority, and that intrigued him.

"Ah, yes, you wouldn't know me. I have traveled a great distance to get here, and am hoping to complete my journey visiting the lands of Tubal-cain." The angel would not lie, as it was not in his nature, but he knew that this was going to go south quickly if he allowed the man to think too deeply on any of his answers. So, he quickly added, "Do you know how I might get there? I came to you desiring to learn something of the lay of the land and the situation in this region, since I see that there are armed men about."

At this, the soldier softened considerably, his attitude brightening as he described what seemed to him to be an exciting set of events. Prior to now, the region and indeed this very village had been overrun with armed bandits who roamed the land in small groups terrorizing the villagers. The people, unable to defend themselves in the face of such unexpected attacks, had given in to the exorbitant demands of the bandits and begun to starve. They were helpless. Then, one day everything changed.

A large group of villagers determined to journey to Tubal-cain and seek help while the bandits were away. He was rich, and had both weapons and men, so it was their only hope. The soldier speaking to Micah was one of those who had volunteered to go, and he was clearly star struck by the wealth and power he had experienced that day. In the end, Tubal-cain himself had agreed to send a band of mercenaries that he employed to their rescue, and the bandits had been driven out of town. All that he asked of the villagers in return was their loyalty, and that some men among them would choose to become a part of his army to protect the village from future attacks. He would supply the weaponry, of course. The villagers were beyond thankful and had agreed wholeheartedly, immediately becoming Tubal-cain's subjects.

Thanking the soldier for the information, Micah took all this in slowly, turning it over in his mind and sending up prayers to the Lord in his spirit for discernment of the situation. So, it seemed that this once-simple blacksmith had grown some rather grandiose ambitions. These people were under his protection, and he was, practically, their lord. This was a highly cunning, manipulative way to maintain control of territory, and, somehow, Micah doubted that this plot was developed in a vacuum. This had the signature of that age-old serpent written all over it. He was sure that if he pressed in further, he would find that Satan was the puppet master and Tubal-cain his oblivious dancing toy.

Unable to glean anything further from the little village, the angel took to the air again, all the more eager to get to Tubal-cain's territory. He'd been right. The answers were there.

Lucifer was enjoying himself. Lounging complacently on a large, silken cushion intended for Tubal-cain, the demon prince sat surrounded by his evil cohorts. They had come together here, in the mountain fortress of the iron-workers, to plot the conquering of the world - or, rather, to goad unwitting humans into doing it for them. In the very same room, a lackluster banquet hall, were gathering the so-called rulers of the known world. In reality, the kingdoms of the south and west represented throughout the room were under the tyrannical rule of Lucifer's underlings, however little they knew of the matter. There was no kingdom on earth free of their influence.

Leaders began to enter the room and take their seats, filtering in one by one with far less fanfare than they were accustomed to, since there were no subjects to supply the praise. The level of wealth and power on display was in stark contrast with the humble setting, a fact that Lucifer reminded everyone was soon to change.

"I do apologize for this less-than-luxurious backdrop to our most ambitious efforts yet. My puppet is not yet ready to forsake efficiency for extravagance as most of yours have done, but this is good at the present time, as there is much work to be done. A whole army needs outfitting, and that takes time and resources that ought not to be wasted on pretty trivialities. I will strip this quality from him when it suits me at a later date, so that he can face the sure and steady destruction that endless pleasure affords." He wasn't really apologizing; he never did. The others knew this. He was simply turning a setback into an opportunity for boasting; they'd have done the same.

"Now, you may fear that the humans will balk at the idea of entering into an alliance with someone so seemingly poor, but I believe that we can use this too to our advantage. Tubal-cain is on the path to greater riches than the world has ever seen, and these men know that he has the means to achieve his goals. When they hear his plans as they eat, the simple surroundings will make them all the hungrier and become for them yet another reason to reach out and take what they deserve." Lucifer said smugly. "Remember the plan. I know that each of you has a special fate in mind for the kingdoms under your control, but we must all be willing to sacrifice our own agendas for the sake of the ultimate goal: foiling the plans of the Enemy. If we can achieve a united front among the human lords, we can direct them as one to follow our purposes. Through them, the entire world will be subject to our rule and the swift, sweet destruction that we long to bring to those dreadful image-bearers of the Enemy."

To his right, Moloch motioned to speak. The demon lord was fearsome in spirit form, appearing as a cross between a massive bull and a man. Taut muscles rippled down his chest and thighs, interrupted here and there by patches of coarse raven hair. His face was that of a mighty steer, horns stretching a few feet above his head, and his eyes blazed with a deep, sickening satisfaction as he spoke, " I don't know about the rest of you, but I am doing quite well on the destruction front. My people are so enamored with earning my favor that they sacrifice their very own children to me - at least two per week! And one or more of the parents inevitably succumbs to the pain of their child's passing, taking their own life or else ruining whatever future the family might have had with a deep depression. They are firmly under my thumb."

Through this outburst Lucifer just listened quietly, staring at the brutish creature so hard it seemed his eyes would bore through it. Rather than speaking, however, he simply nodded slightly at Bacchus, another of his cronies, and the demon spoke his mind, "Yes, yes, brother, that is all well and good. I myself have a whole kingdom of fools tramping about killing one another in a perpetual drunken stupor as they waste themselves on food and strong drink. And yet, these are such small victories! We must quit wasting our time on minor achievements and focus on attacking the heart of the enemy's plans."

Then Lucifer finished his thoughts, "The redemption of mankind. Ever since that fateful day of our first victory over these insipid dirt clods, the Enemy has been working to gather a people for Himself who will obey Him and continue His reign on earth in freedom. We have, due to our significant efforts, caused irreversible damage to those plans and the people with whom He might carry them out. Yet, our victory is not yet complete. We cannot stay holed up in our little corners of the world with our heads stuck in the sand, or we risk being caught by surprise when the day comes that the Enemy moves forward with the next phase."

He rose out of the chair at this, taking a few slow, deliberate steps towards the bull-demon. Then, as if having changed his mind, he turned to face the wider group, "Do we not all remember the promise that our Enemy made to the man and woman on the day that they fell? What was it again?" He waited for an answer, his back to Moloch, who eventually replied, embarrassed in the face of the silence, "The seed of the woman would one day crush the serpent."

"Yes, that was it." Lucifer said as though he had actually sought an answer. "The serpent, of course, represents every one of us, all those who would lie in wait to deceive His precious humans." He turned swiftly towards Moloch and looked him in the eyes. "Does it not, therefore, stand to reason that we might make it our highest aim to thwart said plans? Or would you rather experience whatever creative form of crushing the Enemy has in mind?" He was making an example of the fellow, of course, but Moloch could see the sense behind his words. He was the leader for a reason, after all: the most cunning and the most cutthroat among them.

"No? I thought so." Lucifer smirked. "Then let us unite this rabble so that we may rule unquestioned, watching every corner of the world where our Enemy might attempt to raise this would-be serpent-crusher. Let us turn our attention to the matter at hand. You all know your roles."

By this point, Tubal-cain had finally entered the banquet hall and was moving to take his seat, utterly unaware of the unholy characters already crowding around his table. The other leaders had waited out of respect for the lord of the land to arrive before being seated. If there had been any doubt before about the wealth or taste of their host, it was summarily dismissed when he arrived. Dressed in full battle regalia, his new armor gleaming golden in the torchlight, the ruler cut quite an imposing figure.

"Sit, sit my friends." He bellowed good-naturedly, "There is no need to stand on ceremony for me. I am a simple man, with a simple goal. I want to make us all very, very rich." Bursts of laughter abounded at this bold declaration. He had their attention. Lucifer was beaming, impressed with his work. The man couldn't have started better; he was doing exactly as instructed.

"As some of you may know, I am a man of efficiency. It is my firm belief that time is a commodity, just as is gold or silver, a good that can be traded, lent, or spent. Unfortunately, I have considerably more gold and silver than I have time, especially as the years wane for me, so, the former is considerably more precious. And I imagine, - " He cleared his throat, pausing for dramatic effect, "-that you all are facing a similar dilemma, whether the younger men among you are aware of it as yet or no. With this in mind, I bring before you my humble attempt to increase our share of all three."

He gestured towards his servant girl Rhoda who was waiting in the hall with a map, and she hurried inside, placing it carefully on the table before fleeing from the lecherous gazes of the leaders. As she passed back into the hallway, she noticed a servant standing near the doorway whom she did not recognize, and wondered where he had come from. Certainly though there must be a number of new faces on such a day as this, she supposed, what with the gaggle of gentry and their corresponding attendants. She dismissed the thought and moved right along, not bothering to question him. There was something special about the man though. He had had a sort of healthy glow about him, and this stayed on her mind until long afterward.

CHAPTER 8

An Uninvited Guest

MICAH WAS IN A BIND. Upon entering Tubal-cain's territory, he had seen the gathering of kings and their vast entourages down below and knew that he'd found what he was looking for, but in his excitement had nearly flown straight into a demon guard. It shouldn't have been a surprise, but he thanked God that the fellow hadn't seen him, and that escape had been relatively easy. He was not interested in making a scene, as exposing his cover would most certainly assure that he did not discover what the gathering of minds was plotting.

Now, he stood in the doorway of what appeared to be a world council of leaders, disguised as a servant, and he had no idea how he was going to keep from being caught. If it had been just humans, there wouldn't be a problem; they were blind because they chose to be. But the room practically seethed with demon spawn! At the elbows of every single one of the monarchs was an evil spirit, whispering lies. Not only that, but these were not minor players; in that room were some of the most diabolical minds of the age. One or more of those figures had authored every conceivable form of corruption plaguing the world. Micah believed the Lord had sent him, but he felt like he was in over his head. The chances that his identity would not be discovered were dismal. It was a miracle that it had not happened already.

Out of the corner of his eye, the angel saw a demon head turn in his direction, and he quickly ducked behind the towering oak door. Had he been seen? He was worried: not for himself, but for the mission. It was imperative that he learned what happened in that room. Moments went by without any event, so he thought perhaps danger had been averted. Whether he had been discovered or not, it was too late to change that now, so he settled back against the wall to listen to the master smithy speak.

Tubal-cain gestured towards the general area of Assyria on the map and began, "My kingdom lies here. Now, my sons and I have already made significant progress in purchasing the allegiance of the Assyrians. They are a simple people. We offer them tools and protection, or in many cases simply provide them with the means to protect themselves, and they bow to us in moments, feeling as though they owe us an eternal debt. All villages and cities within a day's march have sworn fealty to our banner. Our only obstacle at this point is King Tudiya, the leader of the barbarian tribes immediately south of our location. However, this is a minor detail, as we have far superior weaponry and a greater force, without even eliciting the help of you fine fellows." Enjoying the rapt attention, the leader's voice grew more confident with each word.

He pointed his sword at the sprawling map and jammed it into the region marked Havilah, "Our first order of business is to line our pockets with gold, as promised. Now, we have - "

"How exactly do you propose we do that? Havilah is heavily guarded. I won't risk my men on such a fool's errand," sneered Obed, king of one of the smaller regions to the southwest. Shortly after he spoke, however, an evil spirit was hissing into his ear. Dagon, the fish god, was eager to see this plan move forward, and was not about to let his pawn ruin it with his big mouth. A few lies later, Obed was looking rather more amiable and open to the idea.

Unaware of that event, Tubal-cain continued as though he had not been interrupted, not feeling the comment worthy of his attention, since all would soon be revealed. No one would be scoffing when he was finished. "As I was saying, we have here massive stores of iron and coal, as well as a limitless supply deep in the mountain, waiting to be brought up. We increase our holdings every day. Were we to form a partnership, I could assure you all that we have more than enough supplies to outfit every one of your soldiers with weapons and armor the likes of which you have never seen. What's more, for us, mining has been our longtime trade, and we have special tools that would allow us to quickly and effectively mine deep into the heart of the Havilah mountains, mountains that we all know are bursting with gold."

"And what of Queen Arissa? Will she sit idly by while you tromp into her lands and steal all of her gold? She has a sizeable force of mercenaries, gathered over many long years by means of the gold of which you speak. She has already long accomplished what you seek to do, buying the loyalty of those within her lands." It was Barak, lord of the great city of Arnon and its surroundings who spoke up this time. He was not one to be trifled with. However, Tubal-cain thought that he detected a glimmer of intrigue in Barak's blue eyes. Perhaps he had only issued the proclamation to challenge the smithy, but expected a solution to be forthcoming.

"Yes, well, we have thought of that as well," He waved a hand towards his sons who were standing behind him out of deference. "I am not foolish enough to think that Arissa will gladly part with her hard-won wealth. With that expectation, we dispatched scouts to determine the approximate size of her force, and we are now certain that if we have the help of even five of the dozen or so kingdoms in attendance tonight outfitted with our weaponry, we can easily overwhelm her defenses for a decisive victory." He slammed his gauntleted fist on the table with these words, intoxicated by the possibilities.

Then, in a far more composed fashion, he spread wide his hands, looking at each world leader in turn, "My proposal to you is this. Join us in this venture, and together, we can fill our kingdoms with gold, enjoying wealth beyond our wildest dreams. And this is only the beginning. Once we have conquered Havilah, the real prize awaits. For that information, however, there is a price. We are about to start the feast, and anyone who stays to dine with us will demonstrate by partaking of our food that he has chosen to take part in our enterprise.

Anyone who wishes to leave may do so now, at this time. I will assure that you and your men have provisions for the journey home."

Here, Lucifer stalked over to the leader, touching his shoulder in a familiar way that implied absolute ownership, and gave him a curt command. Looking at his henchman, he winked. Whatever he said must have highly motivated Tubal-cain, because a moment later, the man said slyly, "And if any of you does choose to miss this unique opportunity, remember that those who remain will be your considerably wealthier, more powerful neighbors when the mission is finished. So, I trust you should sleep well, knowing that they will be near at hand."

Needless to say, not one of the men left the room. There was a considerable level of shifting in seats and furtive glances around the table to gauge the general feelings of other leaders, but not one of them rose from their place. With such tremendous stakes, none of the monarchs could dare risk missing out on the opportunity. To refuse would have been political suicide in the near future. Tubal-cain was ecstatic; everything was going according to plan. That veiled threat at the end had sealed the deal. He was proud of himself for thinking of that one. Now it was time to reveal the pièce de résistance.

Just outside the door, Micah's thoughts were running wild. After hearing all this, he wanted to burst into the room and stop these fools before they played right into the enemy's hands. They thought they were just building their own kingdoms, but in truth, they were building Satan's, and none of them knew just how diabolical the fallen angel could be. To that fiend, everyone was expendable, and he would most certainly use them as long as they were needed, then throw them away without hesitation. The room was still yet teeming with enemies, however, so Micah could only sit back and pray while their fates were sealed.

Soon enough, servants began to stream past the angel laden with food. The feast truly was a sight to behold. What seemed like countless silver platters poured into the banquet hall, carrying everything from simple honeyed oat cakes to boiled vegetables to tureens of stew. It seemed the ironworker had brought in dishes to represent the cultural cuisine of every kingdom in the room. That smacked of Satan as well, the infernal flatterer. From the midst of the cacophony of scents arose a strong, rich smell, and as Micah turned, he saw that they had even roasted a huge boar, tusks and all. The angel was reminded of the beginning, when God had set man in the garden and told him to eat freely of every plant. It seemed the sun had long set on that day.

Peeking around the corner, the incognito angel looked on the faces of the so-called leaders, glowing with greed as they dreamed of gluttony and promised conquest. How very far mankind had fallen. God had given them everything, and they still lived out their pitifully short days scheming to take what was already theirs by right. If only they would trust the one true Leader, the Good Shepherd of their souls, they wouldn't have to. Realizing his musings had taken him a moment too many, he pulled back. Just a bit longer and he would hear what he needed. Then he'd be out of there.

The table set, the slew of servants were sent away with a harsh command to leave them in peace for the evening. Whatever Tubal-cain was plotting, he didn't want a word of it to leave that compound. Micah merged with the servant stampede and slipped into a side room off of the main thoroughfare until he heard the great oak doors slam shut. Only then did he venture back into the empty hall to finish spying on the gathering. Unfortunately, it wasn't entirely empty.

As soon as the angel sidled up next to the doors to listen, he felt a foreboding presence in the spirit realm. He immediately slipped out of his physical body, wings whirling, but before he could even register what was happening, a crushing blow hit him in the back of the neck, stunning him, as enormous, beastly hands latched onto his flailing limbs. In that iron grip, he struggled to turn his head to catch a glimpse of his attacker. It was none other than Moloch, the bullish beast, and the demon wasn't alone. Six more hands were grappling for purchase on his wings, pinning them tightly so he couldn't move. He'd been had. Micah was strong, stronger than any one of these brutes in a fair fight, but, as always, fighting demons was never fair, and they'd played their hand well. God help him.

Noah was exhausted. Since the angelic pronouncement, he and his sons had been hard at work for days preparing the wood needed to build the ark. Their backs were aching; their palms were raw, and the axes were already growing dull. They'd already cut through a dozen trees, some so large that they'd needed the angels' help. Thank God that the family were already carpenters by trade and had the tools they needed for such a job. As the head of household considered what it would take, however, to fully realize the project, he knew that there were still yet tools they would need that they had never used, things that possibly had never been made - at least not on a scale equal to the task.

With this in mind, he eventually called the men together to make the needs known. One of the most important items he wanted at hand in the near future was an auger. They had several already that they had collected over the years, but none even near the size that they'd need to drill the holes he had planned. The two old men hadn't helped nearly at all thus far, and he could hardly fault them for it with their ancient backs, but that made them an easy target for errands. "Good work everyone!" Noah exclaimed, truly thankful for a productive day. "It's about time that we take a break." He laughed, looking at Methuselah and Lamech, "At least, those of us who have sweat today. As for you two, I have a special mission in mind that I am only willing to entrust to your capable hands."

His father and grandfather exchanged glances. They knew what that meant. The old fogies had to take a shopping trip. "Very well," Lamech said, "What's the idea?"

"Well, we've been cutting away trying to stockpile some wood to get started on the work proper, but sooner or later we are going to have to get going, shaping and joining pieces. When it's time for joinery, we will need to drill holes - big ones - large enough to put an entire tree limb through. So, we need an auger roughly the size of a grown man." He smiled wanly. "Think you can handle that?"

The old man was dumbstruck. "You can't be serious. Noah, there isn't a tool that size on God's green earth!"

Noah was quick to reply, "Then it's a good thing its God's earth, because He is just going to have to create one." That all sounded well and good, but the reality was another matter. He really didn't know how he expected his father to find such an item.

Nathan had been hovering above the bunch, listening until this moment. He dropped down among them and said, "I must remind you, my friends, that the God who gives the call provides what is necessary to fulfill the call. It is His mission, and He takes on responsibility to see it carried out. We are all just a part of it. It does not depend on us. You may not know how He could provide, but provide He shall."

They all knew the truth of his words, surely, but the doubt lingered still. Methuselah got up from his grassy seat at this point, remarking, "Well, we will just have to step out on faith, then, into the unknown, as our forefather did." They all knew what he meant. Time and again he had told the story of his father being taken up from the earth, and he referenced it without fail anytime they feared the future. "Off we go," he proclaimed, taking Lamech by the arm as he headed to hitch up the ox and cart. The other man's eyes lowered in consternation, feeling as though he hadn't been given much choice in the matter, but he couldn't argue with truth.

Once on the road, the two men quickly found themselves squabbling over where on earth they might find what they needed. "We need to find some traders," Lamech was insisting. "If ever such a nonsense item as a giant auger exists, the traders will have it. Perhaps we might find someone traveling from the great mines of the north where a thing like that could be useful."

"And why, my wise son, would they bring it way down here to a place with a sum total of *two* sizeable mountains? They say *I* weave tall tales. At least my stories have sense to them!" Methuselah quipped. "No, a tool as Noah has described cannot be found. It must be *made*. We go to the iron-smiths of the East. Only Tubal-cain and his ilk could satisfy such a request."

"You want to go to *Assyria?* That's probably a week from here! And only the southern border, at that. There is no telling how long it would take us to reach Tubal-cain's lands." Though they had left Boaz behind - he was yet young enough to do a little hard labor - Methuselah felt like he was all too close. He could tell where the man got his impetuousness; it came honestly, straight from his father!

"I'm patient. I can wait." Methuselah said in a self-satisfied manner.

Lamech was positively fuming. "That's two weeks at least that they will be waiting on us! Do you really think Noah meant for us to take a vacation?"

"They'll have plenty to do. They'll probably take the better part of a year just cutting the wood. It should work out just fine." Methuselah was immovable when he had made a decision, especially if it made the most sense. Never mind that he always thought his own thoughts made the most sense.

Just then, they heard what sounded like a shout from behind a nearby hill to the side of the road. "Hey, quit jabbering and listen."

Methuselah whispered. Lamech immediately retorted, indignant, "So you get to wag your jaw until you're satisfied but I have to shut mine as soon as you have a new idea? I have already listened quite well - thank you - it's time for me to speak."

"No," his father pointed at the hill, "you need to shut your trap so we can hear what's going on over there. There may be danger afoot."

As he spoke, a sheep-dog crested the hill, running full tilt as though it were trying to escape from something. It wasn't long before another form appeared behind it, this time a human, hard on the chase. "It's just a shepherd chasing his spooked pet, are you happy?" Lamech said smugly. "Now, what was I saying?"

He didn't make it much further than that, because Methuselah wasn't there. The carpenter had already hopped off of the cart and was halfway towards the fleeing canine. He had in his hands a piece of fig that he had cut into so that its juices were dripping to the ground invitingly. Kneeling in his woolen smock, the old man paused directly in the dog's path and held out his sticky treat. Sure enough, the beast slowed its pace and ambled over, sniffing curiously. Once it was close enough, Methuselah grabbed hold of it and held onto it until its owner could catch up.

Shortly, the fellow came huffing and puffing up to Methuselah, struggling to both breathe and thank him simultaneously. "Thank you, kind sir, I can't tell you how important this is to me. That's my one good sheep dog, that is. I dunno what I would do without him." The man was a considerable height and admittedly had run what seemed a significant distance, but he also had the look of a man who spent a great deal of time sitting and eating when he wasn't following his sheep, being nearly as round as he was tall.

"It's no problem at all. How else were you going to catch it? Goodness, how far have you been chasing it?" Methuselah asked.

"Not sure, but it's been most of the morning. The sun is getting pretty high in the sky there and it wasn't hardly over the tops of them mountains when it first ran off." He replied, pointing at the peaks of southern Assyria to the east.

"And where is your flock then?" Lamech piped up, adding, "I'm Lamech, by the way, at your service."

"Oh they'll be a ways from here now. I come from Cush, out on the plains, you know, like most shepherd folk. Are you headed that way? I would dearly love a ride." He patted his stomach fondly. "It's hard to run so long when you've gotta lug this lot around."

"Well, we're actually headed - " Methuselah started, but Lamech interrupted him, seeing his opportunity, "Sure we can help! We have what we have by God's grace, and so it is available to you." He knew that his father wouldn't stop him if he blessed the man. It wasn't God's way to turn down those in need. And perhaps this could lead to a meeting with some traders. "Hop on!" he said, grabbing the man's arm to help him onto the cart.

"Don't mind if I do." The shepherd was beaming, clearly thankful for the chance to rest. He still hadn't quite caught his breath.

Methuselah didn't say a word for a few minutes, as he was frustrated about the change in plans but knew that his son had done what was right. He eventually repented for his attitude, accepting that God always reserved the right to change the plan, and struck up conversation with the man. He might as well be good company. "So, what's your name and who are your people?" Methuselah asked, white beard wagging.

"I am Timor son of Hanoa, and I belong to the clan of Jabal. We are a shepherding people, as you can see," he said happily, pulling at his drab sheepskin tunic. "We settled long ago in the land of Cush, and have built our homes and our cities there, on the plains and in the hills. Most of us farm as well, for wheat, corn, and the like."

"Yes, I know of Jabal," The old historian was intrigued, because Jabal was one of the three sons of innovation along with one Jubal and their other brother Tubal-cain, men who had formed entire civilizations by their God-given trade. He wondered if the man was still alive. He decided to see what else Timor knew. "So, is old Jabal still alive?"

"Oh, yes sir, alive and well! He lives on the plains with the rest of us. The sheep and other animals are his longtime companions. He's not far. I could take you to him, if that helps you. You have done right by me, after all, and more than right."

That sounded like a plan. The brother of Tubal-cain might well lead to just the sort of folk they were on the hunt for. So, they set off.

Two hours passed rather uneventfully. Timor, it turned out, while friendly, was not overly talkative. It seemed that shepherds weren't using to having to speak all that often. Seeing how long it was taking, though, the older men had to respect the shepherd's determination if not his personality; he really had chased the beast quite a ways! At long last, however, the horizon began to shift, losing the vague, shapeless quality it had maintained throughout the journey as small structures began to appear. They had arrived.

Jabal's historic settlement Elon was not much to look at if one was hoping for grand, sweeping city-scapes, but it was certainly a hub of activity for the region. Homes and shops of every type sprawled across the countryside, rising and falling with the rolling plain. The road that had been relatively empty prior to sighting the city quickly became busy with traffic of every kind: shepherds making their way into town for errands, craftsmen traveling to deliver their products, slave traders with their miserable cargo, and, thankfully, Lamech noted, merchants lugging their wares into town to make a sale. He spotted one fellow who looked particularly promising, carrying several cast-iron farm implements on a horse-drawn buggy, and turned the ox-cart to intercept him.

"Hullo there!" He called to the merchant, clearly startling him. He apparently didn't often sell things while moving. "My companion and I are looking for an iron auger. Do you have one?" To his delight the man slowed the buggy and proceeded to pull back a tarp, assuring them he had just the thing. Lamech chuckled slightly, winking at his father in an I-told-you-so sort of way. His chuckle, however, quickly turned into a grunt of dissatisfaction when the trader pulled out a fine piece of craftsmanship roughly the size of his forearm. "Ah, no thank you. We need something a bit bigger," he grumbled, slapping the reins to get the ox back in motion.

"Why did you leave Lamech? That was perfect - if we wanted to build a model ark to see if it will float!" Methuselah laughed good-naturedly.

Timor had been in the back sleeping by this point, but awoke with a start when the cart ground to a halt. "Are we here already? My, your ox is fast." He muttered sleepily. Father and son exchanged wry glances, and the older responded, "Right. So, where are we headed? We need to drop you off and find Jabal."

"Oh, you've already passed where I live by about a mile." He looked so innocent, unaware of how much their blood pressure was rising. He stretched, "Anyway, it's no bother, I can walk. I feel nice and rested now! Anyway, what's all this about finding Jabal? Is it to do with that 'ogre' thing you fellows were talking about with the salesman?"

"It's called an 'auger', but yes, we want to speak with him to see if he knows of any of Tubal-cain's kin who are nearby. We need an ironsmith to make a very special tool." Methuselah answered him.

"I see! Right, well, I will lead you to him. I know where he lives." The shepherd responded cheerfully. It seemed like the best plan available to them, so the two gratefully accepted his offer and rolled away into the heart of the city. Perhaps God was leading them, Lamech thought. He did like to do these sorts of things, surprising them with answers to their prayers where they weren't looking for them.

CHAPTER 9

It Takes Two

DARKNESS SURROUNDED MICAH. Though his enemies had covered his eyes before transporting him here, he could feel the moisture in the air and drop in temperature, and he knew that they must have taken him underground. There were countless mining tunnels laced beneath Tubal-cain's lands, so he had no doubt he'd been deposited in one of those. Not even a trace of ambient light could find its way that deep into the earth. He was slightly concerned about the situation, but not for his own safety. He would endure any trial for the sake of his King, but he feared being away from Noah and his mission too long. With these thoughts in mind, he sent up a prayer to God, eagerly asking for aid.

A hand suddenly grabbed hold of the blindfold around his eyes and ripped it away, revealing, at first, nothing. Then, the room exploded with light as his foes assumed spirit form, first one fallen angel bright as a star

- and beautiful, at that - then the all-too-familiar horned silhouette of Moloch, glowing red-gold like the embers of a dying fire. The first appeared to be the one known as Beelzebub or Baal, the so-called "lord of the heavens". Demons really were a pretentious lot. These two were followed shortly by another pair of shining forms that he did not immediately recognize.

For a few moments they just stared, baleful eyes boring into him. If it was intimidation tactic, it wasn't working. He had faced their kind on innumerable occasions and did not fear their wrath. He spoke first, "So, are we waiting for tea or is there a better reason you're all sitting there ogling at me? This is hardly a way to entertain guests. Surely your master taught you as much. He schmoozes with the best of them; does he not?" He said this last with more intention than perhaps the demons realized, aware that they were not fans of being called the Satan's servants. Each of them saw themselves as the absolute pinnacle of creation, and it irked them to no end to be thought of as lesser than anyone.

Moloch wasn't one to take insult well, so he couldn't help himself. He immediately retorted, "We are no slaves. We are lords of our own domain, and all flesh serves us. The world obeys our will."

"Are you sure? From my point of view it sure looked like you jumped when Lucifer said jump at that meeting tonight." Micah was enjoying himself - just a bit - but, more importantly, he was playing for time.

"You miserable worm, I will crush you!" Moloch boomed, bounding across the room, sword in hand. Micah dodged the intended blow, slipping to the side, and planted a kick right in the small of his massive back, sending him careening into the rock wall. The demon picked himself up, furious and ready for another pass, but he was stopped by the voice of Beelzebub, calm and cold. "Stop. We didn't bring him here to have a wrestling match. He has information that we need." Moloch was practically snarling by this point, but he paused, chest heaving, and stepped to the side, seemingly content to wait for his revenge.

Micah chuckled. They could not kill him, and if they thought he was going to reveal anything to them, they were even bigger fools than he would have imagined.

Beelzebub heard the angel, and responded confidently, "You do not fear us? Oh, but you should." He smiled. "We are far more inventive than you might imagine." He snapped his fingers, and one of the other demons took to flight, streaking towards the entrance into the darkness. At this point, Micah did feel a stab of worry. This was not going as he had expected, and these enemies were ruthless; their evil knew no bounds.

Shortly, the demonic errand-boy arrived back in the room, but he was not alone. Behind him tromped a young girl, shivering and frightened. Micah was certain it had been one of the same serving girls he had seen at the leadership gathering. What were they planning to do with her? Then his heart sank. Following the girl was a large, burly soldier, eyes gleaming with unholy desire in the light of the torch he carried. The scene of his shadow and hers playing along the wall was reminiscent of a nightmare, like a child being chased by a ferocious beast. The demon stopped, whispering into the soldier's ear, and he stopped as well, satisfied that the two were at last out of earshot from the mine entrance. The soldier unsheathed his weapon, running his finger along the edge of the blade to test its sharpness. He was intimidating her, but there was no telling what he was about to do.

Micah tore his eyes away from the ghastly display, aware he had only moments to act. His spirit was in turmoil, and he prayed earnestly but could not help but feel the pressure to do something himself rather than wait for God. "Leave her be," he said, forcefully somehow despite being bound. "What do you want?"

Beelzebub raised an eyebrow. "Not so confident anymore, are we? As I thought. Your pathetic sympathy for these human scum makes you weak. This was almost too easy." He motioned to his minion who began to spew words of guilt at the soldier that had already come so far towards his attempted conquest. Micah could hear some of it. "You pitiful wretch! Stooping to treason to satisfy your urges! This servant belongs to your King! You call yourself a man of honor. You can't even control yourself..." and on it went, stopping the man long enough for Beelzebub to interrogate Micah. How typical it all was. Their ilk could manipulate a man to make himself god one minute, demanding worship from the world, then move him to such depths of self-loathing that he ended his own life the next. It was despicable, and, the humans' response was so tragically predictable.

"I'll get to the point then," the lead demon drawled. "We know that the Enemy is forever scheming to destroy our plans, however much He seems to fail at it. As evidenced by your presence here tonight, he is certainly aware of our current venture. So, despite my severe doubt that

He can do anything to stop us, Lucifer and others, myself included, would like to know what your Master is working on. You know, the best defense is a good offense, and all that. We feel we deserve a sporting chance to counter-attack."

Micah's own mission was now at stake, and the lives of Noah and his family would be in danger if he spoke a word of God's plan. Was it right to open all of them up to harm in order to save one girl? These were God's chosen to rebuild the future, after all. This girl would surely perish with the rest...But then there was God's spirit in him again, forever crying that He loved the people, her included. Every last one of these humans made in God's image was precious to Him. So what was he to do?

Meanwhile, Moloch and his cronies were growing impatient, looking more eager for blood by the second. Micah feared they might just kill the girl for the sick enjoyment of it. "I'm waiting," Beelzebub said, tapping his foot. "My friend here can only *influence* the decision of the soldier - remember - not stop him if he decides to act. The fellow does look rather confused at this point, doesn't he? There is no telling what he might do!" His thin lips split into a frightening grin.

Just as Micah was about to burst from anxiety, a burst of light illuminated the room, and the demon who had been tormenting the soldier flew from his feet as if hit by a bolt of lightning. There, standing next to the man was Nathan, clothed in white light and forming a living barrier between him and the servant girl. It was a good thing too, because at that moment, the man swung his sword, enraged by his guilt and confusion to a point where he wanted to destroy the source of his frustration - her. His sword stopped in mid-air, parried by Nathan's light dagger, and it must have seemed a miracle to the man, who panicked and dropped his weapon, unable to see the source of his failure. He muttered something about the girl being cursed by the gods and fled the mine with the torch, leaving her to fend for herself in the darkness.

As Beelzebub stared in stunned disbelief, a fiery axe came flying at him from high overhead, and Micah knew Gurion had arrived as well. God had answered his call! The lion-angel's axe missed its mark as the demon sidestepped, but it was only a distraction. Strong hands gripped Micah's bonds at just that moment and wrenched them apart, freeing him for battle. Now it was a fair fight. The lead angel would have embraced his brother, but there was no chance. Enemies were already swarming towards them. Tossing him a light spear, Gurion rushed to meet the onslaught.

Micah hefted his spear, called out to Nathan, "Take the girl to the surface! We can handle this until you return," and dove into the fray. Nathan had seen the young woman cowering in the corner, weeping and crying out for help. She could not even see enough in the cave to make her way towards the exit. The kind angel went to her, telling her spirit the way out. Then, knowing she would probably think it was her own thought, he flew ahead, shining enough light to show her where to go.

Micah rushed to head off the stunned demon and his heretofore inactive partner as they attempted to chase the serving girl. He caught the first by surprise just before it reached the foot of the tunnel, crashing into it so hard it was knocked from its feet a second time. Then, aware he had milliseconds before the other demon was upon him, he turned just in time to parry a blow aimed right at his head. Returning blow for blow, he swept the shining demon's legs out from under him and thrust him through the heart, slicing deep into his ethereal form. Now, angels could not die, but they could most certainly suffer. Holy fire coursed through the weapon forged by the Lord's word, and it latched onto the demon's body, tormenting him like a physical wound. That one would surely flee when he was able, so Micah turned his attention behind him.

There, beset on both sides, was Gurion, whirling about with two axes now as he faced the wrath of both Moloch and Beelzebub. He was holding his own, but the tide seemed as if it might turn soon enough. These were demon lords, and their strength was not to be underestimated. The moment Micah looked, he saw a blow land on the lion's shoulder, though he did not flinch, and the angel knew he had to help his compatriot. Acting in the quickest way possible, he hurled his spear with all his might just as Beelzebub's back turned towards him, and it met its mark, striking him square in the shoulder blade. The demon howled in pain, and Gurion took the brief reprieve to turn on Moloch, giving him his full attention.

The two warriors battled fiercely, weapons whirling for several minutes, neither able to gain the upper hand. Micah was not worried. Gurion had never been bested in single combat. He wouldn't start now. He looked at Beelzebub and made his way towards him. The demon lord had immediately grasped the light spear with both hands and yanked it out of his body. It seemed he would not fall so easily. Sword at the ready,

Micah advanced, a dreadful gleam of confidence in his eyes. He knew when he had won. Beelzebub seemed to know as well, because he took one step towards Micah as though he was going to throw the spear, then, feinting, sprinted out of the cave. The fiends were forever eager to save their own skin. True comradeship was foreign to them.

At first, Micah wondered what had brought on the sudden surge of cowardice, but he didn't wonder long as another light settled down beside him. Nathan was back! He gave him a thankful look, communicating more than words could say, and the two moved on to help Gurion finish the job. Above, the two arch enemies were locked in perpetual combat. Seeing Gurion's face flushed with excitement, the angels actually wondered whether they should leave him to it. Nathan shouted up at him, "Hey brother! You look like you're enjoying this a bit much! Have you finally met your match?"

Gurion, thankfully, was too focused on gaining the advantage to look down at them, but he replied boastfully, "Not hardly. We are just having a bit of fun." Seeing the lion's teeth bared with concentration, they laughed. At the sound, Moloch paused momentarily, looking away long enough to see them below - it seemed as if for the first time. Then, barely missing his head being clipped by Gurion's flailing axe, he ducked under the big angel and fled as well. He was the only one of his party left in the cave, and even in his manic anger he appeared to have recognized defeat. Panting, Gurion dropped to the ground to join the others.

"He got away. Have you lost your touch? Gone soft?" Micah quipped, slapping Gurion on the shoulder. Gurion winced, reminding Micah of his wounds, and said embarrassedly, "No, I let him go. Just letting him recover so we can go another round when he's fresh. He does fight better than most of those imps."

"Right...right. Well, let's be off. Duty never sleeps, my friends." Micah looked at Nathan questioningly. "You took care of the girl?"

"Yes, she is safe and sound in her bed, though perhaps a bit the worse for wear. I do fear for Noah and the family, however. We need to get back."

As they had journeyed into the heart of Elon, Methuselah and Lamech discovered just how different a city could be in the land of Cush. One moment they would be right in the midst of the hustle and bustle of traffic and trade, then the next few they'd travel across vast, open acreage with nothing but livestock-laden plains as far as the eye could see. After what seemed like ages, they arrived at their destination. Jabal's home was an astonishing array of colors, a patchwork display of blues, greens and golds. Vibrant tents spread out in all directions with sheepskin-clad residents spilling out of them in far less garish clothing. Street vendors hawked their goods on the corners, accosting the people with a variety of fantastic fare, while the occasional goat or sheep ambled through, munching on stray morsels. "There she is. Our leader's camp." Timor sighed. "Beautiful, isn't it?"

"You could say that..." Lamech sounded noncommittal. "Why is it so...bright?"

"Because it's pretty, of course. Jabal likes pretty things - and food: only the best food." The shepherd grinned, patting his belly, "We all do!"

And he paid a pretty penny for it too, no doubt. So that was why all the merchants were passing through. They could count on this Jabal character to buy the finest textiles and delicacies that any land had to offer. Methuselah just hoped that the leader also had a penchant for buying custom-made iron tools for his farms; a cute tent and a bite to eat wasn't going to help them build an ark.

It was time to cut to the chase. "Alright, so where do we find your fearless leader?" Lamech asked before Methuselah had a chance. His hair was shining silvery gray in the light of the setting sun, and his father was reminded just how old they both were getting. Truly these were the twilight years of their lives. Perhaps he should be more understanding of the haste he found in Lamech and Boaz. Maybe they just wanted to make life count before it passed them by.

"Oh he's right over there." Timor pointed a thick finger vaguely at a massive canary yellow tent that rose several feet above the rest. Then, he promptly hopped off the cart and started away towards the street vendors. "I wish you fellows well," he called over his shoulder. "It's time to eat!"

The two looked at each other. *That* was why Timor had been so eager to take them to Jabal. He wanted a free ride to stuff his gullet. Selfishness knew no bounds. Methuselah broke the silence. "Let's get moving then. No time to lose." His son smiled, and they made their way towards Jabal, leaving the cart outside with the dog in the back. Timor must not be too worried about losing his dog again if he was willing to leave it behind like that.

In the yellow tent, the duo were surprised further still by what they saw. The walls were festooned with tapestries, each depicting a different aspect of pastoral life, and dyed silk drapes covered every entryway. More interesting still was the populace. The tent was alive with every farm animal known to man: pigs, cows, asses, hens, and, of course, the ever-present sheep - all with human attendants to feed and stroke them. What an odd way to live! The unique environment had Methuselah wondering just what sort of man it was they were about to meet, but he wasn't left waiting long. Behind the curtained entryway to their immediate right a bawdy voice cried out, "More cake!" That sure-enough sounded like someone in charge to them, so they followed the voice.

They were soon greeted with yet another intriguing sight. A robust, jolly fellow with auburn hair was stuffing his face with a golden-brown cake, eyes glazed over with bliss as his fingers dripped honey onto the table before him. "Mm, delightful, simply delightful!" He mumbled through mouthfuls of cake, crumbs dropping to the floor where eager piglets awaited to clean up the mess. "We will have to make this a regular affair - yes indeed!"

Servants were scurrying to and fro juggling half-finished dishes and other treats, while a sizeable gathering of folk ate around the large circular table at which Jabal sat as the head. Fearing they were interrupting something, the carpenters considered leaving until the meal was finished, but the leader spotted them from his raised seat and bade them enter before they could make a decision either way. "Come in, come in. I don't believe I have seen you before! Are you traders come to sell me some special item? I do enjoy traders." He called from across the room.

A bit taken-aback, Methuselah did some quick thinking and responded, "Greetings! Ah, no, not exactly, my lord, we are actually on a search for a special item ourselves. But on our journey we found one of your citizenry in distress, a shepherd named Timor who had lost his dog, and we brought him home to Cush." The leader looked at him for a moment as if sizing him up, and said, "And the dog?"

"Ah, I'm sorry my lord, the dog?"

"Yes, what happened to the dog?"

"Oh, yes, well, he is just fine, sleeping in the cart. We fed him some fruit and he passed right out. He'd been running all day it seems." The carpenter was mystified. He'd said all that and the man was concerned about a dog?

"Excellent! Then I welcome you to our great city with open arms!" Jabal exclaimed, clearly relieved and thankful. He motioned to a servant, "Go and take the dog. He has a new home now." The servant then scrambled off to see it done. What an oddball. The man practically worshiped animals.

"Come, join us for a bite to eat and a story 'round the fire. Perhaps then we can speak of this special item you seek." Thankful for the man's graciousness, though still a bit flabbergasted at what had prompted it, the two older men accompanied him and the dinner party outside to an already roaring fire, no doubt prepared by the servants who had left while they'd been speaking. Jabal waved towards a fallen tree trunk that served for seating and said, "Sit, please, and hear a tale of our people."

As soon as everyone had settled, a gaudily-clad servant leaped over the log into their midst and began to weave an incredible yarn about how the city had come into being. It started with a man called Abel offering a sacrifice of the first of his flock to God, so Methuselah's interest was piqued, as he thought perhaps they had a genuine story of history that he could record for the future. However, the experience quickly turned sour as the man spoke of how Abel in his great wisdom had then tricked God into blessing him above his brother Cain. Furious, God had stricken Abel down in judgment and given the riches of Abel to Cain and his sons, one of whom was Lamech, Jabal's father. Jabal had then grown in power and wisdom all his life, becoming such a friend to the animals that it was said he could speak to them in their very soul, and he had built this great empire which they now saw, following the way of Abel, his ancestor, who had been smart enough to trick God.

"What a load of utter nonsense!" The historian muttered to his son, seething with anger. "Abel was not a trickster, and Cain was cursed because he disobeyed his God. These fools would destroy the truth!" Because it looked as though he was about to get up and make a scene, Lamech grabbed his father and tried to calm him. "Father, please, quiet down. Do you think you will be able to change their mind? This is *their* history, true or not. They will believe as they always have."

"There is only one truth. God's truth! Man ruins everything. *Everything!*" Methuselah would not be put off. Seeing that there was no way to stop him, Lamech instead decided to reason with him. "Father, listen, if you get up there and give them a slap to the jaw that isn't going to change their minds, and, what's more, it's going to get us thrown out or killed, and where will God's mission be then? Noah needs us. If you want to obey God, you need to stop and think about what matters most here." His father's breathing slowed as he considered these words. Then, Lamech had a sudden idea. "You know, if you want to influence them and give them some truth, you could volunteer to tell them a story. It wouldn't be offensive, because this is the arena for that. Perhaps it would ingratiate us with the big one over there," he said, gesturing towards the rotund form of Jabal not far from them, laughing merrily at the story he had probably heard a thousand times before.

Methuselah liked that idea. He was about to ask Jabal for permission to do just that, when the jovial leader turned and accosted him first. "So, about this 'special item' you seek. What exactly are you looking for?"

They hadn't expected him to stop the festivities to ask them that, but it seemed like an opportunity, so Methuselah spoke up. "Well, you see, we are carpenters by trade, and we have a very...um...large project that we need to complete. For this, we need an auger, and it needs to be approximately the size of a small man. Therein lies the trouble in us finding it. We hoped that you might - "

"Oh, I know an iron-smith who can take care of that for you. Tubal-cain is my brother you know!" Jabal interrupted him to say. Before Methuselah could even thank him, however, he brought up what might have been expected. "How do you intend to pay for such an item? And for this, ah, service I have provided you in helping you find it." There was the rub. The two men had brought enough money to secure their prize but had not expected to have to bribe a portly aristocrat on top of it.

Lamech was the one quick on his toes this time. "We did bring some carpentry tools in the cart. Perhaps we can make you something? Anything you desire, if you provide the wood. We are masters of our craft, as you appear to be a master of husbandry." Jabal pondered this offer for a moment, then his fat face split into a grin. The flattery must have gone a long way. "That sounds perfectly reasonable to me! I have long desired a new chair, a throne of sorts, if I may be so bold as to say." He cast a quick, baleful glance around at his subjects as if daring them to say anything, since he was not, exactly, a king, then turned back towards the carpenters and dismissed them with a wave. "Go ahead, fetch your tools and you can begin. I look forward to this!"

Methuselah stayed, doing his best to appear entertained for his host, while Lamech hobbled off to get the tools. However, it was not long before he returned empty-handed, and Methuselah knew that they were in deep trouble. Lamech had stepped in unnoticed at first, so he whispered to his father, "They're gone! Some fool from this infernal land of color has stolen our tools! What do we do?" He sounded desperate, having surely driven himself into a panic the entire trip back to the fire.

The older man was silent for a moment, then winked at his son as if having had an epiphany. "We use what we've got." He got up just then, seeing that the gathering had reached the end of yet another bout of entertainment. Signaling to Jabal, he sidled over to him and told him what had happened. "They've stolen our tools, sir, so, regrettably, we cannot build you your throne. However, I am renowned in my land as a storyteller. I am, in fact, the first historian of all mankind. Might we propose a trade? Your connection with the metalworkers in exchange for the most fantastic story you've ever heard, and a true one no less!" He bowed with a flourish, and awaited the leader's answer. Lamech laughed to himself at this absurd proposal, even more so at the veiled jab his father had made about the falsehood of the other stories in relation to his "'true'" one. His laughter didn't last long though, as he realized they'd likely be hanged if this did not go well.

Jabal eventually gave Methuselah a curt nod, his curiosity clearly piqued. The storyteller wasted no time, eager to impress the gathering before he lost the leader's interest and to gain their prize. He then introduced himself to the crowd, "My name is Methuselah, and I am the oldest man alive and the world's first historian, the keeper of its deepest secrets." He clearly couldn't know if this was the case, but it sounded good, and he'd never met anyone older - or another historian, for that matter. Lamech admired his boldness. "Now, sit back and enjoy the fire while I regale you with the greatest tale ever told." He had their attention.

"In eternity past, before all things, there was God, the greatest and most powerful of beings. He was there, Father, Son, and Spirit, three people as one God, forever in community, forever in love. They had everything they needed, even though nothing had yet been made. Now, as we all know, " Methuselah looked about the room at each person, "all good things are greatest when shared. And so, God decided to share the love and community that he had with beings of his own making - his children, if you will. This is where we come into the story. God made the first man, Adam, and his wife, Eve, to be a unit of love together and to share His love as He poured it out on them in immeasurable generosity. He gave them the whole world, everything you see around you: the trees, the sky, the rivers upon which we all depend, and the animals for whom we care so deeply." He leveled this last comment directly at Jabal.

"They had everything they needed for a good life, and he even put them in a garden where there was no death, no pain, and even a tree that would allow them to live forever. Can you imagine that?" He said to the audience, touching his white hair. "What's more, God gave the man and woman authority over the earth to do with it as they saw fit, to take care of it and to subdue it. Everything God had was theirs for the taking. As are all relationships, his relationship with them was built on trust. So, he gave them a choice, allowing them to choose against him, or for him. He told them there was a tree of which they should never eat, or they would surely die."

He paused, then said, "Now, I don't know about you, but I think I would listen to the God who made me and choose not to eat of a tree that would kill me. But, instead, they doubted God, and trusted themselves more than Him. In fact, they went so far as to trust a serpent above the God who made them, allowing a beast of the field to beguile them into believing lies. That great enemy, Satan, lies to us still today, stealing life and joy from us with half-truths that invade our minds and hearts." He let this sink in.

"Needless to say, the outcome was disaster. God found them whilst they hid from him in shame, already experiencing the broken fellowship with one another and with him that God had promised would follow such a choice. They would never again enjoy unblemished communion with each other again, but would forever be destined to argue and lie, to steal and to cheat, to blame one another for their faults. Because they had authority over the earth, the world and all that fills it was cursed along with mankind, never again to be a paradise. So, in order to protect the world from being forever ruled by evil caretakers, God cast the man and woman from the garden, away from the tree of life. There it stands, guarded by flaming swords covered in God's holy fire even to this day, a forever reminder of what we have lost. God did not leave us, though, without a promise. Now, we wait, until that day when our Lord will himself send a servant, the seed of the woman, to crush the head of the great serpent Satan."

The historian was exuberant by this point, filled with passion for the subject he most dearly loved, but he resisted the urge to yank the rug out from under their Cain and Abel story. The two carpenters had made it a long way towards their goal, and that would surely ruin the whole effort. So, he finished reluctantly with, "And so we come to the other story of the night, the tragedy of Adam and Eve's first children, Cain and Abel, that your people related so...creatively." He bowed again and took his seat.

Silence reigned for a time, and Lamech wondered whether they hadn't struck the wrong chord. Eventually, though, Jabal began to clap, an action which was followed quickly by a smattering of applause from all around the campfire. Thank God! They had enjoyed it! At this moment, however, Methuselah began to have thoughts that would not quite ever fade, deep thoughts that moved his soul. Clearly these people did not remember the old stories, had not had them passed down from generation to generation as had the line of Seth, their forefather. No wonder they were steeped in lies! No one was there to tell them the truth. Understanding this, the historian's heart moved from judgment to pity.

Jabal lifted a hand to command silence, and announced, "Truly, you have kept your word. That was a most fantastic story, and one I have not heard the like in a great many years. It does remind me of something..." His voice trailed off as he became lost in thought, but he caught himself quickly enough, and said what they had longed to hear. "You may have your iron-smith. I will see to it that work begins on your requested piece immediately. You shall have it by tomorrow evening, if not sooner." Then, yawning, he finished, motioning to some servants, "Now, I'm off to bed. Make sure that these honored guests have accommodations for the night."

So that was that. Father and son rejoiced together aloud, unashamed, as they were led to a small, makeshift tent that it seemed had been erected in a relative hurry. "That was absolutely amazing, Father!" Lamech gushed. "God is so good. You gave them the truth, and they *loved* it! He must really be behind us in our mission." Methuselah was ecstatic, but pensive about the state of Jabal's people. "Yes, son, He is. He absolutely is. Let's get some rest, I'm sure it's certain to be a long day."

CHAPTER 10

Casting Stones

THE DAY AFTER THAT EVENTFUL EVENING with Jabal's court passed in a blur for Lamech and Methuselah. They spent most of it searching for their stolen tools without much luck, before eventually meeting with some good news in the form of a servant sent by Jabal. It seemed that the metalworker of which Jabal had spoken was an avid fan of good stories and had been present at the campfire gathering the night before. He had been so inspired by the tale that he had rushed home immediately and gotten right to work on their auger, unable to sleep. What good fortune! God was blessing them yet again.

Eager to see their trophy, the companions hurried behind the servant through the streets back towards the smithy which seemed to be near that great yellow monstrosity of a tent. Of course the pampered fool would have an iron-smith ready on hand. He had everything else available to him. On the way, however, the men were stopped by a ruckus taking place in the street outside the tent.

A young woman was kneeling in the midst of a crowd of angry men, her face and hair bowed to the dirt. Her dress was torn and she was covered in dust, obviously having been tossed to the earth rather roughly if the scratches were any sign, but was yet stunningly beautiful. Her tanned skin and dark hair framed a face flowering in its youth, and Methuselah could see that her rich brown eyes had both sadness and strength in them. What was going on?

At that moment, the crowd parted, revealing none other than the great leader Jabal himself. It seemed that he also had a bone to pick with the woman. Looking at her with utter disgust, he abruptly turned his gaze away, towards the people, and spoke to them as though she was not present. "This woman has been found guilty of adultery and whoredom. By the laws of our land, she is to be stoned without mercy, and it is the duty of this people to see it carried out." His words stirred up the crowd, and they cried out for her blood. These people were sick. Did they have any proof of this?

Methuselah spoke up, and Lamech knew that their brief period of favor with the lord of the land was going to end shortly. "Ahem! What of witnesses? Do people get stoned in this land without the evidence of two or three witnesses?" The bold proclamation startled Jabal, but Methuselah softened it by adding, "I am a foreigner, after all, and do not understand your customs."

Jabal didn't even have to respond. Immediately, two men came up ne xt to him ready for a

fight, both of whom Methuselah remembered from the dinner table the night before. They battled to speak first, with one - a rather ugly fellow - shouting, "She was betrothed to me! And she was seen with a man last night, only weeks before we were to be wed!" The other quickly followed up with, "I saw it! I saw the two in the act!" Methuselah was old, and had seen many men like these. He didn't believe them for a moment.

"And where is the man with whom she was found?" He questioned them. What utter hypocrisy to have her stand trial alone if there was a man involved in the act! Methuselah doubted there was at all, however, and that was the point. The two men looked flabbergasted, annoyed at having their swift and certain execution put off. They had clearly not expected to have to defend their conclusions. The second witness piped up, "Yes, well, he ran when we found them, and we have been unable to locate him." The other added, "And it was dark, so we did not see who it was. But justice must be done!" He shouted, hoping to rile the crowd back up. So these two had it in for this woman, for whatever reason. No doubt the fellow shouting about his betrothal had another woman on his mind and wanted to be rid of this one.

Methuselah could see that the people did not take much convincing to desire bloodshed. So, he did the only thing he could think of at the moment. "What if she were to be wed to another? What if someone could forgive her, and take her as his own wife? Then he could redeem her." Even the crowd grew silent when they heard these words. It was evident that no one had ever made such a wild proposal. Jabal finally spoke again. "And who would be so foolish as to shame their name to accomplish such a redemption. You, old man?" He laughed, but it was forced. It seemed he also was not eager to see this woman dead, but was playing his part as leader, and that was more important to him than her life.

"Well, no, not exactly." Methuselah laughed right along with him, just to lighten the tension. "But I do have three young grandsons, and I can promise you that one of them would gladly take this lovely young lady as their wife." He then threw in some humor, "It's hard to find a good one in our neck of the land. Small towns and all that..." Lamech was sweating at this point. They were playing a dangerous game here.

The two men who had put themselves forward as witnesses were fuming, but they dared not speak out whilst Methuselah addressed Jabal directly. Jabal's reply was slow and deliberate, "Very well. You may have her, but I want you all gone from this place within the hour. It brings us shame even to look upon her!" With that, he turned and stormed back into his tent, leaving the crowd and so-called witnesses gaping in disbelief. Methuselah and Lamech were ecstatic! They were alive, and had successfully accomplished a daring rescue! Talk about God's favor!

It didn't take long for the crowd to dissipate and return to their daily grind. Apparently a public execution was prime entertainment, but once the prospect of violence had passed, no one cared a whit about the woman involved. Walking up to her slowly, Methuselah offered her his hand. She looked at him with tired eyes, and he thought he could see the mistrust in them. Still, she took his hand, standing to her feet.

"My name is Methuselah," the old man said, face crinkling into a smile. She didn't think she'd ever seen that many wrinkles on a person in her entire life. "And this is my son, Lamech," he said, gesturing to a bent, graying man who looked nearly older than he did. She wasn't sure about these two; she had been betrayed so many times, she doubted anyone had truly honorable intentions. She had learned this well over her short life. Seeing kindness in the eyes of the one called Methuselah gave her hope, however, enough that she decided to see where this would lead.

She spoke, carefully at first, "I am Naamah. Thank you, for your kindness." As the men didn't immediately request something of her, she continued, more boldly this time. "They would have killed me without hesitation, the savages, and my brother wouldn't have batted an eye."

"Your brother?" Methuselah was confused.

"Yes, Jabal is my brother. You know, the fat one, ruler of the city?" She said cynically. Seeing their dumbstruck faces, she continued, "Surprising, is it? Sadly, it shouldn't be. He lives for himself. He cares more about what he's having for dinner tomorrow than he does about me. I wouldn't doubt that he'd pick up a stone and join them if he wasn't a coward."

After taking a moment to let it soak in, Lamech replied with considerable compassion in his voice. "Then it's a good thing we came along. God has spared your life this day, because you are precious to Him."

Naamah didn't know how to take those words. He could tell that she wasn't used to hearing such things. Her reply was noncommittal, "I don't know of any God who cares for me, or any person, for that matter." She didn't want to sound ungrateful, but she could not find it in herself to believe him.

Methuselah saw that they needed to get to know her a bit better. She wasn't easily persuaded. "Was the man lying a moment ago? About being betrothed to you, I mean?" He asked.

"No, unfortunately. I was to be married to him in two weeks as he said. It's hard for a woman in this town. You need a man to have a place in society. He was a pig, but he was my ticket to a better life. Then he turns around and drops me for another tart who laughs more at his sick jokes. But he can't be seen committing adultery, so he hangs his sin on me. Sound about right?" She looked hard at them for a moment, no doubt slightly angry at them just for being men as she aired out her frustrations. "You know, I was almost glad it happened, because I knew I wouldn't have to be saddled to that beast the rest of my life." She sighed, "Thank you again for your kindness. I wish you well on your journey," and abruptly turned and began to walk away towards the open road.

Methuselah was torn. He was sure God had brought them here for this precise moment, to intervene in this woman's life, but he knew it was absurd to ask her to travel with them across the countryside, two utter strangers, and *men* at that. What else could he do?

"Wait, Naamah." He called out, before she had gone far. She turned towards him, expectant, but didn't move from her place. "I wasn't lying about my three grandsons...They are the sort of men who would welcome a woman like you into their lives, and not just them - the whole family would."

Her response was cold. "I don't think you know me very well, then. Besides, I'm not interested in being married off to someone I've never even met. I can only imagine how that will turn out, if *this* is what I hand-picked." She motioned vaguely to the yellow tent where her previous suitor had fled.

Abashed, Methuselah blushed, and quickly stuttered, "I didn't mean that, my dear. I simply want to offer you a new start, somewhere where no one knows your name or sees you as less than you are. You can make your own impression, and be judged by your actions instead of your reputation. If you aren't interested in any one of my grandsons, nothing would change. You could leave us and start a life in Kadish or wherever else you like, and we would help you however we can."

There was a glimmer of hope in the young woman's eyes, but he could tell that she thought it sounded too good to be true. Still, he prayed that God would give her enough faith to step out and see. They would take good care of her.

"What do you say? Can you tolerate a couple of old fogies on the road? We could drop you off anywhere if you decide you want that, and you'll have had a free ride." Lamech reached out a hand towards her, beckoning. He knew this was right, too.

Naamah was still filled with doubt, but as she thought on what was next for her, she knew she had no better options. Why not take a risk? She was pretty certain she could handle a couple of old men if they gave her any trouble. She was independent and would not appear weak, so, gathering whatever strength she had left, she replied assertively, "I will go."

Clapping his hands in excitement, Lamech shuffled over to help her onto the ox-cart. She softened as he neared, thankful to be appreciated.

"Lamech was my father's name, you know. But he was not a good man...he only wanted sons. And I only wanted a father." Methuselah winked at Lamech, and shouted jovially, "God is a good Father. The best! You'll see. Now, let's see that smithy and be on the road! I've had more than enough of this town."

After the cart was hitched up and the trio began rumbling down the road, Methuselah couldn't shake the feeling that this was the beginning of something. God had given a person hope through them, and hope was scarce in the world. People needed that. Perhaps his purpose was to provide that to them, to give them the good news of a God that cared for them. Maybe God was only judging the world because people didn't know how good He was. If they only knew Him, they would follow Him, surely.

Noah was tired: tired of doubting God's word, tired of believing it, and tired of pouring countless, sweat-laden hours of work into the ark he was supposed to build. He was tired of trying to convince everyone else it was the right thing, as well. His sons came to him often asking him hard questions: What if the flood didn't come? What if it did, and they didn't find wives first? Noah didn't know what to do any better than they did. He just knew what God had said. Judgement was coming, and they needed to get this ark done to save themselves. *That*, he could get behind. Protecting his family was nearly all that mattered to him - and honoring God. That was important. It was.

If it wasn't for the fact that God had sent actual angelic messengers to confirm his word, they would have probably quit already, but He had, and who could doubt their own eyes? Yet, day to day, they were beginning to doubt even that. They had not seen the lead angel since the day of the visit, and they hadn't seen any of them since the first few days after that. Noah knew that God was not in the habit of letting angels hang around chatting with humans all the time - or, at least, he thought that was the case - but he couldn't help but feel as though the family needed the extra support of their eyes to believe. Besides, those angels had been incredibly helpful when they needed them to lift heavy pieces of the ark - and that was becoming more and more often.

Still, every time he wanted to quit, God would remind him of all that He had done for the family. He was their hope, their refuge, their very present help in times of trouble - and this was such a time. His wife would tell him the same. Leah was forever faithful, always speaking a word of encouragement in the darkest hour. Yet, even she was beginning to waver in her own heart as she considered how much her sons were going to suffer if they had to leave everything they had ever known and watch it be destroyed. How would that affect them? How could she trust that everything was going to be alright, when, literally, nothing was going to be alright except they themselves and some animals, according to God's word?

The only ones who seemed to have any sort of joy around the compound was Tabitha and Japheth, as their newfound love blossomed before everyone's eyes. It was a continual source of encouragement for the whole bunch as they all stumbled in, weary and bone sore for dinner each evening. Nothing could stomp out love, not even the threat of losing all they knew - and that message raised spirits. Yet, it comforted only those who had experienced love themselves. For the other two brothers, the romance was rather a continual reminder that the world was ending as they knew it and they had not found love. It made it hard for them to believe as well.

It was during one such evening that Ham spoke up. "What on earth are we doing?" He had hardly touched his meal, and his father had noticed that his work had been less than stellar earlier in the day. Looking around, the young man saw confused faces, but received no response. "I say to you, what are we doing, laboring day and night to build a massive ship that could hold an entire city when there isn't even a lake nearby - let alone an ocean that might cover the earth?" His face was livid. "This makes no sense, and I'm tired of it. I'm tired of long days and rough, aching nights, of having to eat like paupers because we spend so much time building that we don't have time to farm."

Noah responded, dejected but attempting to lead him, "Son, we are trying to obey the Lord's will. That is what's best." Ham's retort was instant, "What's best, huh? What's best is what we *had*, not this! If this is obedience, I don't want any part of it." At this, he abruptly stood up from his place, preparing to storm out into the night, it seemed, but his brother Japheth stopped him. Noah was too discouraged himself to do much about his son's outburst at this point; he felt much the same.

"Don't leave, Ham. We need to be thankful for what our God has done for us, and focus on obeying his word and on the good things." He glanced over at Tabitha, hardly suppressing a grin. This was not lost on Ham, whose eyes darkened immediately. Fists clenched, he seemed ready to erupt with jealous rage. Then, before anyone could do a thing, he leapt across the room, flinging himself at his brother in wild-eyed fury.

◆ ◆ ◆

The angelic trio was speeding through the night, sailing through the sky towards Kadish like shooting stars. They knew in their spirits that something was wrong, and that their absence had not gone unnoticed. Up ahead, the ark was becoming visible, which meant the family had made considerable progress. That, at least, was encouraging.

"They haven't given up yet!" shouted Nathan with glee, clearly thankful that they had stayed obedient to the call with their absence. Micah knew the angel; he would have felt tremendous guilt if the project had failed while they were gone. Still, Micah was certain something was not right, and would not be surprised if they didn't like what they found when they arrived.

Alighting on the ground in unison, the three saw that it was dark in the fields. The family must be at dinner. Stepping towards the house, they began to hear what sounded like a quite a commotion: raised voices and muffled grunts of pain. They hurried their pace.

The scene that met the angels as they entered the home was horrifying. There, in the living room, Japheth was lying on the floor with Ham on top of him. Veins in his neck bulging, the older brother was straining to keep his attacker at bay as Ham tried to throttle him. And that was not all.

Next to Ham was a demon, mouth twisted in evil delight as he spat filth into the young man's reddening ears. What's worse, he wasn't the only one! Across the room, another was grasping Noah's arm, and they could hear some of his words, "This is all your fault. You're a great fool, and you're destroying your family. Look, your own sons hate each other, and it's all because of a foolish dream. The angels aren't real. Who does that? Who endangers their sons' well-being because of a dream?" Another was across the room, flitting from one member of the family to another, assuring them that there was nothing anyone could do, that the boys just needed to be left to fight it out.

As all of this hit them at once, the angels were furious. These fiends would set themselves against the Almighty God's plan and their own mission? They would pay dearly! Gurion zoomed across the room without a second thought, fiery axe gleaming, and swung it straight into the closest foe, silencing its poison mid-breath and sending it sailing away from Noah. Following close behind, Nathan ran to seize the villain spewing apathy at the family, and Micah darted towards the wrestling brethren.

At this point, Ham was looking far too fondly at a knife resting on the table as he struggled with his brother's strong grip, and the archfiend at his side was urging him on with a passion, wooing him to murder. It didn't last; Micah barreled into the brute with abandon and gave him a taste of his sword for good measure. Those rascals weren't near the caliber of the adversaries they had faced in Assyria, and promptly fled, screeching in pain as they went.

Once the demons had been vanquished, the room immediately began to calm. Everyone looked confused, but Noah came to himself enough to go to his struggling sons and pull Ham off of his brother. Shem moved to help Japheth up from the floor, and he was promptly beset by his mother and Tabitha, crooning over him with abandon. Ham must have realized what he had been about to do, because he suddenly sagged against his father, the fight gone from him, and went into a fit of soft but uncontrollable sobbing.

Up to that point, the angelic trio had been scanning the room for further threat, with Gurion rushing outside to see that the enemies had truly fled. Now, they took human form right in the midst of the sad gathering, appearing from nowhere and shocking everyone near to death. "Hello friends! I see you have been having quite a time of it." Micah said with a forced smile to set them at ease.

Noah, who had been nearly convinced by this point that the angels were a figment of his imagination, was overcome with a mixture of relief, exasperation, and shame as he realized just how far he'd come from fully trusting in God's word. "It's about time," Boaz said wryly, clearly fed up with having had his own doubts grow over the past days.

Micah winced, "Yes, I do imagine it's been difficult without us here for the past few days. I apologize. I was...detained." He glanced at Nathan, uncertain as to whether they needed to know the details. The other angel nodded and spoke to him in spirit, "They need to understand that we didn't abandon them - that *God* didn't abandon them."

Micah was less certain that this business with Tubal-cain was a matter that concerned them, and he felt no push from God's Spirit to reveal such things - it would only frighten them further. He did, however, concede that it was important that the family know enemies had been present in the home, as they needed to become aware so that they could be on their guard in the future. So, he gave them what he thought was fitting, "As I say, I was detained for a few days on a mission for our Lord, and, in order to see that I could return to you, God had to bring Nathan and Gurion to my aid. But now we are here, and you will be protected from this point forward." Ham interrupted him, "A few days? It's been far longer than that since we saw any of you." There was still some frustration in his voice.

Micah was unphased. "If you all would listen to me a moment, I believe the Lord wants to make some things known to you. I assure you that Gurion and Nathan only left their post long enough to assist me, and it has not been more than a day or two since they left. You see, there will be times when you will not see us, because we only reveal ourselves when commanded by our God, but that does not mean we are not there." Nathan chimed in at that moment, "This is when your *faith* comes in. You must *trust* your God. He does not leave you or forsake you! Never for a moment. Faith is the evidence of what is not seen!"

He stopped as the lead angel waved a hand, "Yes, faith. There is much in the world that is unknown to you, including enemies. You must trust the Lord through our word, and understand that there are those out there who would see you harmed. We do not wrestle against flesh and blood, but with the spiritual forces of darkness ruling over this present age. These adversaries plot day and night for the destruction of God's plan and His people, and they will see your lives in ruins if you allow it. So, be on your guard, and trust our God to protect you, but pray to him that you do not fall into temptation."

He set his eyes on Ham, face grim. "What you have experienced today is the result of such an attempt. You have allowed the enemy to bend your hearts towards evil and faithlessness as they whispered lies into your ears all throughout the day. You must learn to watch your thoughts, and take captive every stray, hopeless, envious thought to the word our God has given you. Let your thoughts submit to His word; do not submit His word to your own wayward thoughts, as you have done."

Nathan saw that the family, eyes wide, were struggling with Micah's harsh words, so he stepped in to help them. "There is no need to fear. These enemies have been at work since the foundation of the world, as your father Methuselah has likely told you in his stories. Yet, you have survived until this day. Though our adversaries come against us, there is no weapon formed against us that will stand if we put our trust in the Lord of Heaven's Armies. He is the King of kings and He rules over this earth and these demons who come against you. Nothing happens that is not known to Him. If you find anxiety in your hearts, make your requests known to God in prayer, and His peace will guard your hearts and minds."

Then, his face lit up with sudden joyful inspiration, "What's more, you can have hope in the midst of these trials! Your God wants you to know that, just as He promises to save you from the coming judgment, so, too, He will one day save you from your own corrupt flesh and from death by resurrection, and you will be raised to new life in the Kingdom of our God where righteousness dwells. That day is coming. When trials come on you now, as they surely must, you can look to that future day and know that there will be a reward, a rest from all of your weariness and toil. You must receive it by faith, however, until that day. You will soon watch the cities of the world fall to ruin, but you must look to a better city, prepared by God, a city not made with hands."

Through all of this, Noah and his family listened in amazement, overwhelmed by such lofty thoughts. They did not know what to make of it all, but it had the ring of truth. Their spirits knew that much, and they were certain that their own words and actions throughout the day had been influenced by some malevolent force. They would be on their guard, most surely, from this day forward. Boaz said as much, Nathan's words of hope largely lost on him in the face of what Micah had said first. "So, you're telling us that we are surrounded permanently with evil beings we can't see that constantly want to kill us? And we are supposed to be able to just accept that and keep on with business as usual?"

Micah couldn't help but laugh to himself at the man's tenacity. He gave the old man a bold reply. "No. You do not. You change your life to fit the word God speaks to you. You throw away your old way of living to make way for a new way of life, lived with the constant pressing presence of the unseen." That put the cynical old coot in his place, sure enough.

Just then, Gurion flew back into the room, converting to human form as he did so and nearly bowling over Ham and Noah with his size.

His face was bright with satisfaction, "The coast is clear. I have driven the enemy as far as Beth-Aven, and they will not be eager to come back! Get some rest while you can everyone, knowing we are on guard."

There was nothing left to say. Everyone headed off to bed, eager for a new day. The angels, however, were left wondering just how the enemy had found the small family in the first place. At the meeting of the minds in Tubal-cain's lands, Moloch and Beelzebub had been completely unaware of what was going on in Kadish. Now though, the demon leaders wouldn't be in the dark for long. This battle was only the beginning.

CHAPTER 11

A Heavenly Calling

THE NEW DAY DID NOT bring an end to the family's troubles.
The rising sun could not dispel their worries as easily as it had
banished the darkness of the night, and yet, as it ascended into the sky,
washing the land with its warmth, the cold hand of despair did begin to
thaw and release its iron grip over their hearts, giving way to rays of
hope. God's word had given them some hope.

The sun was not the only visitor on that new morning, however.
Dawn also brought with it the familiar sounds of creaking wheels and a
tramping ox. The grandfathers had returned! The three sons, already up
and getting to work, were the first to hear the party coming and rushed
to meet it, shouting as they went. "Sabba! You are back. We missed you!
We have such stories to tell!" said Shem. Japheth, ever the practical one,
got right to the point. "Did you get the auger?" he yelled, smiling still,
but clearly concerned that they might not have found what they sought.

Ham came last, not eager to have to recount his deeds over the past days.

All of this caused quite a ruckus, which brought the rest of the bunch outside to see what was going on. As Shem drew near the caravan first, he realized that there was someone sleeping in the back of the cart. Or, at least, they had been sleeping. Now, the mystery passenger had begun to stir, raising its slight form up into a sitting position. As the hood fell back from their cloak, Shem stopped in his tracks, his breath stolen by the sight. Before him sat the most beautiful woman he had ever laid eyes upon! Hair shining in the sunlight, her lightly bronzed skin and dark eyes captured him, holding him fast as surely as if he'd stepped into a net. From where had this vision come? Behind him, the family was equally surprised, though perhaps not quite so enamored. The old codgers had gone for a tool and returned with a woman!

They had achieved their goal as well, though, Shem saw soon enough. In the cart, rocking back and forth next to Lamech was a massive, curling iron monstrosity that looked like it could bore a hole in a mountain if one only had the strength to wield it. The Lord had delivered yet again! - and more than anyone had bargained for, it seemed. The young man looked again at the woman. God had said they would all have wives...Could the Lord have prepared her just for him? Would anyone so enchanting even want to look upon him?

Lamech called out to Shem excitedly, "Ahoy there Grandson! It's good to see you! I feel as though we've been gone for ages! I can't remember the last time I've been away from you all." Shem ran to hug him, but it was brief and distracted. Methuselah received similar treatment, but was all too aware of what had caught the boy's eye. He nudged Lamech and pointed behind them. After a moment's disappointment, the old fellow turned and saw what had stolen Shem's attention. He was besotted with the girl! His great-grandfather's lips crinkled into a wide smile as he thought about the Lord's grace. It was so fun to see it at work. When he had told the girl she might find a husband, he didn't expect it to be the first person she met!

Methuselah took the initiative to help this match along, hopping down to introduce Shem personally while the other family members made their way to greet them. "Good morning, son. Let me introduce our new friend here." He took her hand to help her down from the cart, a gesture she promptly refused before slipping to the ground in one fluid motion. Shem was enamored. She was graceful as well!

"This is Naamah." Methuselah said, a twinkle in his eye. Her name meant "pleasant", and she was certainly that. Shem couldn't restrain himself. "What a lovely name!" he said, almost shouting. "It suits you. You are the most pleasant sight these eyes have met in all my years!" He bowed, nearly touching her feet. "I am Shem, and you may ask of me anything you desire during your stay with our family." Though the young woman had resolved to remain poised and aloof in these first interactions, she couldn't help but blush at his effusive praise. Methuselah laughed to himself. This was going to be easier than he'd thought. No lady could resist such bold overtures for long! He was impressed.

Noah and the others met them at this point with laughter and hugs all around. Each, in turn, met the new arrival and expressed their own personal promise of hospitality. Naamah enjoyed Leah the most. She had never had a real mother who loved her for who she was. Her birthmother, Zillah, had been brainwashed by her father to only desire male children, and so when Naamah, their only daughter and youngest child, came along, they had cast her off like trash. She was left to the care of her father's other wife, Adah, who was struggling to survive in that family as it was. Eventually, when she was past childbearing age, Adah had taken Naamah to join her son Jabal in the city that he had founded. Now, meeting Leah and her friendly family, she felt like she was finally receiving something she had yearned for her entire life. She still didn't trust anyone, but she felt like she just might be able to live here.

"So, it looks like you met with success, grandfathers, and more than that! How did you fare on your trip?" Noah inquired, eager to share his own struggles as well. Methuselah responded first, "It was a blessed journey, no doubt about it! We got on the road and boom! - we were right where we needed to be for the Lord to provide what we needed." He winked at Lamech, remembering just how hectic the decision about where to travel had been. "We ended up traveling to the plains of Cush, where a...ah...ruler of sorts ordered the tool we needed from his personal forge in exchange for a good story." He wagged a finger at them. "I always did say my stories were worth more than you gave them credit for!"

"And where did this lovely young lady come from? I daresay heaven, but it's always good to check." Shem asked, beaming.

Naamah's eyes darkened at this even as she blushed, a fact that did not go unnoticed to Methuselah. He glanced at her reassuringly and did his level-best to tell the absolute truth without revealing anything at all about the actual circumstances of their meeting. "We found each other, quite by surprise. She was eager to be moving on from that dreadful place, and we happened to be on our way out. So, we proposed she come and stay with us for a while. Everyone could use a change of scenery every now and then." For the family, that was good enough, though Noah and Leah knew their grandfather well enough to be sure there was more to the story. If he had brought her back, then they could trust there was good reason for it. Naamah, on her part, breathed a deep sigh of relief, and thanked the God that she wasn't sure existed for this kind old man and his sensitive words.

"Let us have breakfast then! Inside, you all. Come, come!" Leah said, rescuing the young woman from any further probing questions. And that was that.

The ladies couldn't help themselves, and began fussing over Naamah like two mother hens, Tabitha saying, "You'll room with me, and we'll be fast friends! I've always wanted a sister. I haven't always lived here either. God brought them to me at a time I needed it most, and they made me a part of the family," while Leah made sure she was ready for what she was getting into, admonishing, "You may feel a bit out of sorts at first, living with a load of men. And they can be difficult, I'll attest! But soon enough you'll grow used to it, and even appreciate the lot of them to some extent. I daresay they're alright for their kind. We women run the household, however. You'll find your place with us helping us keep this place together. We work hard in this house, but we also find regular rest, as our Lord would have it. He never intended us to work nonstop." These things and more poured from them like an incessant fountain of concern, but for Naamah it was music to her ears. She enjoyed having others concerned about her.

While the women grew acquainted, the men ate their fill with abandon, finally feeling cheerful enough on that fine morning to have a strong appetite. Around the table, conversation moved towards more pressing matters. Noah, eager to bring someone into the loop who might help bear the burdens and give him some encouragement, began to regale his father and grandfather with tales of the tragic adventures of the past several days. They had made progress on the ark, but had been attacked, apparently by demons, of all things!

Methuselah's response was measured, and he did not seem overly surprised, as usual. "Son, I should have thought to warn you of these things before I left. It is just this sort of evil that took your grandmother from us those many years ago. We have to always be on our guard, because the enemy is out to steal, kill, and destroy, and he has many laborers under him who do his evil bidding, spirits who have lived for many years watching mankind to learn their ways and see how to best make them fall. They watch for an opportunity to devour the good in our lives, to wreck our relationships and steal our hope - and our lives, if they can manage it." He sighed, clearly upset that they had not been there to help, but Noah thought he could see something else bothering his grandfather as well, something he was not telling them.

At that moment, the angels walked in on them, Gurion sitting right down to eat and slopping a huge portion of stew onto his dish as the other two greeted the family. Micah slapped him on the back of the head, "What are you doing you great elephant? You don't even need to eat!" He responded in kind, "Who said anything about needs? I *want* to eat! This stew is good!" The lead angel could only shake his head at this, turning back to the men and Nathan in dismay. "It's alright," Boaz said. "There's plenty - and that woman's food is divine, I must say."

Nathan, for his part, didn't seem to be paying attention to any of this. He was staring at Methuselah, transfixed even, as though looking through him at something they could not see. Lamech tapped his father's shoulder, letting him know he was being observed. Methuselah had been lost in thought himself and hardly noticed that the angels had even entered the room. Now, he looked up and caught what was happening, returning the angel's intense gaze. Something unseen must have passed between the two of them, because a moment later, Methuselah spoke, not to Nathan, but to the rest.

"I have something I need to share with you all. During our journey, God did something in me, partly because of Naamah over there." He gestured towards the women, smiling as he did so. "When we met her, she was in need. Suffice it to say that there was great injustice being done to her, and we realized that God had placed us there to bring her hope and rescue. In that moment, when we invited her to come live with us, I realized that we have the hope the world desperately needs. We have hope, yes, of being rescued from death and judgment through the flood - or at least you all do." He said, pointing to Noah and his sons. "But we also have the hope that our God will never leave us or forsake us, that

He is everything we need, and we have hope of a day when our bodies will be brought to life again, long after they have ceased to breathe, when His Kingdom comes on earth. This is a hope that must be shared with the world. Naamah needs it. The people need it."

They could all see that he was heading somewhere with this, and they weren't sure if they would like where it was going. He continued, "I realize now that right then our God was speaking to me. He was giving me a heavenly call. I believe I am called to give the good news of our God's grace to the people so that they might repent."

The men were astounded. He would leave them all right now, when they had an ark the size of a small mountain to build? Noah began to worry, feeling once again the shaking of what little confidence he had that they could accomplish the work. Japheth spoke up first, "Grandfather...I understand that you feel for these people who are suffering, but did God not say that only our family would be saved? It is His way...who are we to say differently?"

"Yes, yes he did, son. Yet, He led me to Naamah, and she needed to be found. He knows our hearts, and He knows who will choose Him, and who will not. It may even be that there are those out there who, like me, will not live through this flood, but will yet choose God before it comes. I know him, after all, but His plan does not include me living through the next part of the journey. I do not understand it, but I submit to it as His will, and as right." At this, the young man quieted, unsure what else to say. He saw the reason in his great-grandfather's words.

Boaz had been listening to this, however, and he had far more to say. He was practically fuming, " You would leave us all at a time like this? Do you understand how much your influence holds this family together? How much we need you to stay encouraged and move towards the goal? If God has already spoken, and I, yes even I, finally believe that He has through His angels, then should we not do what has clearly been given to us, and see this ark completed?" His words said one thing, but his father could see his heart, that he did not want to be left alone in this time of difficulty in his faith. Boaz, too, had not been mentioned in the prophecy about the near future.

"Son, you know I love you. I'm proud of you for who you are and for your acceptance of what God is doing right now, but I can't do anything but what the Lord tells me. His plan is always best. He will sustain you. He is your rock, your fortress, your deliverer. He will be your guide and encouragement. You don't need me for that."

Lamech, his other son, spoke up now, "Father, as much as it pains me to say this, I want you to understand that I, too, have felt God at work since we met the young woman, and He has given me a sense of release for you, to let you go so you can accomplish the work he has given you to do. You, as keeper of history, know more than anyone about what God has promised to the world. It must be you to do this. I will miss you, but, I think, we shall not be parted for long. None of us will be here beyond the flood." He motioned to Boaz as well as he said this. "But we will be with one another soon enough, with the Lord as we wait for the day of His Kingdom."

At that moment, something seemed to have clicked in Boaz, because he stood up suddenly, eyes wide, and said, "You're right. You're all right. I've been wondering what God was doing with us, why I wasn't included in the Lord's word, and I think I understand now. We have lived good long lives, and our time is at its end. What better way to end it than to go out reaching far and wide to spread the news of our Lord? He is worthy of every man's praise, and we have only a few short years left. Surely this is the purpose for which I have sought?" He sat down next to his father, teary-eyed, then whispered, "This is my calling..."

Lamech's grizzled cheeks raised in a wide smile, and he said, "Now, lest any of you young folks start thinking there won't be a gray-beard around to run this show, think again. I will be staying. The ark does need finishing, and I know a thing or two about crafting the joinery you'll need to bring this thing together. I know I'm old, but I still have enough strength in these arms to swing a hammer."

Micah watched all this in amazement, awed by the difficulty the humans had with grasping the word of their God and impressed by the rapidity with which their minds could change. They were highly emotional creatures, truly. He did not expect what came next, however. Nathan, happy as could be with Methuselah's decision, made an announcement of his own. "I'm coming with you. You'll need someone to watch out for you on the journey, and our Lord is releasing me to help. It has always been my place to go to those in need and help them find hope."

Gurion, until then lost in stew, perked up in alarm. "You what? An angel never leaves his post!"

Nathan was unphased. "You're right, my friend, but an angel does respond when His Lord calls him onwards." His words had a hint of rebuke in them, a reminder of how reluctant Gurion had been to obey the Lord when they'd brought him from Eden. "And I am needed elsewhere. You and Micah can hold the fort while I am away. I also have a feeling that we will return every now and then."

Micah was slightly put off by all of this sudden change, but, then, they were dealing with people, after all, and their Lord was a mystery to boot. He shrugged his shoulders, not sensing in his spirit that God was saying otherwise, and said, "There we have it then. You all will set off at first light, and we will get to work on this ark in earnest. There is much to be done!"

The victory was total. Not one person had been left alive who was not immediately enslaved or imprisoned, and Lucifer was ecstatic. This was no quaint hamlet either; Huron was a significant stepping stone to conquer, a mid-size town known throughout the region for its independence and fierce home-grown fighting force. Considering this, their defeat was remarkably swift. The immense army formed by the coalition of kingdoms had decimated Huron's force with relative ease, leaving the city overrun within half a day. Now, cries of pain from the wounded cut through the night amidst the crackling of a thousand campfires and the tramp of booted feet. War and ruin. It was music to his ears.

It had taken some significant coaxing to assure the leaders of the twelve kingdoms that annihilation was the best plan of action for Huron. Tubal-cain kept going on and on about "annexing" so as to keep peace and minimize loss, but Lucifer had quite a keen interest in *maximizing* destruction, and several of the other rulers had been of the same mind. He was proud of his work, if he did say so himself!

Finished was one of the very first steps to their ultimate goal, and the demon leader was eager to keep moving. Everything thus far had worked extraordinarily according to plan. As he surveyed his forces, he could see a number of demons flitting in and out of tents to keep the soldiers on their toes, causing an odd brawl or backstabbing every now and then. There wasn't much else afoot, except - there! He saw Beelzebub gliding toward him in the night, looking uncharacteristically hurried, and wondered what bad news he was bringing now. He had nearly torn the demon's head off when he heard about the escape of that angel who had been peeping in on their meeting. There had been nothing to do, however, and the Enemy was not ignorant of their dealings anyway. He saw every blasted thing the demons did. It was infernally irritating. Lucifer had brushed it off, confident that the humans were so entirely under his thumb that nothing could derail their plans.

As Beelzebub neared, Lucifer could see that there was another, less familiar demon accompanying him - clearly no one of importance, but rather an underling of his underlings. The two of them winged their way to his side and immediately began blabbering as fast as they could something about angels and arks and some place called Kadish. It was rather unintelligible, as the unknown demon clearly had the details but was nervous and Beelzebub was trying his level best to control the fellow but instead was speaking over him. It seemed he was eager to get credit for something to redeem himself after the angel escape incident. "Shut up you fools!" Lucifer roared, shocking them into submission. Then, as if nothing had happened, said coolly, "You, with the unfamiliar face - introduce yourself and tell me your news."

The demon was visibly flustered by the lack of recognition and respect but was scared to death of getting on Satan's bad side so he did as he was bid, "Yes, my lord, I am Andros, and I am stationed in Kadish, a small land far to the south, by the sea. I have news that might interest you."

Satan was unimpressed. "Out with it then."

"Well, some days ago, my fellow and I were making our rounds near the border of the town, and we saw what appeared to be two angels soaring off in some great hurry from the direction of a nearby farm. Knowing this to be a local farm of a man who fears the Enemy, we thought we had best look into the situation. When we arrived, we saw him and his sons building the beginnings of what looked like a colossal structure. We are not sure what it was, though it looked rounded at the bottom, as though it might be a boat. But never on the earth has there been such a vessel, if that is the case. So, we set to work disrupting their efforts, attempting to turn them upon one another."

"I'm waiting to see how this is important. You *thought* you saw an angel, and you stopped some fellows from building a boat that could never float." Lucifer was perennially sarcastic when he had no need to be flattering, and his disdain was coming through loud and clear.

Andros hurriedly finished. "We nearly had them beat. The brothers were at each other's throats about to commit murder when we were interrupted."

"Interrupted? By whom?"

"By angels. *Three* of them. That doesn't usually happen, especially not in Kadish. These men are up to something, and the Enemy has an interest in it. We thought you should know, my lord."

The Devil did not respond with the enthusiasm Andros was looking for. In fact, he looked positively irritated. His answer came swiftly, "It could have simply been an answer to prayer. You know how dreadfully attached the Enemy is to the humans, and there are so very few of them that actually pay attention to Him; He can afford to be lavish and send three angels to one family." Truthfully, Satan was simply weighing the matter, deciding if it was worth his time, but he *detested* it when the Enemy threw a wrench in his plans. He decided. He would have the place watched, in case there was something of note to this situation, but he would not sacrifice any of his own time to the task, or that of his generals, until something truly concerning came to his attention.

While Andros hovered there looking sullen, Lucifer turned to him at last and said, "Go to your regional overlord, Wormwood, and make this known to him. I want the home and activities of the family watched. If you catch any news of the Enemy's actual plans, you make sure I am the first to know."

✦✦✦

Meanwhile, two days march away, Tubal-cain was miserable, feeling older and grayer than he ever had as he sat on the edge of his enormous oak bed with his head in his hands. His plans at the meeting of the minds had proceeded spectacularly, but he had not realized quite what he was getting himself into. Many of the men with whom he had made a pact were twice as shrewd and five times more wicked than he himself was, a fact that came to his attention all too quickly. He had proposed that all the lands of Assyria on the journey towards Havilah be annexed diplomatically, sure that the people would be willing to bow before his superior force without bloodshed. He had not anticipated that his warlord allies were not only power-hungry but bloodthirsty as well. Though they gave their verbal assent to the specified terms of engagement with Huron, a group of leaders including Obed - that sniveling weasel - had said that *if* the people put up a fight, they would have the right to destroy them so as to save loss of life among their own men. The ironsmith had agreed, sure that the people of Huron would bow rather than die.

Yet, just days after his sons marched out with the coalition army, a messenger had returned with news that the city was being laid waste and whatever women didn't die were being hauled off as slaves. This was not what he had envisioned when he decided to do this. He just wanted peace and security for his own family and for his kingdom, a peace that couldn't be taken, and a legacy that would last, that he could pass down to his sons and their sons after them. Now, whatever legacy he hoped to have was forever tainted by the barbaric tactics of that day - and it was only the beginning.

He now knew that he couldn't control the monster that he had created. His only choice was to help guide it towards the intended goal. He couldn't give up now, or his own kingdom would be devoured, and he wasn't quite ready to pay as high a price as that. He just hoped his sons hadn't been hurt in the battle.

As he battled inside himself, an unknown presence slipped into the room. It was Ashtoreth, the demon who prided itself in destroying men through wanton lechery. He often presented himself with a female form, because it worked so remarkably well in luring them to their fates. Angels were not made both male and female, as mankind, so he had no qualms about the process. The end justified the means.

Within moments, the demon had slinked its way to Tubal-cain, joining him on the bed, and began to entice him towards forgetting this whole mess about guilt and shame. He deserved better. He was a king, after all! There was no need to feel any of these things. Diversions awaited him that would be far more interesting and worthy of his time.

Tubal-cain was too lost in his own mind to even pay attention to these attempts at coercion, so the demon switched tactics. This required direct attention. He knew well how to shift a man. Lucifer had left him there for just that reason, to keep an eye on the tame warlord. Reaching out an icy hand, Ashtoreth began to touch Tubal-cain's spirit with darkness, afflicting his body in the process. For the humans, spirit, body, and mind were inescapably connected. It wasn't long before the man began to cough and shudder feverishly.

If he wasn't going to distract himself, then Ashtoreth would do it for him. Sickness always worked. It would keep the ruler from having any direct involvement in the affairs of the army at least until he had a change of heart, or until Lucifer returned with his uncanny charms to help the process along. As Tubal-cain sickened, the demon embedded his mind with the powerful notion that he was making himself sick with worry, and hammered it home with these words, "When your anxiety kills you, where will your sons be then? You must give in, and let be what will be. This is out of your hands now; you can't turn back. Just hold on to what you have."

CHAPTER 12

On the Road Again

METHUSELAH WAS ON THE ROAD. The ladies had spent the morning preparing a delightful pack of provisions, and he'd had the young men load up a pair of horses before starting the day's work. It was time to save the world! For what seemed like the first time in his life, he actually felt rushed. Someone could die tomorrow who did not know about the hope that he had and the God that He followed. As for Noah, he had at first been disappointed by the fact that he'd be losing two good workers and sources of encouragement (Boaz didn't count in that regard) but God worked on him through the night, helping him to see just how much it would help their spirits to know that they weren't condemning the world as they worked. Their family had been chosen, but he did not want to imagine that he was sentencing the world to death personally by keeping his hope to himself.

Boaz, on the other hand, couldn't help but drag his feet a bit, however much he had said he was on board. It was difficult to look forward to countless days spent uncomfortably, on the road, sometimes sleeping out in the open - and that was only the beginning of his worries. What with all of the stories of the world growing darker by the day and beasts beginning to turn vicious, he was beginning to fear they wouldn't make it more than a day's journey without being eaten or robbed and left for dead on the side of the road. He didn't seem to have stopped to think about the fact that if God had sent them - and with an angel at that! - then He would surely also take care of them on the way. Nathan, on his part, had mysteriously decided last-minute to stay behind and confer with the other angels about matters of importance, promising that he would join them by the close of the day wherever they might be found.

So, with heavy hearts unsure of the future, the family had said farewell to the duo and sent them on their way that morning. Father and son were now seated astride their horses, Shemer and Hephzi, trotting along at a respectable pace. The former was a light gray gelding dappled with dark spots, and the latter Boaz's longtime companion, a snow-white mare that he'd raised since she was a foal. Her name, chosen in one of Boaz's softer moments, even meant "I want her".

It was nearing evening, and they had made considerable progress towards their destination, though it was yet several days journey away. They were headed to Eshcol, a massive city renowned for its entertainment and trade. Seated at the Northernmost border of Cush between the two rivers by the sea, it was a regional hub of activity between Havilah and the southern Cush plains where they'd met Jabal.

On this trip, they would skirt those lands entirely, as Methuselah was not eager to rendezvous with the ruler again after the narrowly-avoided conflict involving Naamah.

Why they were headed to such a god-forsaken place Boaz was still yet unsure, but his father insisted that it was because God had called him to this task while in Cush, and, so, perhaps, it was the people of Cush who most needed to hear about His grace. "If this Eshcol place is known across the world as a pit of sin," he'd said, "then we are likely to have an easy time finding sinners, are we not?" Boaz couldn't argue with his logic, of course, but that didn't help. So, they'd set their course following the Euphrates River north as it flowed from their home of Kadish up towards the mountains of gold in Havilah. They would take its path right along the border between Cush and Assyria until it met the Gihon River and meandered west to the sea.

Boaz's father had assured him that there would be plenty of settlements along the river as well because of the proximity of fresh water, and that meant they wouldn't have to sleep out in the open all too often, a fact that did much to garner his son's approval. Yet, the sun had already long ago crested in the sky, starting its all-too-swift descent, and Boaz still couldn't see a sign of any settlements in the distance as he squinted down the river. They had better hurry. "Father, we ought to pick up the pace a bit; I still don't see any of the hundreds of settlements you promised," he jested, but his father knew that behind the wisecrack he was as serious as could be.

Methuselah looked at his son's dark green eyes and lined forehead,

marred by years of worry, and he couldn't help but feel some slight pity
for him. The boy had just never known how to trust God. He always had
to *know* things: see them with his own eyes and experience them before
he would believe. He wasn't a boy anymore, though, and the aging man
before Methuselah needed to grow some faith before it was too late. He
spoke up, "I suppose I can speed up a bit, but you know - "

He didn't finish. Just then, a slew of armed men burst from the grove
of cedar trees to their immediate right, swooping down upon them like a
swarm of hungry locusts. It looked like there were near a dozen of them,
and all of them were mounted, so there was not going to be a swift
escape. Curiously, they did not all ride horses. Some were on camels,
which was not unusual, but others rode a variety of reptilian looking
beasts that ranged from about the size of a small horse to as large as two
oxen stacked atop one another. One had small forelimbs that didn't
touch the ground, complete with three sharp talons on each, and it was
covered in leathery, hairless skin from the tip of its extensive tail to its
bulbous head. Other, larger beasts were similar in appearance but had
conical bone formations protruding from the backs of their skulls
toward their riders, and their hind legs were near the size of tree
saplings. Methuselah did not recognize these particular beasts, but they
reminded him of creatures he had heard of called "dragons". Dragon was
a name often used to refer to any of a number of larger reptiles, but they
were known by unique names in the different regions in which they were
found. The historian and his son, however, had much bigger problems
than what to call these strange animals.

One man had ridden forward ahead of the others atop a large

brownish-green dragon with dark, beady eyes and feet that just might could crush them if lifted high enough. He now sat high on its back glowering down at the two travelers with an air of deranged confidence. Boaz could see that these bandits were no strangers to violence, and by the demented gleam in the leader's eye he doubted they would hesitate to harm him and his father if it pleased them. This was exactly what he had been afraid of going on this foolish trip! Of all the things that could happen...and the first day at that!

As Boaz quivered internally, Methuselah spoke up, brazenly breaking the silence between the two parties, "Hello there, my fine fellows. What has you out on this lovely afternoon? I must admit, I find your mounts to be positively splendid, an example of some of God's best handiwork." He was trying to keep the situation light, but Boaz couldn't imagine what he was hoping to achieve. The party clearly meant them harm, and wouldn't be put off by pleasantries.

The man snorted derisively, "God? I don't know where you came from, but there is no god in these lands. I caught this beast myself in the wilds. I trained it and beat it into submission. I'd say it was my handiwork." He spat to the side, nearly hitting Boaz in the process. "Anyway, I ask the questions. Where are you two headed all by your lonesome?"

Boaz was flush with anxiety, planning feverishly for a way of escape, though without success. He was not in the least confident that they wouldn't die. There was a reason they were not included in the prophecy to Noah and the family. Methuselah, on the other hand, decided he would keep the conversation going. They were on their God's mission, after all. "We're on our way to the land of Cush to spread good news to the people!" He replied. He wasn't willing to lie to the man. God could take care of people who honored him by speaking truth, but he wasn't a fool either, so he was not going to give them the exact destination and risk them being followed if they ever made it away.

The man's face was blank. "Good news?"

Here was his chance, so the old man went for it. "Yes, the good news that there is a God in heaven, the one true Creator of heaven and earth, the creator of all of us, and He wants to know us and be known by us! He is willing to be a Father to us, and allow us to be His children, if we repent of our way of life and turn to Him to follow His way. If we believe in Him, He counts our faith as righteousness, goodness that we didn't earn - "

At that, his message was cut short by the startling crack of the lead bandit's whip. He had anger in his eyes, and Methuselah could see that this whole notion of a God above who judges had struck a nerve. Several of the other men had begun to inch towards them as well, eyeing their saddlebags greedily. Boaz was busily searching his luggage in his mind to figure out if they had *anything* remotely resembling a weapon. The situation had instantly gone from bad to worse, and he couldn't see how they'd get out of this with their lives.

Yet, the expected climax never came. The bandits appeared to be waiting expectantly for their leader's command, but he didn't give it. He seemed conflicted: eyebrows drawn, face stuck in a grimace, restlessly stroking his chin in concentration. Something had disturbed him, and

Methuselah hoped it was God working on the man's heart. He was trying hard to have confidence that their Lord was with them in the work they'd been sent to do.

The man's cracked lips began to move as though in conversation with someone, perhaps himself. Then, without warning, he spoke up, "These old fools aren't worth our time boys. Let's get moving. I want to get to the city before dark." The whole lot of them stood stock-still, clearly dumbfounded and hesitant to miss out on such easy pillaging. "I don't know about you, but I'm tired of sleeping on the ground, and if anyone wants some company tonight, its best to get to the tavern early before the best ones are taken." Without another word, he rapped his mount with the whip and rode off into the night. These last words seemed to get their attention, and, slowly, one-by-one, the other bandits followed suit, still unsure about what had prompted the sudden change of plan but eager to not be the last ones to the tavern.

When the last of the brigands was out of sight and the cacophonous thudding of their mounts had begun to fade, Boaz finally breathed a sigh of relief. He needed to *know* they weren't coming back. Methuselah had already been praising God for deliverance for several minutes by the time his son stopped watching the dust cloud and turned to look at him. In that moment, a bright figure materialized between them, shocking both near to death. As it took shape, however, they recognized Nathan and could breathe again.

"You make quite an entrance, you know," Boaz huffed. "Something a little less dramatic would be nice." Nathan's cheeks lifted in a slight smile. "Be thankful, my friend. God has given you great favor today. If I hadn't arrived at that precise moment...I hesitate to say what would have happened to you. Those men were hungry for blood."

Boaz was nonplussed. "That precise moment? I'd say you were about ten minutes late!"

The angel laughed, shaking his head. "I swear, Boaz, your unbelief really does amaze, sometimes. Do you think that whip-wielding fiend just decided to leave of his own accord?" Seeing the abashed look on his face, Nathan could tell that this was exactly what the man had thought. He continued, "I've been here for quite some time, coaxing the fellow to leave you two alone."

Methuselah took the opportunity, "We have to learn to expect God to be at work, son. He is never far away, and all rescue comes from Him. Even if the man hadn't been influenced by Nathan, we could give the credit for any change of heart to our Lord who knows men's hearts and turns them whatever way He wishes."

The younger man, to his credit, took the rebuke rather well. He had to ask, though, "How exactly did you persuade the brute to leave, then?"

Nathan's face fell somewhat. "I reminded him about his late great uncle that he loved dearly. The man raised him for much of his life, and the depression following his passing was one of the more significant reasons for the bandit's descent into depravity. Once his heart was convicted by that powerful memory, it wasn't difficult to suggest he leave you two alone. Methuselah bears a passing resemblance to the old fellow, after all. " The angel's compassion for the marauder was evident, and Boaz couldn't help but feel guilty that he'd never considered for even a second anything beyond saving his own skin.

Methuselah was thankful for how God was beginning to speak to his son. There was more to this journey for him than met the eye. They needed to get going, though. "Alright fellows. Let's be off. However little he actually meant what he said, the bandit was right about how soon night is approaching." He pointed at the sun that had nearly disappeared behind the trees.

"Actually," Boaz interjected, "as much as I absolutely detest the idea of sleeping in the wilderness, I think we would do well to stay away from the city where those pirates plan to make their lodging tonight."

Nathan nodded. "He speaks wisdom. Though the Lord delivered us the first time, we shouldn't invite a second encounter. We can make a path that swings out wide of that city, and we should just make camp for tonight. I will watch over you, so you can sleep in peace."

The next several days went by without incident as the party meandered across the countryside towards Eshcol, stopping off in several smaller settlements along the way. At each inn, Methuselah shared stories of the creation of the world and the fall of man, hoping to awaken the populace to the God who was there, who provided for them day to day, making his sun shine on the just and the unjust. Boaz played his part as well, chatting up those with more discerning minds who raised objections. He could understand why they resisted such flighty notions of reality. He, like they, preferred his truth to submit to the careful inspection of the five senses. However, as he watched person after person reject the God that He knew had cared for his family for their entire lives, he began to see just how jaded his own view of the world had become. He was not, it seemed, a man of faith. He did not trust implicitly. That was something that could use a change.

Now, the morning of the tenth day, they were within walking distance of the great city itself. They had made it to the outskirts the night before, but had chosen to stop so they could meet the city in the light of day and take advantage of the opportunities for conversation that a bustling roadway would provide. This had been a wise decision, it seemed, because the dirt road had soon transformed into a colossal highway teeming with life, the street pounded smooth for near twenty paces on either side of them by countless thousands of tramping feet - not just human feet, either. The animals that they'd seen days earlier carrying bandits were in abundance, accompanied by large beasts of burden resembling rhinoceroses that stretched several times their size and had wide, flared skulls with bony protuberances along their rims. These scaly monstrosities were hauling everything from carts to carriages with ease.

If that wasn't impressive enough, a leg the size of a tree trunk nearly squashed Boaz flat as a lavishly dressed individual thundered by on an enormous creature with a long, muscular neck rising several paces into the air. His muffled yelp of terror was drowned by the resounding crash that followed, and Methuselah was certain that if he'd needed to relieve himself beforehand, he didn't any longer. Though his family had never seen such a wealth of wildlife in Kadish, the old historian had heard tell of the larger dragons. It was quite another thing entirely, however, to see them in person. Yet, no one else seemed to even bat an eye. Apparently, in a place so inundated with culture, this impressive display was the stuff of everyday. One irate merchant even wagged his fist menacingly at the gigantic dragon as the shaking of the ground disturbed his carefully stacked wares, sending some tumbling.

There were traders and artists, craftsmen and priests, day-laborers and slaves, not to mention a healthy portion of sailors this close to the coast. Every occupation and nation under heaven it seemed had come together in this hub of civilization. Nathan had his work cut out for him as he soared through the air keeping watch on the throng below. With such a mass of humanity in one place, there would without doubt be a corresponding wealth of demonic activity. He could already see the prodigious spires of worship centers rising above the crenelated walls of the city, menacing heralds of what was to come. Methuselah would certainly find plenty of people with which to share his news, but the angel feared what else they might find.

CHAPTER 13

Dragons, Demi-gods, and Demons - Oh my!

A S THEY ENTERED THE CITY GATES, Methuselah and Boaz couldn't help but gasp in awe at the spectacular architecture. Necks craning to see how high it went as they passed under it, their attention was first captured by a titanic stone archway that left room for even the most massive of dragons. Then, when their eyes moved ahead again, they were stunned still further by yet another gargantuan structure, taking up what looked like the entire center of the city. It was several stories high, a marvelous montage of columns and arches that together formed a sort of stadium that rose three levels. It must have seated thousands, a modern marvel if they'd ever seen one. Even from this distance, they could see myriads of people perpetually streaming in and out of it. What went on in there? They wondered, but weren't sure if they really wanted to know. This city was a den of debauchery, according to their most reliable sources.

The duo had to dismount and lead their horses on foot in order to make their way through the crowded streets - it was *that* congested. In doing so, they subjected themselves to innumerable bumps and bruises as people rudely shoved their way past, sometimes carrying rather large or dangerous objects which the men had to hastily avoid. The press of people did not bring quite so much opportunity as they had hoped. It was more of a nuisance keeping them from connecting with anyone. Accordingly, they decided they ought to scout out a place of business where they could sit down and perhaps meet with better luck. Looking every which way for a semi-accessible eatery, the country carpenters couldn't help but notice the turmoil that reigned in the taverns. Men were bursting out of them, fists flying as they bawled drunken epithets at one another. One or two were even bleeding from cuts about the head or abdomen, making it clear that weapons certainly weren't against the law in this place. It seemed as if the city was in an ever-present state of upheaval, and the worst part was, *no one seemed to mind.* Truly, the city was well-named. Eshcol meant "cluster of grapes", and evoked images of free flowing wine and carousal, a fitting moniker for the scene before them.

What's more, behind all of the kerfuffle, the men could hear a faint but persistent melody serenading the masses in the midst of their commotion, even seemingly playing in concert with it. Every sort of instrument seemed to be working together in harmony, and - somehow - it was not unpleasant, but it was disturbing because lovely music did not pair well with such a scene of drunken revelry. Instead of comforting the conscientious travelers, it fueled their fast-growing dislike for the city. It was as if the conductor was actively arousing the desires of the populace and instigating indulgence. Methuselah exchanged a wary look with his son, eager to be out of the city already, but aware they needed to keep going. Boaz returned the look, then leerily pointed towards something new that had stolen the attention of the passersby.

A street magician had set up his show among the crowded lanes of traffic, and, miraculously, the sea of people parted before him like water before a ship. Apparently entertainment was priority in this place. The man was dressed garishly in swathes of multicolored silk, covered from head to toe except for his eyes, and he wore a dark green turban on his head, as though somehow that increased the aura of mystique about him. He was dramatically dancing about, telling everyone about the "limitless powers of the mind" that he would use to discern the most secret facts of the heart. "Come, come everyone to have your mind opened wide by the mystical power of meditation. I can tell you anything about anyone by linking our minds together through this ancient practice."

One young man stumbled forward sheepishly, clearly pressured into the matter by his friends, but looking as though he was willing to give it a go rather than deal with the embarrassment that would follow should he refuse. The enchanter seized his chance, leaping towards the man with a flourish of his cape. He took the fellow's head in his hands, and said, "What is your name? Gershom? Good. Now Gershom, I am going to enter your mind, but you must assist me. You must meditate by focusing on becoming one with the universe and opening yourself up to its influence. Breathe deep, and let all other things flee your mind. Forget your friends - " he pointed at the gaggle of guys laughing behind him, "and lose yourself in the vast greatness of the universe. Every tree, flower, and person is part of it, and it calls to you. This part is very, very important. The mind is a gateway to the soul, and you must *allow* me entry as a part of the life force that fills us all."

Gershom looked decidedly uncomfortable by this point, but couldn't back down, so he gave his best effort to play along, genuinely moving through the breathing techniques and submitting himself to the "power of the universe", and, in response to the magician's urging, granting him access to his mind. Methuselah and Boaz had never seen a display quite like this, so the debacle had their rapt attention, though Boaz doubted heavily whether any revelation of genuine import would arise from such a foolish undertaking.

Then, the magician spoke, "Go on. Grant me access. Your mind is under your authority, and you choose what you allow into it...Yes...there we are...I have it. You are feeling guilty, I see. Last night, you were with someone...someone you shouldn't have been with, and you are afraid that your friends will discover this fact and shun you." Gershom's eyes were closed, and he did not speak, but he began sweating profusely at this point, betraying the truth of the soothsayer's words. "In fact, that person is among us today! Perhaps I should reveal to the audience just what sort of secret you have been keeping? Hmm? And oh, it is a *particularly compromising* secret, is it not?" The conjurer was gaining far too much enjoyment from the sick spectacle, and Methuselah was fighting the urge to speak up on his behalf.

During this charade, Nathan had been watching warily from above, ready at any minute to intervene on behalf of his charges if needed, but otherwise not inclined to get involved in the situation. Magicians were a dime a dozen in cities like this, but what concerned him was a fact of which no one else was aware. There was a demon running the show.

When the would-be wizard had appeared, he had been accompanied by an evil spirit. Such spirits regularly walked unseen in the world of men, stalking individuals, studying them for weakness, and pouncing at the right opportunity. If it didn't already know all it needed to know about the young man, Gershom, it would be easy enough for it to goad him into giving it away. Then, all it had to do was pass the information along to its human counterpart, the magician. Nathan could see that the demon was now fervently flooding Gershom's mind with guilt and shame over the things it was discovering about his recent transgressions. However, in the second that the seer was about to reveal the secret to the masses, the demon stopped cold, shutting its mouth, and turned to glare at Nathan. He had been seen!

The next moments flew by in a blur as Nathan swooped down to join the masses, changed into physical form, and unceremoniously yanked the two unsuspecting carpenters into a nearby building. To their eyes, nothing of note had occurred, except perhaps that the performer's dramatic pause was taking entirely too long. After being whisked inside by Nathan, whom they had heretofore not been aware of, Methuselah and Boaz were befuddled, to say the least. "What was all that for?" the younger asked.

"That conjurer was acting under the influence of a demon, and it saw me! I couldn't risk it alerting other evil spirits in the city to our presence, so I fled before it had time to make a move and catch a glimpse of you two." Nathan responded in hushed tones, suddenly all-too-aware of where they were standing. The building was a place of worship, and it wasn't for the God they served. In his haste, he had pulled the men out of the frying pan and into the fire. Boaz though was still stuck on the unbelievable performance. "So that's how he did it...You mean demons know our every thought?" He inquired.

"Not exactly. All angelic beings live primarily in the spirit realm, and humans are primarily spiritual creatures, though you have bodies that are inseparable from your spirit substance in a way that we do not. Because angels live in the spirit, they can interact with people's spirits, sort of like the way you and I are interacting now, and they can observe and ask questions and pry to get answers, much like in conversation, but far more easily, as the human is unaware of the interchange, and typically do not even know that demons exist, much less that they are studied by the fiends." The angel sighed, "Anyway, we do not want evil spirits following you around about town. Hopefully, since it was a brief encounter and the spirit was busy, it won't bother with looking for me again. We need to lay low from this point forward."

Behind Nathan, a throng of men in long, tan robes were gathered in rows all throughout the vast room, which appeared to be a temple sanctuary of some sort. They were all seated with their legs crossed and hands outstretched towards a golden image set up at the front of the temple as they chanted in unison. The image was that of a scantily clad woman with two pairs of arms and several legs branching out from her body. The front pair of arms was raised with the hands clasped together in a prayer position, and a flame rested in between the image's fingers. In the glow of that flame, the image shone with a ghastly light, making the scene seem all the more disturbing. This was not the place they wanted to be to escape demonic activity. Methuselah well knew that false gods were demons in disguise. Like Satan, they yearned for the glory of God Himself, and preyed upon unsuspecting humans to give them the praise that they felt was their due, since no other creature would do so willingly.

At first, the trio thought that their presence had gone unnoticed and that after a few minutes they might exit without incident, but it was not long before they heard a voice from the right side of the temple that spelled the doom of that hopeful notion. A middle-aged man was heading towards them garbed much like the rest of the gathering, but with one distinction. Nearly everything on him was pierced: his nose, ears, eyebrows, and who knew what else. He carried a ragged looking scroll in his hands, and was eyeing them with an air of disapproval. They had interrupted his service.

When he reached them, he looked at Nathan first, perhaps sensing something unique about him, but then turned to what must have appeared to him to be the older men, and addressed Methuselah. "Sir, you have entered into the temple of Ishtar, her holiness. She is the being from whom all blessings flow, the god of fertility and plenty, and we here are her humble servants." He bowed.

If there was anything that was obvious to them concerning the man, humility wasn't it. He had an arrogant way about him, strutting around as though he owned the temple. Methuselah responded in kind, "Great to meet you! We are humble servants of the Most High God, Yahweh, the Creator of heaven and earth, the sea, and all that is in them." These words grated on the man like an iron file, and they could see that he was not pleased to have them speaking so loudly of such things during the chanting session. He held his tongue, however, responding, "We respect all faith traditions. Your god may be one of many, but he is certainly not the only one. You are mistaken. You all seem like you are from a distant land. Perhaps you have not experienced the wealth of worship practices in the city before. Yet, do not let me stop you. By all means, worship your god as you see fit. Just don't push it on us." He looked as though he was about to return to his post, but paused, as though trying to determine a good excuse to usher them out.

Methuselah wasn't giving up that easily. "I beg to differ. I am a historian, and I can tell you that ever since the foundation of the world there has been one God, perfect and unchangeable, and only His way is right. People know about Him. Even you do, because his eternal power and godhood has been clearly seen all around you in the things that have been made. People are without excuse. Although they know there is only One True God, they do not give honor to Him, but they worship and serve the creature rather than the Creator."

Though he practiced a serene exterior, the monk was clearly unsettled by what he was hearing. He took a few moments, then retorted, "I have heard you, but I do not see how you hope to please a god that is perfect. Our gods are like us, flawed but powerful. We offer them what we have, performing the rituals they require, sacrificing our bodies as necessary," he lifted his sleeve to reveal an ugly mass of scars all along his forearm, "and they bless us with sunshine and good harvests and healing. If we do as they ask, we can earn their favor and perhaps enter into a better life through reincarnation."

Nathan spoke up at this point, using the man's name which he had not given. "Amos, I don't think you understand what my friend here is offering you. There is a God in heaven that does not demand enough good works to please Him, to curry favor with Him. This God has all that He needs. Everything under the whole heaven belongs to Him. No one has given to Him that He should repay them. Even you do not have anything that you did not receive. He offers favor as a gift, by faith. Trusting this God alone is all He asks of you, and He will count your faith to you as righteousness."

The man looked like he was about to break at this point, but a young woman came out to meet them dressed in such a way as to draw the eye and interrupted the holy affair. She was dark skinned and wore a shimmering golden dress, much like the image of the false god, that contrasted beautifully with her skin tone. Methuselah looked at her eyes, and he knew she was imprisoned, spiritually if not physically. She had given herself over to something that was only ever going to take from her. The woman nodded at the men, offering a slight half-curtsy, and whispered something urgent into Amos's ear. His face turned sour, and he reprimanded her harshly but quietly. The men heard just enough to catch her name, Amaris. After that she hurried off, and the priest followed suit, but not without turning to the men and ushering them out the door, conveying a thinly veiled threat as he did so. "You men need to watch what you say while you're in this city. There are those who would not be as...welcoming as I have been."

Considering that their reception in the temple had been far from what one might call "welcoming", they took his comment as a word of warning. Eshcol was not going to be a walk in the park. Nathan was just thankful that the Lord had provided a place for them not frequented with demons, which was surprising given that it was a pagan temple. That priest's case was tragic. Humans were so willing to believe that they could earn divine favor that they didn't need anything beyond their own thoughts to keep them captive sometimes.

Once outside, the trio found the enchanter gone and the hordes of people flowing ceaselessly yet again. Relieved, Boaz was about to head out into the street when he realized that their horses, too, had moved along, and the chances of finding them in such a sprawling monstrosity of a city were slim to none. Unphased, Methuselah just held up a foot and said, "Good thing God gave us these! More important is what has just happened. We must pray for those poor souls God has brought into our path. They are worth the loss of the horses."

He closed his eyes while Nathan kept a lookout, and began, "Lord God, we come to you as your servants, knowing that you brought us here for just such a moment as this to give your good news to these people. We pray now for Amos, asking you to wake him up to the foolishness of what he believes. Open his eyes to see that he can't do enough to find favor, because only You can make a man right before You. Lead him to wake up to your presence in his life, because you knew him before you formed him in the womb, and you have a plan for him. Lead him to surrender. We also bring Amaris to you, not knowing her situation, but knowing that you love her and want her to meet you and walk with you, because you created her for that. Protect her from the enemy and set her free from the slavery of her own choices. Let your will be done in their lives, on earth as it is in heaven, so they can find abundant life. Thank you, Lord."

The old fellow looked up, brown eyes shining bright in the afternoon sun, and he saw that Nathan had left them, though he was no doubt nearby and aware as ever. Boaz, on the other hand, seemed a bit agitated. He was shifting his feet back and forth and looking uncomfortable. "What is it son?" he asked. Boaz just looked at him, but the look said enough. He was afraid. He spoke up, voice strained. "I just don't know how to do this. This faith thing. We are telling others about how much we trust this God of ours, but I doubt Him myself so often, it feels false. And then there's you, so brave and bold. Aren't you afraid at all that we are literally facing ageless demonic forces with near unlimited resources who are intent on our imminent destruction?"

The old historian smiled. "I am afraid, yes. But, I know Him in whom I have believed. He is at my right hand, that I may not be shaken. With Him, we need never be moved. Our hearts can be firm, trusting in our Lord, and we need not fear until we look in triumph on our enemies." He patted his son's shoulder. "He's with you too. You've only made it this far because of him." Boaz nodded, then looked around, his gaze settling eventually on the colosseum. "So, should we go see what all the fuss is about?"

Methuselah was nervous already, but didn't see the point in saying so. "Sounds like a plan. Maybe if we can see what gets this city so excited, we can figure out what good news looks like to them, and communicate our message better." They set off for the stadium, joining the enthusiastic crowd.

When they arrived, the congregation had been squeezed into such a tight space as to make moving nearly impossible, except when everyone did so as one. Boaz was worried he was going to have his pocket picked, but he couldn't even see enough of his bags to do anything about it. After what seemed like an hour, the throng where they were standing finally spilled into an open space and filtered into the stands. The stadium was truly magnificent, a wonder of human achievement. What seemed like the entire city lined the sides of the amphitheater, looking down upon a dirt arena where armored men were milling about as though waiting for instructions. Some of the brutes were nearly twice the size of a normal man! Methuselah had heard tell of such beings, demi-gods of sorts. It was said that they were the offspring of the unholy union between demon-men and human women. The people called them the Nephilim, and they were the men of renown, the mighty men of old.

In the center of the stands on the second level, there was a special section festooned with lavish decor that the historian supposed must belong to a ruler of some sort. Whoever it was, they had not yet graced the place with their presence. Boaz looked around and noticed how full the stadium was getting and commented on the leader's absence to his father, jabbing a thumb towards the royal seating, "Looks like it's going to be a while for the main event. Whoever is throwing this party apparently decided they want to be fashionably late, and we've all got to suffer for it."

What he didn't realize was that the soldier standing right next to him did not take kindly to insults, and he made his feelings known, "You there, stop! Do you know of whom you speak? The Lord Jubal is our founder and ruler. Everything in this city that you enjoy comes from his grace and ingenuity. To speak evil of him is to speak evil of this city and its loyal people, of which I am one." Boaz wasn't quick to pick up on the severity of the situation, and retorted smugly, "We don't come from this city, so...no, 'everything we enjoy' does not come from his lordship." That was a mistake.

"You are not citizens, and you dare speak such slander? You have no rights here. Do you realize that we can do with you whatever we please?" His eyes lit up with wicked glee, and he motioned to two other soldiers. "Arrest these men. They are to be sentenced to death. Perhaps we will throw their bodies in the arena, and see how the beasts like fresh meat."

CHAPTER 14

A Joyful Occasion

THE UNEXPECTED EXODUS OF BOAZ AND METHUSELAH, though far from cheerful, did much to ignite the dormant flame of commitment and obedience that was embedded deep in the hearts of Noah and his family. Because of the old men's willingness to sacrifice themselves for others on a mission to save the world, those at home felt that their task, too was worth giving their very lives, and so they poured their heart and soul into the work before them. Now, the ark was progressing smoothly as the family began to rally around the cause. By this point, the ark had already grown in size so much that they had been forced to make ladders to reach the second and third levels that they were working on, and they'd driven posts deep into the ground(with Gurion's help) to hold up the sides of the structure until the day the flood would come. Like all great projects, the further they dived into it, the more they realized how each of them had a specialized role that they alone could best fill, and that made the enterprise go that much better.

Old Lamech, as promised, had a deft hand for joinery, and so he set to work carving out mortises and tenons on the ends of all of the wood they cut so that it would fit together so snugly a drop of water wouldn't even try to get through it - never mind the gobs of pitch that would coat the joints to ensure the same result. The young men, on the other hand, served as muscle, spending their days in the woods chopping tree after tree until their hands bled, scarred, then bled again. Once a significant portion was chopped, they then had to slice it piece by piece with a two-man saw so that it could be planed smooth. On this they took turns - and it was a formidable task at that - scraping their blades slowly along the planks until they actually had smooth enough edges to fit together.

Throughout all of this, Noah acted as designer, supervisor, and joiner. He planned it all as the Lord led him, then put it together himself so that if any part of the ark were ever to fail, the responsibility would fall squarely on his shoulders alone. He did, however, require some slight assistance in lifting which the boys sometimes provided, but occasionally the pieces were so gargantuan that the angels had to lend their considerable strength to the equation to see it done.

Then there were the ladies who were perhaps more busy than the men! They had to both retrieve and heat a constant supply of water with which to steam and bend the wood into the various curved pieces that were required. The heating itself demanded a steady stream of wood which had to be chopped, and the river was, unfortunately, some significant distance from the main encampment where they were working. In addition to this, they had taken on the responsibility of making all the pitch to waterproof the ark, and it was going to take untold amounts of the stuff to do the job. Thankfully, they only had to produce enough at a time to handle whatever joinery was needed for the day at hand. So, they kept a well-stocked pile of pine resin collected from nearby trees and, whenever it was necessary, put it on to boil in a massive pot. To this steaming concoction was added a heaping portion of days-old rabbit dung for filler material and beeswax to keep it malleable. Suffice it to say that these women stayed on their toes. On top it all, they made sure that food was readily available at every mealtime, and it was *actually good!*

It was during one of these times in the household kitchen, preparing for the day's breakfast, that Tabitha began talking to the other women about her wedding. It was no surprise by this time, as she and Japheth had asked for his parent's permission(she had none) and had announced their engagement a week prior during a family meal. The proposal had been met with terrific enthusiasm all around, as a wedding seemed like just what the little community needed during a stressful, difficult season. The young couple's love gave hope in the face of the vague depression that they all felt was pressing its nose against the glass of their fragile lives. Though they were empowered by purpose and thankful for many things, the family still struggled with the notion that, before long, they alone would be left in the world. So, the lighthearted musings of the young Tabitha were a welcome reprieve from the worries of the day.

"What am I going to wear?" She was saying. "The wedding is tomorrow, and I don't have anything but the same two dresses I wear every week that I brought from my parents' home all that time ago." Her face was drawn with worry, a look that Leah met with a motherly smile that spoke volumes about how foolish and unnecessary it was. "My son found you just like this, and he fell in love with you. Are you really worried he will change his mind now because of your clothes?"

"Of course not, but I want to look special for him." Her eyes were shining, slightly moist in the flickering torchlight. Leah brushed a hand across her cheek. "I can try and sew you one perhaps. I do have some skill with a needle, but where we will get the materials, I can't say." That was a problem. Fabric for the sort of dress they might desire would be expensive and difficult to find in a smaller village like Kadish.

Naamah had been listening to the exchange attentively, not speaking because she was unsure of herself, but thinking deeply nonetheless. She still wasn't sure if she trusted these people sometimes, and that kept her fairly quiet. They had been nothing but good to her, but so was everyone else until the day they decided to be otherwise. How could she be sure they wouldn't turn on her as well? Whenever she would have thoughts like these, since she had arrived here, a voice in her mind would remind her that she shouldn't expect to be accepted by them if she didn't accept them first. What's worse was that they *did* accept her while she didn't accept them - or at least that's how it appeared.

She spoke up at last, "I have some dresses that you could use. They aren't the nicest dresses in the twelve kingdoms but they can turn a head. I can promise that. And if you don't like any of them, you could always dismantle them and fashion a new dress from the fabric." She had decided that she would show them she meant to be part of the family, and perhaps then they would keep her around.

Tabitha was beaming, eyes wide. "Thank you so much! Are you sure? That would be absolutely wonderful! You *are* the sister I always wanted." Naamah allowed her lips to curl in an ever-so-slight grin in response. Success: she was loved. "I'll finish supper," Leah said happily. "You two run along and find a dress for this girl. We have a wedding to do!"

The next day at sunset the entire family gathered together under the shade of a terebinth tree to witness the sharing of the vows between the two lovers. The shimmering gold of the sun had begun to fade into a dark orange as the subtle blues of night rose to meet it. By its evanescent light, Japheth began first, gently taking Tabitha's hand in his. "Since I first saw you, I've been in awe of your beauty. The stars that soon tonight will reveal their diamond crowns do not shine with even a fraction of the radiance that you do. They would surely disappear, if you were to join them, as they must day-to-day give way to the majesty of the sun. And within you lie greater treasures still. Your heart is pure as gold, forever willing to spend and be spent for others, and your creativity and imagination know no bounds. I know, without a doubt, that I would gladly give the rest of my life to knowing you more, and I offer myself to you now and forever. I love you." He finished, looking into Tabitha's dark blue eyes, misty from the power of his words.

Then she began. "Until I met you, I had always felt as though the world didn't want me: that, perhaps, God had made a mistake when He made me, and I wasn't what I should be. Then, you and your family came along and showed me that someone could accept me just the way I am, and that God could too, and always had. I saw that you are a man who knows what matters in life, who chooses to serve others and live for a cause greater than his own ends, and who isn't willing to just let life lead him. You make your own path with the Lord, a good one, and I look forward to spending the rest of my life walking that path with you! You are strong, handsome, and I love you!"

With that, the family came around them, tears falling from many a face, and prayed over the couple, committing them to the Lord to be joined together in holy matrimony. It was a sort of commitment for all of them as well, to serve as the witnesses to the union and support its health with their own lives. Next, Noah spoke a blessing over the newlyweds, and they ended the ceremony by accompanying the couple to their first home, built by Japheth's own hands.

The ceremony left quite an impression on them all. For the parents, it swelled their hearts with pride and joy, filling them with thankfulness for God having brought something good in the midst of a time of evil. One day, there would be children from the blessed union that would fill the hills and halls with laughter. Here was the future of the world. Then there was Lamech, who was just thankful that he had gotten to see one of the sons find a wife before his passing, and he hoped he would make it that far for the other two.

Shem enjoyed the wedding immensely, because everyone had dressed up as best they could for the occasion, and Naamah was positively stunning. She commanded his attention the entire time, and he was barely able to draw his gaze away from her beauty long enough to pray for his brother's union. During the vows, he rehearsed in his heart the words he would say to her if he ever got the chance. He desired to be with her, but he was not sure if she reciprocated. He had spent nearly all of his time over the passing days doing woodwork for the ark, and had not had many personal encounters with Naamah since her arrival, though he had done his best to make it known even then that she had left quite an impression on him.

Naamah also was affected deeply by the wedding proceedings. For once, she finally felt *included* in the family, especially since Tabitha had worn her exotic white dress that she had intended for her own marriage weeks before. That, however, was not a fun memory, and it reminded her yet again how little she could trust anyone. As she witnessed the couple say their vows though, she could not help but long for someone to say such things about her, and she did remember fondly what longing she'd seen in the eyes of the brother called Shem. Perhaps he would pursue her...

Ham, on the other hand, watched the entire event with baleful eyes. He alone, it seemed, was to be without a woman to woo. That was about right. Everything else had been taken from them: peace, comfort, rest, *time*; he hadn't had a minute to himself in months since this the ark had been set into motion. And it was all for what? To start again as the *only* people on the earth and work *more* to build a new civilization? It didn't sound like much of a reward for righteousness to him - and now he had to deal with the constant irritation of his older brother's romance. He was fed up.

Andros was ecstatic. His meeting with Lucifer on the battlefield near
Huron had been a great success. Not only had the overlord been willing
to hear him out, but he had tasked him personally with assisting
Wormwood to bring about the destruction of Noah's family - or, at least,
that's how he took it. After speeding back to Kadish, he had immediately
requested a meeting with the regional demon leader, an appointment
which he was now rather impatiently waiting to begin as he sat rocking
in a creaky oaken chair. He'd changed into human form and come to
the agreed upon location, a sort of private library that was chock-full of
the most outlandish books he'd ever seen. Typically, the covers of such a
collection would be coated with dust, but these looked nearly new, and
he'd have mistaken them as such if it wasn't for the worn binding. Every
single one appeared to have been pulled down and perused on a regular
basis. Who read that much? It wasn't like there was anything of note to
learn from the humans anyway. Their life spans were a mere drop in the
vast sea of time in which spirit beings swam.

"I see you've made yourself at home." A cold voice said. He felt a
strong hand grip his chair from behind, stopping him mid-rock. "Did
you let yourself in?" Wormwood asked as he came into view, face devoid
of emotion. "I do so detest unexpected visitors." The man before
Andros was a peculiar specimen. His form was gaunt - frail even - with
voluminous robes hanging across his bony shoulders like a blanket over
a branch. The robes themselves were nice enough, a dark red silk
embroidered with some sort of bright blue stitching that gave them a

mysterious air. Down the front of his robes hung his most interesting feature, a long, extravagant beard that was dyed - of all things - *emerald green*. Most likely it served to take the attention away from his face and eyes, which were devoid of life and warmth. To anyone who might meet him, he appeared to be some kind of eccentric scholar.

Andros gulped and answered, plucking up some courage and feigned indignation as he did so. "Yes, well, I was told to be here at a precise time, and seeing as *you* were not here to allow me in, I did as we always do with human residences, and 'let myself in' as you put it. Is that a problem?" He was playing a dangerous game, but demons were always vying for dominance, and he couldn't let Wormwood think him weak.

Wormwood just looked at him with those dead eyes making him uncomfortable, so Andros changed the subject. "What's with all the books, anyway? Do you actually read them?" The other demon smirked. "You think them impractical? I'll answer you with a question of my own. What would you say is the best way to learn about something?" He didn't wait for an answer. "You study, of course. Now, what is our mission with the humans? You can answer this time." He said condescendingly.

Andros was not enjoying this interrogation, but he replied, eager to get it over with. "To corrupt them."

"Yes! Good work! This involves bending the mind to our will. It is in the mind that all of the action happens. So, what better way to *study* our targets than to *know* their minds." He slapped a leather-bound tome onto the desk. "And *books* are full to the brim with their deepest thoughts.

This is how they communicate the more important notions of their feeble intelligence. If we wish to win, we must know our enemies. Now - ," he held up a hand, "I know that we can glean a considerable amount just by *listening* to them, but the fact is, we do not think as they do, and I find it best to immerse myself in their culture so as to be at all times potent and at the ready." He stepped back from the desk, and gave a command, "Look at me. What do you see?"

Andros was perplexed. "Ah... A feeble old man with an odd sense of style."

Wormwood's face lit up, "Yes! Precisely! So, if you met me on the street, would you see me as a threat?" Andros was beginning to see where this was going. "No! You wouldn't concern yourself with me in the slightest. I'm just an eccentric old man who reads too many books and doesn't eat enough to feed a bird. Deceit: the element of surprise. Therein lies the victory, before the battle has even begun."

Wormwood promptly sat down, satisfied with himself. "Now, why did you come to see me?"

The other demon hadn't enjoyed the lesson, but he had to admit it made sense. He decided to just get things moving, being sure to paint himself as the most important element in the story. "Yes, well, I and a couple of my associates happened upon a family at the outskirts of town who serve the Enemy. We began to antagonize them and make them generally miserable as usual - just doing our jobs. Then, right when I had nearly achieved the murder of one of the younger ones, we were interrupted by a trio of *angels*. They defeated us." He coughed, waving a hand dismissively, "You know, the whole element of surprise thing you mentioned. Anyway, after that point, I took the news to Lucifer and -"

Wormwood stopped him there, slamming a gnarled hand onto the table in fury. "You did *what!*" Andros looked decidedly confused as to why there was an issue, though, so he had to continue. "You are supposed to report directly to my underlings, who then report to me. Why did you take such a small matter to Lucifer? It makes it look like I can't run this operation."

Andros couldn't help but feel a slight twinge of delight at the self-important demon's difficulty, and he answered smugly, "I like to deal with those who actually have the power to act, is all. And it doesn't do me any good to make *you* look good to the big boss. Anyway - ," he moved on as though that conversation was finished, "Lucifer told me that I needed to report back to you," - the demon overlord was leering now - "and *lead* a reconnaissance mission under your guidance. We are to keep watch on them and send word of any significant developments."

Wormwood was fuming, but underneath the perturbed exterior he was also vigorously plotting how to turn the situation to his advantage. "Reconnaissance, eh? I think we can do better than that. We will make sure that those Enemy-loving fools don't ever even have a chance to make any developments. We are going to destroy their family. And let those angels just try and stop us."

Now *that* was a course of action upon which they could both heartily agree. The humans deserved whatever was coming to them.

CHAPTER 15

Is it Victory?

THE MOMENT THE SOLDIER ACCOSTED HIS SON, Methuselah had known there was going to be trouble. Boaz never could keep his mouth shut. Now, they were literally facing the death penalty for his rash words. After their brief interchange with his son, the soldiers had snatched the two of them up like criminals and marched them down into the arena, where they awaited the decision of the ultimate authority in that place, the Lord Jubal. The men couldn't help but wonder where exactly Nathan was during all of this. Was he rushing to rescue them? Staging a coup? Had demons captured him as well? He was a mighty angel, but just one, after all, in a city positively rampant with demons as mighty as he.

As father and son stood forlorn, each manacled to a massive wooden post driven into the ground, they could do nothing but watch the crowds jeering and calling for their blood - and pray. They prayed, both of them, for rescue and for their families and for forgiveness for all the ways in which they had not lived as they should have. They weren't entirely sure they'd make it out of this, but their spirits told them that they still had work to do, and that should mean that God was going to make sure they survived to see it done. Their thoughts were interrupted, however, by a sudden hushed silence. The fearless leader had arrived.

Stepping languorously onto the pedestal in the center of the arena, Jubal radiated arrogance. He had, purposefully or no, made practically the entire city wait an extra hour for the games to start, and then had the nerve to swagger into the stadium as lazily as if he'd just arisen from bed. Looking at him, one could see where the city got its sense of indulgence. He was bedecked with jewelry from head to toe, diamonds and sapphires and gold carpeting his figure as though it were clothing, and his clothes themselves were resplendent. The finest black silk coat adorned his slight frame, trimmed in silver scrollwork with a luxurious gray cloak about his shoulders, all clasped together by a wildly ostentatious silver brooch in the shape of a lyre. His face was nearly gaunt, however, a fact which, in light of such outward extravagance, implied he was likely suffering from drug addiction. The pale eyes, thin frame, and mousy hair did much to further that impression. After he had moved into position, an attendant ran forward and announced, "Ladies and gentlemen, I present to you the father of music, the king of Eshcol, and founder of our festivities, our own Lord Jubal!" Thunderous applause ensued.

It didn't take long, however, for the pompous royal to notice that there were two strange men standing below his elevated seat looking rather confused and not at all excited about his presence. He motioned for the soldier guarding them to explain the situation, which he did in earnest. "Yes, my lord, I caught this foreigner speaking evil of your greatness, and if it pleases you, I humbly request that these two be put to death so that all may know the due penalty for slandering your magnificent name. It would be a fitting beginning for today's games." It was the same soldier that had stopped them in the stands who spoke these words, and he was clearly enjoying himself, smiling broadly despite the unpleasant nature of the situation.

Jubal, on his part, seemed bored with the whole affair. He didn't even blink when the man finished his gruesome entreaty. This sort of wanton bloodshed was apparently commonplace in his city. Methuselah and Boaz were uneasy, to say the least. Then, the order came. "Why not? Let's get it done with and start the games," he drawled, waving a hand dismissively. Their fates were sealed.

Or they would have been, if not for the timely intervention of an onlooker. A young man stepped forward from the stands, near enough to the ruler to be within earshot, and exclaimed, "I will stand for them!" Everyone gawked in stunned silence, wondering what one earth could persuade a person to lay their life down for two practical strangers. He had the leader's attention though, and if the slight smirk said anything, Jubal's interest as well. The lord did love drama.

"What you all want is a good show, is it not?" the young man shouted, revving up the crowd. "I will stand surety for the foreigners, but let me not simply die. No, that would be a waste." He turned to address Jubal. "Rather, let me fight in the arena, and I give my word that I will best any foe that I face, man or beast. If I can do so, let us all go free. If not, let my death be in their place; you will have had your penalty, and some entertainment as well." His words were met with raucous laughter and catcalls, but the vast majority of the crowd were waiting with bated breath to see what Lord Jubal would do.

It was a gutsy move. Whoever the fellow was, he had no need to risk his life for the old men, and Jubal could just as easily sentence all three of them to death if he saw fit. The king, thankfully, did not give such an order. He stroked his chin, intrigued. The young man was fit: an athletic, muscular specimen of significant size - though he paled in comparison to the mighty men of the arena, of course. Jubal wanted to see what he could do, and the audience was enthralled. It was decided. "You may fight," he called out, pointing a bejeweled finger. "What is your name?"

"Call me 'gift', because I have given the gift of entertainment to the people this day." he replied, readying himself to enter the arena. Jubal raised his eyebrows at the cryptic answer, then shrugged and hailed the soldiers holding the old men. "Let them loose and take them into the stands. They can watch while their friend gets slaughtered." He motioned to the announcer. "To your stations everyone! It's time to bring out the gladiators!"

Seated safely in the stands, Methuselah and Boaz were beyond thankful, heartily declaring God's praises despite the angry glares of onlookers who apparently would have rather seen them eaten. They had no idea who their mystery savior was, but they dearly hoped he was a fantastic fighter, or he'd soon be paying the ultimate price for his bravery. Down below, the various combatants were arming themselves from what looked like a wall of torture, a huge mobile armory rack that gave each of them access to a gruesome array of blades and clubs. The young man called 'Gift' had entered the arena by this time, and was rubbing shoulders with some of the most fearsome-looking warriors they'd ever seen. Gift selected for himself a simple sling, a few choice stones, and two daggers, one long like a short sword and the other only about a hand-span in length, little more than a glorified kitchen knife. He did not put on a trace of armor, which, in light of the company he'd be keeping in the arena, seemed like certain suicide. Apparently the man liked to be light on his feet - perhaps a little too light.

Methuselah wondered what such feeble arms could do against giants. Three of the fighters were literally the height of a sizeable house, and carried weapons larger than Gift was tall. They would skewer him with a single thrust if he wasn't careful. Watching the young man prepare, Methuselah couldn't help but admire his tenacity. He held himself with an easy assurance, and he had been so resolute, so immoveable when addressing the king, that the carpenter wondered whether God was not directly with this man. At any rate, they would find out soon enough, because it looked as if the fight was about to officially commence. The contenders got into position, each of them taking a place with their back to the wall, spread out, so that they would have room to maneuver, while Gift just stood in the center of the arena, an easy target. Promptly, the announcer took the stand again, and cried, "Without further ado, let the games begin!"

The three giants were the first to make a move. Heads swollen with pride, they rushed headlong at the other combatants, clearly overconfident in their greater abilities. The first, a rough-looking brute with a horned helmet, nearly trampled Gift on his rampage across the arena, but the young man skillfully sidestepped, leaving the giant open to a swift stab to the gut from the bearded warrior behind him. He was the first to fall, but he was not left without company for long. The second and third giants swiftly dispatched their competitors, one squashing an older fellow flat with a warhammer and the other skewering a slow man who tried to run. Turning about after their conquests, they scanned the arena, seemingly unconcerned with one another, though Methuselah could swear there could only be one victor. Upon seeing their colossal brethren already fallen at the feet of the bearded warrior, they made their way towards him in tandem.

During all of this, Gift was hanging back, shrewdly watching the horrific scene play out before him. He seemed content to allow the other adversaries to destroy themselves, and was not eager to play a part in anyone's downfall. This struck Methuselah as an incredibly sensible plan, and he began to wonder if the young man had a chance. By the time everyone else was through with one another, there would be far fewer enemies to face, and they'd be worn out to boot! However, there was something more than cold calculation in the brave lad's eyes. The old man thought he could see a hint of pain. Had he been injured? Surely not? Or was is something else? Compassion?

Within minutes, the only battlers left in the stadium were the two mighty men with bloody bodies strewn about them haphazardly, and Gift himself. So much for the assailants being worn out. The two barbarians were hardly even winded! With them acting as a unit, no one had presented much of a challenge to them, and, unfortunately, the lord of the evening had no mercy or sense of justice to mitigate the disaster. He and the crowd were just basking in the carnage.

Gift looked ready though, neither advancing nor retreating, simply staring the two men down as though pleading with them silently to reconsider as they stalked towards him. There was no fear in his eyes as they came closer. Exchanging wicked glances, the two warriors leapt into action, springing towards the young man in unison. He just stood there unmoving until the absolute last second, and right when the larger one's hammer was about to split his skull in two, he feinted right, neatly dodging the blow and looking as if he was about to parry the swinging blade of the other attacker. He did not do so, however, but instead dropped to his knees, barely ducking the edge of the broadsword, and cleanly sliced his two daggers into the giant's calves as he slid underneath its legs through the dirt. Bouncing back to his feet, he turned again, ready for more. The one giant he'd assaulted was limping heavily at this point, barely able to walk, and the other had fallen flat on his face after missing his powerful blow.

The loathing in the giants' eyes was palpable, and Methuselah was sure that if they caught the man, they would happily tear him limb from limb. Again, the uninjured one scrambled to strike the light-footed lad, and by this point, the audience was enraptured. They had never seen anything quite like this. This time, Gift went on the offensive, whirling his sling about with abandon and whipping a stone straight into the gut of his adversary. Rather than the expected ping of stone glancing off of armor that the audience expected, however, there was a sickening thud as the missile tore straight through the breastplate of the battle-axe-wielding giant and lodged in his stomach. He doubled over in pain, out of commission for the time being. Neither of the assailants had enough fight left in them to go another round, and Gift was left standing and looking up at Jubal expectantly. Was he not going to finish them?

Jubal was already astonished that the fool had made it so far, but he was not about to tolerate a day of games that did not end in death - and neither was the crowd. They began chanting, "Finish them! Finish them!" with a crazed look in their eyes. It was a nauseating display of human perversion. The young champion was steadfast, however, unmoved by their deadly desire. Not much time passed before Jubal, growing irritated, raised his hand to some guards near the gates of the arena. It looked like their host was going to make sure that there was enough bloodshed for everyone.

However, the guards did not rush to attack or imprison the combatants. Instead, they made their way to a number of large gated pits hidden at the very back of the stadium, and carefully began removing the bolts that held them in place as one of them shook a large, noisy clacker that made the most irritating sound. Up until that time, the pervasive siren song of the city had been the only sound anyone heard above the din of the arena, but now a new sound began to rise over the rest. It was a faint rumbling, Boaz thought, perhaps an earthquake? If so, they were all about to die, crammed together as they were this high in the air.

It was not an earthquake, however, as everyone was soon to see. The rumbling shortly turned into a chorus of low, feral growls, and that was followed by a deafening roar that shook the entire arena. Having finished their task, the soldiers below scrabbled to the exits as if the very hounds of hell were after them, barring the gates shut behind them in terror. The iron covering of the largest pit suddenly burst from its moorings, stricken with such force that it flew nearly half-way to Gift's position before coming to a grounding halt in the dirt. Something had woken.

From beneath the ground arose a creature out of nightmare, standing nearly fifty spans tall with row upon row of serrated teeth, each nearly the size of a human forearm. It had mammoth legs and clawed feet that looked like they could crush a man in one step, and it was covered in thick, leathery skin - another dragon, it seemed. The beast was accompanied by two different beasts that had been set free from the adjacent prisons. Though not nearly as intimidating as the mighty teeth of the first, each still had its own perilous features. The one on the right had a massive, club-like tail the size of three men, and its entire form was encased in bony armor with spikes along the borders, while the other resembled some cross between a tiger and a lion, but was greater in size and sported enormous fangs. Methuselah and Boaz could see the fear in the animals' eyes, and they knew that the natively docile beasts had been bred and trained for violence. The would-be hero was going to need a miracle.

Enraged by the soldiers' noisemaker and enticed further by the smell of human blood, the large monster tore across the arena towards the wounded giants, trampling the giant who had been gasping for breath with a stomach-twisting squelch and chomping his razor-like teeth down on the other. He barely had time to scream before death took him. During all of this, the other enemies had not remained idle. The saber-toothed tiger had bounded across the arena hungrily and was about to pounce on the hapless young warrior. Gift, to everyone's surprise, leapt into the air to meet the attack, slamming into the beast with more force than anyone would have thought possible and sending the pair of them careening into the dirt in a twisted flurry of fur and fangs. Amazingly, the fellow got up from the ground unharmed, dusted himself off, and walked away from what was now the lifeless carcass of the tiger bleeding in the dust.

The man didn't have long to wait for another close encounter, however, because the dragon with the club-tail had surged across the arena in fear, fleeing from both the cage and the violence of the larger dragon. It pounded towards Gift with abandon, and he had to dodge to the side, rolling back to his feet, to avoid a near incident. As he did so, however, he rolled entirely too close to the blood-spattered monster eating the giants, and it turned its ferocious attentions towards him, rushing on him and crossing the distance between them with terrifying speed. Gift crouched, appearing as though he was going to roll out of the way again, but, instead, when the creature was just a few paces away, he sprung high into the air - impossibly high - above the beast's entire body so that it passed underneath his floating form, and he came down hard on top of its neck, both blades pierced deep into its vertebrae. Carried by its own momentum, the dragon continued a few more steps then crumpled to the ground, eventually shuddering to a halt, dead. The audience was awestruck. This was no normal man.

Not quite finished, however, Gift whipped around to face the rampaging armored dragon and set a stone to his sling. He set his sights on the moving target, sling humming as he aimed, waiting for the perfect moment. There it was! He let loose, sending a projectile spinning through the air like lightning a full hundred paces until it finally found its mark right in the beast's only vulnerable organ - its eye. The fight was over. The young man had won. The arena erupted with thunderous applause! Never had the people seen such a stunning victory.

Methuselah and Boaz gazed at the young man, confounded as to how it could be done. What mortal could boast such things? Then, the old man could swear that the one called 'gift" winked at him. Could it be? Nathan? His musings were postponed as the tournament-master Jubal called out to the young lad, hushing the crowd with his hands raised.

"What a feat! You have bested the mightiest of men and beasts. What do you have to say for yourself? What reward do you require? You may have anything you desire." The pompous fool laughed heartily, "After a show like that, I'd pay you to run the kingdom if I didn't think you'd steal it from me!"

Gift smiled graciously and bowed low. "I require nothing but the freedom of myself and the two men I mentioned before. I am glad I could be of service." He paused. "But understand also that there is a God in heaven who has done what you see before you today. He fights

with me, and it is His right hand that gives me the strength to conquer
my enemies. He decides who lives and dies, and He does not take kindly
to men who put themselves in His place, lifting themselves above others.
I say that to you, o king, and I believe you will take my meaning." At
that, he turned and strode out of the arena.

Boaz and Methuselah had made their way out of the stadium as
quick as a blink, afraid that the king was not one to be trusted, and it
was a thankful thing, too, because Jubal did not seem all too happy with
the unexpected message the young man had given before the crowd,
though he did his best to disguise his displeasure. Out in the square, the
two men were considering what they might do next and wondering
where on earth that angel had gotten to, when he appeared next to Boaz.
"Hello friends!" he said, grinning from ear to ear. "What did you think?
Is the arena what you expected?"

Methuselah was no fool. The angel's light mood implied that he had
not been violently detained, and they knew that he always watched them
like a hawk if he wasn't occupied. "It was you wasn't it?" Then it dawned
on him. "Gift! Nathan means 'God gave'. I should have known!" The
angel was beaming, and Boaz looked stupefied. "How could it have been
you? It looked like an entirely different person!"

The angel's response was simple, but direct. "Things are not always
what they seem, Boaz. Angels can take many forms. Our spirit form is
our only true form. We are not bound physically. The important thing is
that God delivered us out of the den of lions!" Literally. "However," he
continued, "there was a price to the victory. In a place like this, the

leadership is overrun with demonic influence, and I can promise you that it did not escape the notice of my evil counterparts that I fought as no man can fight. My changed appearance is a small boon, but I guarantee the streets will soon be flooded with demon-spawn searching high and low to destroy us. We will have to leave the city."

CHAPTER 16

Friend or Foe?

IN THE WEE HOURS OF THE MORNING mere days after his brother's wedding, Ham was chopping wood. He had volunteered to take the job that day, and every other day since the ceremony. It wasn't that he suddenly found great delight in pounding his hands to a pulp, but he did feel like it was the only way he could get away from the ruckus of family life and his brother's irritating romance. He swung the axe with lethal force against the trunk of the tree, intent upon obliterating it. He sometimes imagined that it was Japheth's head he was swinging at, before he caught and reprimanded himself for the outright murderous intent. Things were just not going his way. Was that his fault?

His father had always gone to God in prayer when he was struggling in a similar way, but Ham wasn't sure he trusted God enough to pray to Him. It was God, after all, who had initiated all of this. God had decided all of a sudden that it was time to wipe out the human race, and sent His messengers to interrupt Ham's family's lives. So, Ham figured that his misery was God's fault, and, even though he had not prayed much before when life was good either, he wasn't about to start now when it was being torn apart by God's own hand.

Unbeknownst to Ham, an unseen presence was slipping quietly into the clearing. Andros, the demon who had first wooed Ham nearly to murder, slithered up to him and began speaking into his ear, "It *is* God's fault. According to what you've been told, God knows every one of your needs before you ask anything of Him, and He is choosing not to meet those needs. What kind of God does that? Not a loving, all-powerful one for certain." The evil spirit had spoken to Wormwood about this one, and they both agreed, the young man was the perfect target. It was always best to go after the weak ones, because once they'd been taken, they could be used to destroy others who might not submit to more direct intimidation.

Ham, of course, was completely unaware that the ideas besieging him were not his own. They flowed smoothly from his own train of thought, and he found them highly agreeable. In fact, it felt like he was receiving a revelation of sorts, like he had finally stumbled upon the truth after long searching. Andros laid it on thicker, "God took your family from a perfectly good situation and threw them into turmoil, promising to destroy everyone and everything you care about. Then, as if that news alone wasn't enough, He began laying burdens on you all that you can't possibly bear, making you slaves to this ark project. Look at your hands! What God does that to his children?"

Ham did look down at his hands, seeing the broken, oozing calluses and the blood smearing the axe handle, and he began to contemplate quitting. He didn't have to do this. But Andros wasn't even finished yet, "To top it all off, God doesn't even have the heart to treat everyone fairly. You slave away with no reward while Japheth gets the wife of his dreams. How is that fair?" The young man's blood was boiling. Truly, he was being ill-used - and by God, of all things!

In the midst of his musings, a strange figure approached him. At first, Ham remained unaware, but as the individual drew near, the crack of a twig drew his attention away from his dark reflections. Glancing up from his work, Ham saw that someone had joined him in the clearing, someone he did not recognize. Hooded and cloaked, they weren't easy to identify, but Ham could tell that the person was small and slight of frame, petite even. When the stranger realized that Ham was looking at them, it stopped dead in its tracks, apparently unsure as to what to do next. Ham was also wary, but he was not scared of much, so he didn't feel the need to flee. Then, without warning, the figure removed its hood, revealing the face of a young woman, barely more than a girl. She was pale and slightly sickly looking, but attractive nonetheless, with watery blue eyes and light hair. He wondered where she had come from, and what brought her to these woods. Her dress was conspicuously torn, and she seemed to have been traveling for quite some time without food or rest.

"Hello, I am Ham, what is your name?" He started off, speaking gingerly so as not to give her a fright. She looked at him closely for a minute, studying him, then, apparently satisfied, replied meekly,

"Ophelia. Pleased to meet you, sir."

"What brings you to the forest? Do you live nearby?" Ham questioned.

"No, I do not. I come from a town three days east of here. I have been...traveling."

He raised his eyebrows, "With nothing packed for the journey? You carry no food or clothing. Where could you be going?"

She looked uncomfortable, but went ahead and answered him. "Alright, I'll tell you. I don't know why, but I trust you." She gave him a half smile, then let loose. "I'm on the run. I have been for days. You see, my sisters and I were all to be married off when we reached marriageable age, but I never found a suitor. The others were whisked away to start their lives and I alone was left. I lived with my father, the miller, and worked for him day after day, so that at least kept my mind off of my marriage woes." Ham was enraptured. It sounded so much like his own story, so unfair. They were like soul mates.

"Then, one day when my father was out making deliveries, some men from the town came together and stormed my home. I saw them from afar and locked myself inside, but they had seen me as well. They banged on the door, demanding that I come out to them. When I asked why, they just said that I'd have to find out, but they weren't leaving. I wondered then whether something had happened to my father, because they would know, surely, that he was coming back home. Many of them knew him personally. So, I made a decision. I would run. There was a window in the back that none of them should have known about, so I made my way quietly out of it and stole away. I have been running ever since, certain that if I stopped they'd be close behind." She finished her narrative, breathless from anxiety, and Ham swore to himself he'd catch her if she swooned.

His face was awash with compassion. "Are you hurt?"

She blushed. "No...no I'm alright, but I appreciate your concern."

"Surely you are hungry then. You look as if you have not eaten in days."

That she did not deny. "It's true; the last time I ate a meal was the morning before I escaped. But I wouldn't want to trouble you with that. I'll manage."

He was not to be put off, however. "I will take you to my family, and we will feed you and clothe you. I'll not have a beauty such as yourself left alone to fend for herself." Then, as if realizing that she may be wary of a man telling her what to do, he added, "You can leave as soon as you're feeling better, if you like."

The young woman seemed to float there, suspended momentarily by indecision, then she nodded her head in assent and stepped towards him carefully. "Take me there please."

That was enough for Ham! He promptly shouldered his axe and took her arm with his other hand, setting off immediately for the house. The wood would have to wait. He had found a woman!

Before long, Ophelia spoke up again while they were walking. "You look like you have been working very hard, indeed. Can I ask what all of the wood is for?" She had to have noticed the mass of felled saplings that had surrounded him in the forest. "Either you have something very big that needs building or you have a personal vendetta against trees."

He grinned. She was charming too! Unfortunately, an honest answer to her question would likely put her off completely from any interest she might have in him. They had already mentioned the ark to a small number of people they were fairly close to, and every one of them had thought the family was absolutely mad. People who had previously visited from town now and again no longer did so anymore. Yet, he had no choice but to be honest. She would see the great wooden monstrosity soon enough when they made it to the edge of the trees. So, he told her. "Ah...my family and I are building a very big, wooden ark together, as sort of a communal project."

"That would explain all the wood. It looks like they're making you do all of the work, though. How did you manage to get the short end of the stick?" She touched his raw hand. "That looks painful. Surely they could take turns with you?"

The young man was enjoying the attention. "Oh, I volunteered. Someone has to do it, you know." She looked concerned, however. "I'd say you should let them share the load. It's not fair for you to do so much and them so little."

Then, switching gears, she asked the real question he'd been hoping to avoid. "What's it for? The sea is a fair distance away. Do you all expect a tidal wave sometime soon?" She said somewhat playfully.

Ham giggled awkwardly. "Sort of...yes." He realized then, though, that if there was any chance she would be interested in him, she would find out sooner or later. Though he didn't trust God to give him a good future, he did believe that there really was a flood coming, and they weren't going to be able to keep living the way they had before. He came clean. "Alright, listen. The whole family will be talking about this anyway, so you may as well hear it from me first." He sighed, eyes shifting anxiously as though looking for a way out of the situation. "We believe that God, the One who made everything, is going to destroy the world by water, leaving only a few people behind. So, we are doing as He told us, making an ark to keep us and the animals safe until the water subsides. There, you have it! That's the truth, as mad as it seems." He winced internally, waiting for the inevitable backlash that he knew was coming. But it never did. The strange young woman just stared at him, stunned. Or, at least, he thought that must be what it was, because she didn't speak or look particularly surprised, just intrigued.

She must have realized how funny her expression looked, because it changed abruptly to a sort of concerned sympathy, and she reached out a hand to touch his arm. "You really believe this, don't you?"

He was hesitant, but he'd made it this far. There was no point turning back now. "I do. I don't like it, but I believe it. This world won't be the same for much longer." Just then, they exited the clearing, unveiling a breathtaking view of the titanic structure that the family had begun to build, and she responded in kind. "I believe you too. So, your family gets to go on that. What does that mean for the rest of us?"

Ham responded quick as lightning, "Don't you worry about that. You're here with us now, so let's just take care of you." Then, walking arm in arm for support, he led her to meet the family.

Back at the farm, Lamech was enjoying his new role as master crafter of joinery. He had not done woodworking in years, and it made him feel useful again. So, he spent the days chiseling away at plank after plank of freshly-planed wood. Today, as was his custom, he was at his workbench under the barn facing the rest of the compound so he could watch the family progress when he took breaks. During one such break, he looked out and saw the dark form of Ham on the horizon coming near with a girl on his arm. What on earth? How many times were strange women going to appear on his doorstep? It would have bothered him if he wasn't utterly convinced that God was going to give these boys wives according to his word. Maybe the Lord had sent Ham one.

He went to get the women, aware that they were working as hard as the others, but knowing that their presence would be needed when the newcomer arrived. With Naamah and Tabitha around, the girl would have no trouble feeling right at home. They all looked surprised when the old man gave them the news, but they came on anyway. At this rate, they might not be surprised if the whole town showed up one day unannounced!

The reception for Ophelia was a warm one. Leah was her usual motherly self, and the other two understood what it felt like to be the outcast and were eager to do everything in their power to make the newcomer feel at home. After introducing themselves, Leah ushered the young women inside, proclaiming "It's time to eat!" loudly enough that anyone within a square mile would have heard the announcement. Never mind that it wasn't really a particularly normal time to eat, being the middle of the morning, but if Leah said it was time to eat, then it was *time to eat.*

As it took a while for everyone to make their way inside, largely because Ham had to go elicit the help of the other men to move the wood he'd left in the forest, the ladies busied themselves getting to know one another. Ophelia was charming enough and pitiful to boot, so she soon found the women chatting away freely about everything under the sun as though she were part of the family. Tabitha, freshly married as she was, couldn't stop yammering for a minute about what a delight it was to finally be married, and how she just loved Japheth to pieces.

"That's so sweet that you two have found each other: true love at last. I hope that one day I too can have a story like yours." Ophelia said dreamily. "And you were right under each other's noses for quite some time it sounds like! I wonder what took the fellow so long. You are such a delight after all, dear Tabitha. I can tell and I've only just met you. "
Tabitha could only smile and nod in response. Ophelia was right, of course. A good length of time had passed before Japheth had shown Tabitha any real interest. She had always just put it down to his shyness or lack of confidence that she would respond favorably. He always was intent upon expecting a good outcome before he would try nearly anything at all. Now, though, she began to wonder if there was another reason that he had taken so long. If a stranger had noticed, was she being naive to think differently? He *had* been less focused on her and their new marriage than she had hoped so far, being entirely too interested in his work. He seemed eager to be up in the morning and away from her, off to work on that blasted ark, and he came back late in the evenings sometimes as well.

Naamah, meanwhile, had finally begun to open up that morning about her romantic inklings towards Shem, and she wasn't about to stop because of the newcomer. It had been too difficult to make it past her fear of speaking in the first place. She was careful, of course, never willing to reveal too much too quickly, but she had begun to ask questions about him, particularly from his mother, who was all too willing to brag on her second son. While Tabitha was reeling from her revelation about Japheth, Naamah, doing her best to seem nonchalant, had asked Shem's mother, "Do you think Shem is going to be looking for a wife soon? I haven't seen him bring any love interests home...and he seems to come right back after short trips into town for supplies. What do you think? You know him best."

Leah was no fool, aware of Naamah and Shem's instant attraction since the young woman had arrived. She was not averse to it, however, so she encouraged the girl as she was able. She responded cordially, "Certainly, certainly, he comes straight home, no doubts about that. I don't know though, I think he may have his eye on someone he fancies, though he certainly hasn't revealed anything to me." She smiled. "You can see there's a look in his eye sometimes, a passion that I don't think I saw in the past. You know, the love twinkle." He did need a wife, and soon at that. She didn't know how long it would be before the chances to find one were gone. At least this one was willing to stay with them and submit to their way of life.

Ophelia though was significantly more brazen. She burst out, "You love him don't you? I can see that 'twinkle' in your eyes when you speak of him!" Naamah's face lit up bright red, which was quite a feat given her skin tone, and Ophelia hastily tried to manage the situation. "Oh, I didn't mean anything by it, just that it's so exciting to see someone in love, and I think you shouldn't be ashamed is all. Surely he loves you back? I mean, why would you doubt it? No matter what your life was like before you came here, I'm sure he would be able to see right past that to the real you that's worth loving." Naamah didn't know what to say to that, so she just made an excuse to leave the room.

"Was it something I said?" Ophelia asked, seemingly perplexed. "I didn't mean to cause any trouble. I just assume that with what Ham told me about God's message to you all, then your sons must be eager to find good wives, and certainly, Naamah would make a good wife."

"It's alright, Ophelia. She's just nervous about such things being spoken of so openly. She has faced much heartache in the past. She will be alright though." Leah said assuredly, though she doubted the words even as she spoke them. Naamah's emotional health had seemed to her to be in a precarious position from the start, and it might not take much to send it tumbling down.

"As I said, she would make a wonderful wife, and I am sure that they will come to that conclusion themselves, she and he both. I only hope that I could be such a wife one day!" Ophelia sighed wistfully. Tabitha was quick to encourage. "Perhaps you will, and sooner than you think! I believe God has someone for all of us." Everyone knew what she meant. Ham was available.

"What of you, though, Leah?" Ophelia inquired. "What is it that you most desire in life?"

The older woman was pensive as she continued stirring the wooden bowl in her hands. "I just want my sons to be happy and live good long lives with the Lord. That's all a mother wants."

The young woman heartily agreed, munching hungrily on an apple as she did so. "You are a wonderful mother, truly. What a sweet heart you have!" Her face grew grave. "But oh, what about this flood Ham mentioned? How did that news make you feel? I imagine it would fill a mother's heart with fear to know that the world was going to come down around her sons heads, and that they would lose everything that once had meaning to them. It sounds like a terribly frightening experience ahead. How can you be sure you can trust this God who told you this?" She hurriedly added, "I mean no disrespect, of course. I do not serve a god myself. You can teach me what gives you so much hope."

Unfortunately, the hope of which the young woman so glibly spoke had fled Leah in those moments as she considered just how much fear was there, lying dormant in her own heart. She had no words of encouragement to give.

Outside, Naamah had fled towards the outskirts of the farm to be alone. She was intercepted on her way, however, by old Lamech, the grandfather she'd never had. He saw her tears and stopped her in her tracks. "What hurts, my dear?" He asked kindly. She wasn't about to trust a man with her deepest fears, so she just looked at him forlornly, contemplating how she might slip away. He continued, unphased, "I don't suppose you've been upset by someone, hmm?" His face crinkled.

Seeing that she was not going to respond anytime soon, he decided he'd just give her some encouragement and let the Lord do the rest.

"You know, I have been alive for over seven hundred years, and I can tell you that I've been betrayed or ill-used at least that many times, and probably more. So, if you find yourself feeling wounded, as though the world was against you, please understand - it often is. But - ," he held up a knobby finger, "that doesn't mean that we can give up on people. God made us all in His image, and we are all beyond valuable to Him. The truth is, God alone is the only one who will never fail you, because all people must fight the selfishness inside themselves. They can't beat it permanently, even if they manage for a while. This is why we need God. We must trust Him, and be willing to give ourselves to others without fear, because when they hurt us, we can forgive, knowing that God has first forgiven us for how we have failed him and others. Only in this can we find freedom." He patted her arm lightly to let her know he was there for her and ambled away.

Naamah just stood there for quite some time, eyes towards the sky, unsure of what to do with herself. She didn't know what to believe. She wanted to believe that she could be loved, but no one had ever showed her that was possible. For the first time in her life though, she looked to the heavens and prayed, speaking to the God who might be there. "God, I don't know what's true about you, but I know that these people have been here for me in ways I have needed my whole life, and I know that they speak about you as though you were everything to them. Whatever you are, I want you in my life. Make me worthy of your love."

Shortly after she finished speaking quietly to herself and to the Lord, she heard footsteps behind her. Someone had come out to join her yet again. She wondered if it was Lamech. As she turned, though, she was astonished and dismayed to see Shem's sun-tanned face looking back at her. He looked right into her eyes, and she returned the look full force for the first time, amazed at the depth of feeling she saw in them. At that moment, they both knew what had never been said. They loved each other. And now that she knew the Lord loved her too, she might just be alright with that.

Later that night, after the family had enjoyed a fairly good, albeit brief dinner, Leah went to bed early. She had been so upset by thoughts of the future after speaking with Ophelia that she just couldn't stop playing out her fears over and over in her mind. Noah came to check on her eventually, asking what had upset her. Leah was never the sort to leave dinner early.

"Noah, I haven't said this to you much before, because I know you can't change anything for us, however much we might want you to, but I need you to know that I am afraid of what is coming." Her face was etched with fear, because she was tired of holding it in. She sagged against his shoulder, sobbing into his tunic. "I just don't know what to do. We are working hard, day in and day out, trusting in a God we can't see for a future unlike anything we can even dream. How can I be sure that our sons are going to be okay? That *we* are going to be okay?"

Noah had been over and over these things in his own mind, and so, while he was slightly overwhelmed by her emotions, the words themselves did not surprise him at all. He understood. "I know sweetheart," he replied softly, whispering comfort to her. "I, too, have feared the same things and more. I fear letting the family down, letting

God down, leading the family somewhere from which we can't return...Sometimes it cripples me, and sometimes I can hold it at bay long enough to keep moving, because I must." He paused, gathering the strength to say what came next. "But I know that no matter what comes, no matter what we have to go through together or what we have to lose, our God is *worthy* of our trust, and we must hope in Him."

He could see that she still struggled to believe, so he took her by the shoulders and looked into her eyes. "Suffering is something that I think we have always thought was only evil, something to be avoided at any cost. But God has been showing me that this isn't true. Suffering is like a fire. It *refines* us, and our faith. We pass *through* suffering to come out on the other side, and God removes from us the dross that did not belong in our lives, like fear and doubt. We are not destroyed, because our Lord walks with us through the flames. We must believe that He is a good Father, and that He will care for us and our children. He loves them more than we do." This last he hardly believed, but it was true nonetheless. Though it would be quite some time before her heart caught up with his words, she did find comfort in them, and she was able to sleep that night and awake anew in the morning, more hopeful than before.

At breakfast, the family gathered around the table in the living area, far more cheerful in general than they had been the day before - except for Tabitha and Japheth. They had endured a rather rough night together when Japheth returned home late yet again, after promising to take care of some finishing touches on the ark when the others had retired for the evening. Yet again, his young bride had waited for far too long to see the face she so longed to see. So, today, they were having some significant struggles, though he seemed unaware of what had caused them. In fact, not long into breakfast, she thrust herself up from the floor and stormed outside. After a perplexing moment, Ophelia, of all people, followed her out to check on her, saying something about how she knew what was wrong.

The family stayed inside and finished eating, purposefully taking their time, but eventually, after a knowing nudge from his father, Japheth figured out that he should probably go check on her himself, since it was his fault she was upset. He was met with a decidedly unfriendly welcome as Tabitha shouted his name. Ophelia was standing next to her, and his wife was positively livid. He had never seen her like this, and was more than a little afraid.

"Ah, dear, I'm not exactly sure what I did, but I'm certain that I'm sorry for it. Just tell me what's wrong." He stuttered nervously.

"What's wrong? What's *wrong* is that you don't care about me at all! All you care about is work! Ophelia understands. She sees it too."

"Um, I mean no disrespect, but hasn't she been here for all of one day? I don't think she's the best person to consult on our marriage, my love. I do care about you, very much, but I also care about the work we are doing. It is for the Lord, after all!" He was being entirely earnest, but was honest to a fault. She didn't look happy.

"You are *such* a man! Do you think I want to be compared to your work? I married you because I wanted to be the most special thing in your life. I thought I mattered to you that much. Was I wrong?" Her face was so red he was worried she might explode.

He responded abashedly. "I'm sorry, I really am. I didn't realize you felt this way. I will do my best to change it. You can trust me on that. And when I fail, you can remind me, and I will listen. Alright? I mean it. You mean more to me than all the world!" The look on his face was so genuine and desperate that she knew he meant it, but she wasn't read to stop being angry yet.

She didn't have much of a choice, however, because that second they were interrupted by a blinding flash of light, and a shining warrior appeared in their midst with armor gleaming like a fallen star. It was Gurion. But why? Surely the angel wasn't afraid Tabitha would hurt Japheth. That seemed a little dramatic, and the young man was certain that his terrifying appearance was doing more harm than good. He covered his eyes, trying to address the blazing figure, but Gurion did not heed him in the slightest. His fiery eyes were on...Ophelia?

Japheth didn't have to wait long. The angel's voice rang out like the roar of river rapids, so deafening that he could hardly imagine it was the same simple giant they had met months ago, and it filled them all with fear. "Show yourself, you demon-spawn! I know your kind! I have seen through your lies."

Ophelia had the most bewildering look on her face. She wasn't scared, for one, or hiding her eyes. Instead, she was staring fiercely back at the angel, eyes aflame with the reflection of his brilliance. As quickly as Gurion had appeared, she disappeared, transforming into an eagle as black as night, the size of a large man, with a man's torso and legs. This figure, too, shone with an otherworldly light, though it seemed unholy next to the glory of God emanating from Gurion. "Wormwood." The big angel spat the name, like so much filth on his tongue. By this time the entire family had streamed out of the house to discover the cause of the ruckus, and every one of them was appalled. They had been harboring a demon?

However, no sooner had they witnessed the evil spirit appear than he was gone in a flash, speeding off into the distance at the sight of Micah descending from above. Apparently he wasn't willing to attempt to take on two angels at once. The whole gathering was mystified, each of them coming to their senses slowly, realizing how they'd been taken for fools.

Gurion was firm. "This means that the enemies are aware of us and your work now, everyone. They will be back. Next time someone wants to come to this place, you speak with us first. We cannot risk this happening again. They will disguise themselves as whatever they must in order to gain a foothold in your lives, and you cannot allow it. You must be on your guard!"

Ham, on his part, was destroyed inside. His only hope at finding a wife had been ripped from him, and his love interest had turned out to be evil incarnate. Now he was sure he could not trust God.

CHAPTER 17

It's Not About You

AFTER THE SURPRISING TWIST at the gladiator games in Eshcol, Methuselah and Boaz were faced with the difficult decision of where God wanted them to bring his news next. It couldn't be terribly close by, because, as Nathan had warned them, there was a strong possibility that demonic forces would be after them every step of the way in that place. So, they planned to cut a wide berth around the city and move further afield to more rural areas. Which direction were they to go, though? People were in need everywhere. Nathan was not willing to give them that sort of direction, as he stood solidly by the truth that God would tell him when he needed to speak, and he would not speak until such a time as that. He assured them though that God would reveal to them what to do, if they asked.

Methuselah was no stranger to asking for help from the Lord, so he and Boaz agreed, stepping into a sort of park in the midst of the market.

It had a patch of grass and some benches, so the two sat down and inquired of God. While they were praying, Boaz's thoughts turned towards that fateful day in the tavern when life had turned upside down. The gold diggers from the north had come down to Kadish, bringing with them the news of impending war. Boaz found that even as his father finished praying, he could not get that thought out of his mind, so he voiced it. "Do you remember those lads in the tavern that night when all of this started? The unsavory lot?"

The old historian scratched his head a long moment, making the younger man wonder for a minute if he was mistaken, then responded abruptly, "Oh, YES, yes I do! They had come from the north near Havilah."

"Right, well. I can't get them out of my mind, and we were praying for a place to go. What if we went there? Perhaps gold-diggers and the like need to know about God's love as well. Seems as good an idea as any." Boaz mumbled, unsure of himself. He had no experience in these matters to base his choices upon, and he felt entirely foolish voicing things when he had no foundation upon which to stand. Yet, as he had said, it made as much sense as anything else.

"No, it's not as good an option as any. It's the *right* one! My spirit is in agreement. I believe God is leading us that way. If there *is* war, or was, then there will be devastation as well, and those people will be in desperate need of hope, having lost much of what meant most to them in life. Good work son! We go north!" Methuselah slapped him on the back excitedly - a little too excitedly, his shoulder blades told him. Boaz hadn't thought of it that way: misery and ruin. It already sounded like a far less pleasing idea than it had on first blush, but there was no going back now. His father had already left his seat and was pushing his way through the crowd.

"Wait up, you excitable old fool!" Boaz yelled after him, scrambling to catch up. This had to be the first time in their lives that the father was getting ahead of the son, and for all Boaz used to say about his father hurrying up, he wasn't sure he liked the change.

They had, unfortunately, lost nearly all of their provisions when the horses had run off during the fiasco with the demon-inspired magician, and so they now had to find a way to re-supply themselves for the coming journey. They didn't have much money, so they fetched what little food they could get from the market. It was there that a merchant informed them that there was a well on the northern side of town that the locals used to draw their water. So, they set off through the city to fill up their water skins and head out. They could never have expected what they'd find.

It was late in the afternoon by the time the men reached the well after a considerable trek through the immense city, and the men could see from a distance that the well was fairly free. They were thankful, because they really needed to get watered and get moving. They could not afford to stay at an inn, and planned to find a good spot to camp for the night before nightfall. The only traffic they could see by the well was a lone woman watering her animals, stroking their backs as she did so. Since she was alone, the two were careful not to stare at her as they approached. However, the closer they got, they began to notice that one of the animals she was stroking so diligently was a gray spotted horse, and the other was purest white. Then it clicked. She had Hephzi and Shemer!

What's more, the woman was also familiar, but they had not met any women in the city. Had they? She was dark from head to toe in every feature save her clothing, which was simple: a light tan woolen tunic. To them, she appeared to be a serving woman or something of the sort. Whoever she was, she had their horses.

Methuselah hailed her as they strolled up, "Hello there my dear! I see you have a couple of very fine horses there. How did you come by them?"

The young woman looked slightly startled, but not scared exactly. They were incredibly aged after all, so he supposed that took away some of the intimidation factor. She answered slowly. "I came upon them by chance... they were eating the carrots we had planted at the back of the building where I work. Why do you ask?" She looked prepared to flee if necessary, but he also thought he could detect a glimmer of recognition in her eyes as well.

"Oh, no reason. They just happen to be *our* horses." Methuselah said glibly, smiling as broad a smile as he could muster. "We'll have them back now if that's alright with you." He moved to take the reins from her, patting Hephzi's head affectionately. She pulled back though, realization dawning in her dusky eyes.

"It's *you*! You're the men I saw in the temple arguing with the high priest!" She was practically shouting, and it was drawing concerned looks from passersby.

Methuselah held up his hands to shush her, nodding towards the perturbed populace. "Yes, yes, but can you calm down, please? We don't want to cause a fuss."

"That's new. You certainly didn't mind causing a fuss earlier in the temple. Amos was furious, and he took it out on me. I didn't hear the end of his tirade until I left and found these horses wandering in our garden." There were hints of pain in her voice. Methuselah wasn't sure that the woman's ears were the only victims of Amos's fury. What the faithful did in such temples was often beyond any notions of human dignity.

Boaz chimed in at this point, unwilling to let her verbal jab go undefended. "We did *not* argue with the man. We just shared our hope with him. It's quite different. An argument implies a conflict. We had no conflict, simply differing views. Although, this priest fellow sure wasn't hesitant to throw out threats as we left the place." He crossed his arms and huffed, satisfied.

The woman softened, clearly unwilling to go so far as to contend on behalf of the man called Amos. "You are right about that...Amos is never unwilling to dole out threats, and he follows through quite often." She had a bruised look about her as she said the words. "Anyway, here are your horses. I have no right to hold them. You can be on your way, and I will be on mine." She dropped the reins and turned as if to leave.

Methuselah was gracious. "Thank you for finding them! You've been part of God's answer to our prayers! What is your name?"

She turned her head, surprised that he had asked a personal

question. What did he care what her name was? "Amaris. And you?"

"Methuselah, at your service." He bowed low. "And this is my son Boaz. Yes, he too is old. You don't even want to know how long I've been around."

Amaris forced a smile. The old men made a curious pair. "Perhaps not. What I do want to know though, is why you think God used me, a temple priestess, to give your horses back to you. What makes you think this was not chance?"

"There is no such thing as chance. The one true God who reigns over all things knows all and is involved in all of the affairs of men. Now, he does not cause all things," he wagged a finger, "no, mankind does much of that, particularly the nastier bits. But, every good and perfect gift comes down from above, from the Father of Lights. We call Him that, because He spoke all light into existence when the world began. It is He, most certainly, who brought our horses back to us today and allowed us to meet such a lovely soul as you. He, too, it is who promises that he appoints the times and places where people should live so that they would feel their way towards Him and find Him. Perhaps you have met us today so that you might find Him."

Amaris was stunned. She had never heard of such a God, but she was stricken in her soul with the sense that He was both real and interested in her. Why though? Why would any god choose to pursue *her*, as it sounded like this one was doing?

The historian could see that she wasn't moving, and that had to mean that some of what he had said was sinking in. He pressed further, "You, like all of us, are made in God's image, and made *for* Him. It means you are *valuable* just as you are. The trouble is, we soil that image by giving ourselves over to worshipping things that we are not meant to worship, things that do not fulfill us. God calls these idols. We worship and serve the creature rather than the Creator, and for that, we are judged. You have served idols all of your life, haven't you?" He asked her, voice low.

She was still a moment more, but soon cracked, spilling with emotion. "Yes, yes I have!" She cried, weeping.

"You feel like a slave, don't you? I could see it in your eyes when we met in the temple." The old man continued, softly but firmly. Amaris could only nod between sobs. "But you don't want to be anymore?"

She stopped, looking at him with watery eyes, and said breathlessly, "I don't. But what can I do?" That was all Methuselah needed to hear.

"You give yourself to Him! Give your life to the One who made you, and you will find His love, blessing, and protection surrounding you like a living garment, a constant companion for the rest of your days, and when they are over, you will be with Him in Paradise!" He nearly shouted the last words, overcome with joy that his good news had finally found a home in a ready soul.

"I will. I trust Him! You must teach me to walk with this God." She said, eyes shining.

"Oh, we shall, my dear. I am happy for you! But first, we need to get some rest. Do you have a place we can pass the night?"

She smiled. That was no problem at all. "Follow me!"

The most natural thing for Amaris to do would have been to lead them back to her own dwelling, but it was attached to the temple grounds where she had served Ishtar, and that didn't seem like an overly good idea to bring these men who served the True God to spend the night there where they were not welcome. What's more, it was the wrong direction. So, instead, she led them further north to the outskirts of town to spend the night with a friend of hers, Ehud the tanner.

He was a kind, middle-aged man, and his home was little more than a thatched hut, but they found it to be a tremendous blessing after a difficult but rewarding day. The animal skin on his dirt floor was near as good as the clouds of heaven on that night. They thanked God that He was so willing to care for them. Not only had He given them a place to stay when they needed it, but He had also returned their supplies and horses! While they bunked down with Ehud, Amaris headed back to her own place for the night, but she promised to return in the morning packed for travel. She wanted to go with them and guide them on their journey, as she knew the land thereabouts.

Dawn came bright and early, and father and son rose feeling refreshed and ready for a journey. Ehud was already up and getting ready to start the day's work as they did, so they thanked him for his hospitality and departed. Once outside, they took the horses and made their way towards the northern city gate, where Amaris had promised to meet them.

They arrived at about the third hour from dawn, but she was nowhere to be seen. Boaz was skeptical as usual, and it didn't take long for him to start muttering. "I doubt she'll make it. She probably just had a moment of weakness yesterday where her emotions took over, but then she went back to that temple and I'm sure she went right back to what she was doing before. People don't really change. We don't need her anyway. We don't even have a definite destination..." Methuselah ignored most of this, having far more hope for the girl than did his ever-optimistic son, but after an hour passed, and then part of another, he, too, grew concerned. They needed to be on the road before it was too late or they most certainly wouldn't make it to any of the rural villages by nightfall, and she was aware of that. So, what was keeping her?

Eventually, even Methuselah's patience began to wear thin, though he wasn't convinced she had changed her mind. He *knew* what he had seen in her eyes the day before. The change was genuine, and she wouldn't go back, however, that devious monk Amos was another matter entirely. Could it be that he had discovered her plan and done something terrible to stop her? He feared that might be the case.

Just as they were about to get up and leave, or (in Methuselah's mind) go back and find the young woman, they heard a familiar voice. She was alright! Coming around the bend in the road towards them was Amaris, fitted for the road and guiding an impressive black Arabian stallion that would make a prince jealous. Before she even reached them they could hear the apologies tumbling from her lips. "I'm so sorry you two! Amos gave me a little trouble before I left, but, strangely enough, when I spoke about the God you all mentioned, a strange look came over him and he just left me alone. I don't know what that was about but I believe this is a *powerful* God we serve!"

Methuselah was gracious. "Yes He is! The only One! It looks like it may have taken you a moment to procure *that* as well," he said, pointing at the stallion.

"Oh, right," she beamed, "this is Hadassah, the fastest horse in the realm! - according to the merchant that sold it to me. To be fair, he probably would have said that about a sick pony with three legs if he thought it would get it sold. It took me nearly all of my earnings I've saved for the past few years to buy him, and that's after we haggled for over a half hour. But I'm proud of him!" She said, patting his cheek lovingly. "So, where are we headed?"

Boaz was quick to reply, "We go towards Havilah until we find a place where people are suffering." Seeing what had happened in Amaris the day before and how wrong he had been about the superficiality of that change, the cynic in him had begun to fade. At every turn, God proved him wrong about what he thought he knew about the world. In fact, he was beginning to think that a man's knowledge meant nearly nothing, except so much as he knew the God who made him.

The young woman looked slightly confused, however, and reasonably so. "Um...what do we expect is going to bring suffering to the villages near Havilah?"

"We have reason to believe that war has broken out in the region, or that it is going to do so, at any rate. So, we want to be there to help whoever is left."

"Oh. Alright, then off we go!" She said simply, not aware of any war in those parts but ready to submit to his directive regardless. They had brought her plenty of news that she didn't expect already, and it had changed her life. "We will head towards Ophir. It's a small town near the mountains that suffers enough on a regular basis from poverty and transience. I am sure someone there will need your news. It may take more than a day's ride to get there, however." The course was set, and they rode away into the high noon sun.

After passing the night on the road and journeying for another few hours the following morning, the trio sighted the small village of Ophir nestled in the hills. It was probably a half day's ride from the mountains looming in the distance: dark, forbidding mountains lined with the world's most precious gold. They entered the town without incident, passing by a number of thatched cottages without meeting a soul. In the distance, they saw a gaggle of children along with a few women here and there, but there was a conspicuous absence of adults, men in particular. Methuselah felt a sense of foreboding, perhaps the Lord's warning that suffering had indeed already made its mark on Ophir.

Just after the old carpenter felt the sharp jab of apprehension, Nathan appeared next to him in plain brown clothes, smiling as he materialized. "Hello old friend. I know this town! I left here when the Lord assigned us to protect your grandson's family. There is someone here that I need to see!" He then glanced over at Amaris as he said this, jabbing a finger her direction, "And I see you have picked up a passenger. You should probably introduce me to this one before she takes me for a marauder or something."

As he said this, Amaris happened to look over and noticed the strange man walking next to Methuselah's horse. "Greetings! Are you one of the locals?"

"Yes...after a fashion," the angel replied cryptically. "I lived here for quite some time. My name is Nathan. Methuselah and Boaz are my good friends. And who might you be?" He gave her a disarming grin.

"Amaris," she said sweetly. "And these two old men saved my life! Any friend of theirs is a friend of mine."

Nathan was happy for them. They had finally seen how rewarding it could be to share God with others, and this young woman seemed like she would make an excellent addition to the party. However, the angel was excited to go, so he told them as much. "It was good to meet you, but I've got to be off now. I have an old friend I can't wait to see!" Then he strolled away, eager also to see what had become of some of the young folk he used to help now and again.

The trio ambled on into the village, but soon stopped, unsure where to go next. Perhaps they'd been wrong about war having made it this far. It was just rumor, after all. Even then, the supposed wars had been in the East at the time, not the North, but they had assumed it would have spread this direction if the Havilah gold-diggers were hearing about it that long ago. Every kingdom longed to seize the fabled gold of Havilah. As they sat, pensive on their horses, Amaris noticed a woman within earshot and called out to her for help. The woman, wispy gray hair waving in the wind, was frantically running about gathering clothes and blankets. At the call, she stopped long enough to notice them, looking as though she was considering ignoring them in order to finish what she was doing. However, she soon set aside the pile of fabric in her hands and made her way towards them.

"What brings you to these parts?" She asked warily. She didn't appear too happy about the prospect of strangers frequenting her town.

Methuselah spoke up, eager to put her at ease. "We come to bring hope to the hopeless. Are there any among you suffering or in need of a helping hand? We heard that perhaps there was a conflict in the region, and there seems to be a noticeable absence of young men about."

The woman's eyebrows lowered suspiciously. "You're telling me you came for no reason but to spend your time helping folks?"

The carpenter could see she wasn't convinced, but it was the simple truth. "Yes, precisely. God has sent us to bless those who are in need, and we believe He guided us to your village. So, have you anyone in need?"

At that, the aged lady whipped around faster than he would have thought possible, and motioned for them to follow as she set off down a narrow path between homes. At the end of the path, they found what they were looking for. Scores of men, both old and young, were scattered about in a broad place behind the homes. Most of them were injured, and one or two, by Methuselah's estimation, did not appear to be moving at all. Covered by only a pitifully inadequate piece of canvas, the whole area was strewn with the wounded. It looked like a war zone. So, destruction had made its way this far north.

"What happened?" Boaz cried. He had not expected to see quite so much carnage, and it was taking a toll on him already.

"War," came their host's anguished reply. "An army the likes of which I've never seen in all my years tore through the countryside from the East. I'd swear the men numbered more than the sands of the sea.

They came, killing and pillaging as they pleased - only the sizeable settlements, mind you. They wouldn't waste their time on a little hamlet like ours. But our boys here," she gestured about her, "were called up to serve the landlords further north who had holdings near the larger cities. Many of the men here are indentured servants of sorts, practically the property of the landowners where they work and farm. Even if they had refused for their family's sakes, they wouldn't have had a job to return to, and that wouldn't help anyone, so they heeded the call. They fought, and many of them died."

The woman was teary-eyed, and they could see that she truly did care about these brave souls that the village had lost. She sniffed, wiping her eyes with a finger. "Then, the ones that came home were beat up pretty fierce. So we are doing our best to care for them, me and a few others, but I don't know if many of them will last long."

Methuselah, too, felt some of the woman's sadness, but that made him all the more eager to start showing her God's grace. "That is disheartening news. I can't begin to imagine how it feels to have the people you love hurt, and many of them taken from you. I wish we could change that, but what we can do is offer ourselves to you in whatever way you might need us. We are yours to command." The other two nodded in agreement, still silently processing the scene before them.

The old lady's eyes shone with emotion, and she croaked a thankful reply, "I am called Hannah. Your help means more to us than I can say to you. Please, follow me and I will show you how we are bandaging wounds. All we have are strips of cloth that we've been making from clothing and blankets, but we are short on all of those, and some of the men need the blankets to help them pass a fever once infection sets in. We are doing what we can."

Hannah walked them through the makeshift hospital introducing them to one after another of the injured men. Some of them greeted them back, while others just nodded tiredly, too exhausted to use words. Still others were not able to speak, because they were either unconscious or had damaged their spine in the fighting. Fathers, sons, and brothers all lay still, wondering when their time would come and their families would see them no more.

Boaz, for one of the first times in his life, felt as though he was being ripped apart inside as he surveyed the wretched scene before him. All of these men had lived lives that were far too short, and far too devoid of hope, and they might pass at any moment without having discovered just how much God loved them. Now, it was his chance to give it to them, and he felt the love of God fill him to the brim, overflowing in compassion. He grabbed some bandages with his rugged, weathered hands, and set to it binding the leg of a young man, hardly more than a boy, who was bleeding profusely from a sword wound. The young man was awake, so Boaz asked him about his life, and for once in his own life, he listened. This wasn't about Boaz.

Amaris, too, jumped right into the work with abandon, running errands for the other women and fetching whatever they needed. Methuselah, on the other hand, while entirely willing to join in, had the concern of these men's souls on his mind, and he could see that their morale was so weak it could break at any moment. He knew that a person was, more than anything, a living spirit, and if that spirit was broken, the body could not live long. So, he decided he would tell a story, and not just any story, a story of hope for such a time as this.

The only sounds currently breaking up the oppressive silence were the coughs and groans of those in pain, so he figured the men would welcome nearly any noise at all, and he didn't need any special announcement. He went and stood in the midst of the gathering, his feet between two lifeless bodies, and simply began.

"In a time long past, nearly eight hundred years ago, there was a man called Enoch. He was my father." He laughed. "Yes, I am *that* old." There were a few scattered grunts in response, and he continued. "His whole life, he dreamed of what *could* be, not of what was - what he saw with his eyes - but what he believed might be beyond them. To him, the world alone was not good enough. Working day in and day out, even loving a family, while beautiful, was not all that his soul longed for. He felt as though he had eternity in his heart, that he was made for more." Now even the pain-wracked hacking had stilled. Hushed silence reigned when the storyteller was not speaking.

"In those days, the world still remembered a place called Eden, where peace ruled and there was no war, famine, or pain. There, you could lie in the grass and eat the fruit of the land without fear, and you could live forever, because there was a tree of life with fruit that made one immortal. What's more, the Creator of that place was there too, and he visited with the first man and woman who lived in it. He was the One True God, Maker of heaven and earth, and He wanted to know His creatures. They were His, and He was theirs. My father knew about this place, and he knew that mankind had since then forever ruined their chances of enjoying Eden any longer by turning against their Creator." He stopped, letting the truth of that sink into the audience.

"But Enoch also knew the God in whom those people had first believed, and he believed that God was so good that He would find a way to bring mankind back to such an existence of joy and fulfillment. In that hope he lived, even when one day his arm was damaged by a falling tree. He had always built everything for his family himself, with his own strong hands, and it was a small tragedy, truly, when he could no longer do that for them. But God showed him something. He showed Enoch that for everyone who hopes in Him, He would one day raise them up from death, giving them new bodies, better ones than they had ever had even in their youth! Then, they would build and plant and long enjoy the works of their hands, and there would be no more death, and no mourning or crying or pain anymore. In that day, hope would come to life!" His clear, strong voice rang out across the assembly, filling the hearts of many with hope.

He finished powerfully, eager to share with them the ending to the story. "What's really exciting is that my father did not die, but was taken from the earth in a moment, by the hand of the God he so dearly loved. He had longed so much to be with his Maker, I believe, that God decided to bring him home. Now, he is with Him in glory and there is no more struggle for him, no more disappointment. All that he used to face has passed away, and he will be made new on resurrection day! I will join him there and rejoice with him, because my hope, too is in that

God that He believed. You, too, can have this hope, if you only trust Him. Entrust what little life you have left to Him, and your blessed hope will never die."

The area was filled with the sounds of weeping and laughter and shouts of joy as people hungrily grasped for the hope he had offered them. It was like fresh water for their thirsty souls, and Methuselah and Boaz couldn't get to them fast enough. Almost every person in attendance gave their lives to the Lord, and the wave of elation that passed over them all was palpable, even in the midst of genuine physical agony. In the face of such a hope, suffering could not help but fade. Amaris and Hannah too found themselves caught up in the thrall of joy, and they all spent the night there, among the wounded, talking with them and praying for them. For many days afterwards, too, Boaz, Methuselah, and Amaris stayed and cared for the wounded community. Truly, God had come to Ophir.

CHAPTER 18

Prodigal Sons

TUBAL-CAIN WAS GROWING TIRED. The twelve kingdoms had cut a swathe right through the center of the continent, taking city after city and crushing all resistance. Their victories were always swift and decisive, but at what cost? Every battle brought untold casualties, and even his own people were beginning to whisper of the "tyranny of the twelve kingdoms," not with respect or national pride, but with fear. He knew though that he ought to expect no less; he hadn't created a nation, but a monster, a ravenous beast whose lust for power could not be satiated until the whole world bowed its knee. And the worst part was that his sons were at the middle of it all, leading the charge as they slaughtered the innocent and took what didn't belong to them.

"This is *not* the legacy I wanted for them!" he shouted, pounding his fist on the oaken table where he sat eating. He had hardly touched the pile of food on his plate, but that was becoming normal for him of late.

Unable to see how he could alter the course of events that had been set into motion, he'd taken to staying in his bedchamber and brooding. Day after day, instead of fighting to try and change fate despite the odds, he had grown sickly and weak as he resigned himself to defeat. Even his servants had begun to wonder how long the ruler would last as they took countless plates of cold food away untouched.

That was Ashtoreth's greatest victory. After trying innumerable approaches on the old coward to entice him to join the conquest, the demon had accepted that this ember was not going to be coaxed back to life, and had reported his findings to Lucifer. The devious leader had already found far more willing souls to command on the battlefront in the form of Tubal-cain's sons, so he gave Ashtoreth leave to destroy the man. The dark servant had then set to work and soon discovered the sweet spot of shame and helplessness to cripple Tubal-cain permanently. It worked like a charm, and the fiend was convinced that the would-be monarch wouldn't last long.

Meanwhile, Iram and Oshik were enjoying the spoils of war. After their first battle at Huron all that time ago, they had developed a thirst for blood, and that acquired taste had only grown in potency with every conflict since. Striking down armor-clad warriors had been easy enough from the start. They were just the necessary obstacles to victory and the future that they yearned to build. Yet, they had hesitated when first confronted with the innocent face of a child, unwilling to go so far. It had not taken long, however, for those misgivings to fade as well, as the other soldiers and rulers killed without question, all in the name of progress.

Lucifer had done his part to assure their descent into depravity, reminding them of what it was they stood to lose if they backed down at this point, and forever pointing them to the promise of gain. They would be *kings*, and rich beyond their wildest dreams. Any vacillation was a sign of weakness, and must be squelched if they were to succeed among such dangerous company. But, if they stayed strong and ignored their consciences, they could subdue every enemy and rise to the top of the pack.

On this particular day, the "enemy" on the menu was Queen Arissa of Havilah and her mountain army. The twelve kingdoms' forces had obliterated much of the countryside from the west and south on their march to seize the land of gold, and they were now on Havilah's doorstep. There, sequestered deep in the black mountains, her people had hewn a mighty stone fortress from the base of the tallest peak. It rose three levels into the air, each with a wall where four men could walk abreast, complete with clefts for archers and large, steaming pots of oil placed every few paces. To gain access to the keep, one had to traverse a sloping stone walkway leading up to an arched gateway tall enough to accommodate even the largest of dragons. It looked nigh impenetrable What's more, that was just the first line of defense. Everyone knew that Arissa's kingdom extended far into the heart of the mountain where her people mined, melted, and crafted the gold that was theirs by right. Doubtless, there would be several more levels of security, given the scope of her operation.

Gazing upon this invincible monolith, many of the kings who had accompanied Iram and Oshik on this campaign were somewhat apprehensive, as might be expected. To their knowledge, *no one* had ever conquered the Golden Kingdom, and its wealth and power were respected the world over. So, they had readied their men and called them into battle formation, but remained unsure as to how to proceed. There was one soul, however, who was not concerned in the least.

Lucifer strolled through the ranks of men like an affluent child on holiday, expectant that every little detail of the outing was going to bend to his will. The mountain stronghold *was* impressive, but it was not truly an obstacle to him and his forces of darkness. They could move in and out of its high walls at will. The Devil was the master of espionage, and already his agents were hard at work inside the walls of the keep, clearing the way for the charge that the twelve kingdoms would soon level upon the gate. It was a simple matter of threatening the mercenaries that guarded the doors with the fulfillment of their worst fears, and prompting them in one direction or another when the time came.

What's more, Arissa was more of an old friend than an enemy for his ilk. Her entire kingdom had dwelt in the oppressive shadows of greed and selfishness since the dawn of its being, and Satan's demons frequented the great stone halls on a daily basis. He would have used the queen herself for the mission ahead and skipped the rigmarole with Tubal-cain if it were not for her lack of ambition. She only desired wealth and security, both of which were abundant right where she was, so she had become expendable, a mere nuisance to be dealt with. His right hand man, Beelzebub, was a regular patron of the Queen's company, and was already hard at work filling her with fear so that she would be ready to surrender when the time came. She would never do so, whatever they told her, until she was out of options. There was nothing to leverage, since her highest values were the security that her riches had won her, and that was precisely what they planned to take from her. Only her own life was more important.

Moloch flew in and dropped to the ground next to Lucifer, informing him that all was ready. It was time to raid the mountain. The demon leader and his cohorts went to the council of kings and gave them the go-ahead, feeding them with lies, ambition, and whatever else it took to get them moving. Then Satan went personally to Iram and Oshik, his favorite puppets, as they were the acting leaders by proxy. He liked Iram, the older, because he was wily and willing to put in some effort to get what he wanted, but Oshik had his uses as well.

Raising a gauntlet-clad hand, Iram signaled to the battering rams that it was time for the attack to commence. Quick as a flash, he swung his arm downwards and a stampede of horned dragons surged towards the gate, intending to bust it down with brute force. The mass of flesh slammed mightily into the gate with the sound of a thunderclap, and it shuddered violently, but did not yield. It appeared that the warlords' fears were not unwarranted. Looking about haplessly, Iram signaled for yet another run, with soldiers pulling the animals back to the base of the bridge and replacing those who had been injured by the impact. This blow, too, was not enough to budge the titanic gate. However, no one had considered the strength of angels.

Having no recourse, the increasingly irritated Iram called for a third run, but this time Satan called one of his own to join the charge. Moloch, nearly as large as one of the dragons but with many times the strength, prepared himself to join the onslaught. In tandem with the battering team, he shot towards the gate full force and his bullish bulk smashed into it with such incredible force that it shattered into a thousand pieces, loosing a torrent of dragons into the unsuspecting fighters inside. Men were tossed aside like ragdolls and the way was clear for the invaders to venture in un-opposed.

The army advanced to find the following levels of defense already in disarray and quick to surrender. Satan's spies had done their work well. Before long, they were tramping through wide stone halls, armor gleaming in the torchlight, on their way to confront the queen. As it turned out, she was waiting for them in a room of gold, a barbarian princess hardened through age and avarice. The sight of her was impressive. Flaming red hair framed a stern, unyielding visage costumed in shining black jewelry. That was the other treasure under the mountain: onyx stone.

Despite the fearsome facade, Arissa was clearly defeated, and she didn't wait for the ignominy of being asked to surrender. Instead, she rose from her place and strode out to meet them, intent on making a deal. Lucifer, however, had plans for the young princes, and he was not willing to risk them turning out like their spineless father, so he ordered Oshik to strike her down. He was eager to assert himself as a man of action, so he obeyed without hesitation, lunging at her with surprising speed and plunging his blade deep into her gut. As she slid gasping off of his sword, the other men got the message: this young man was willing to get his hands dirty. More importantly, they were all filthy rich.

After the fiasco with Ophelia, Ham sank deeper into the depression that had already slowly been forming over him like angry storm clouds. He had only wanted someone to love him, but God apparently wasn't interested in giving him that. The young man couldn't believe that he had practically fallen in love with a demon! The whole spiritual battle nonsense in general was getting ridiculous. His whole life before that he had never heard of angels or demons except from one of his great grandfather's stories, and now the invisible irritants were practically part of everyday life. If that was what following God brought, he wasn't interested in it. So, he began planning his exit. He wasn't going to stay in Kadish where no one cared about him. He'd go find his fortune and a wife elsewhere.

The rest of the family, too, had been shaken by the horrific Wormwood episode. That fiend had found his way into their midst undetected so easily - spreading his lies like the plague - that it scared them. It made them wonder what else was prowling about of which they were unaware. However, not everything was bad.

After the events of that fateful day, Japheth and Tabitha had begun to work through their issue with his work and were decidedly more at ease with one another. Shem and Naamah had struck up quite a romance after their chance encounter as well. Then there was Noah, who understood his wife and her fears far better now and was more equipped to battle for her sake in prayer, though she was still understandably unsteady. Lamech watched all of this with a thankful heart, knowing that His God had turned all of the evil of their enemies towards good for those that He loved.

The old man himself was feeling more and more tired of late, but his spirit was better than it had ever been as he watched the family band together to accomplish a mission that was so much greater than any one of them. He was glad that he had gotten to see the young men grow and find love, though he was worried about Ham. That boy just hadn't been the same since the prophecy had come to the family. Lamech wondered what he could do about it. He decided he would invite Ham to work with him so they could have a good chat.

So, the day after his musings, Lamech hobbled out to Ham's hut early in the morning and banged on the door. No answer. So, he knocked again, adding a few extra raps for good measure. The lad sure could sleep! Goodness, the rocks would wake up with that much racket. Then, without warning, the door swung open and Lamech practically fell inside, as he'd been leaning on the frame for support between knocks. Ham's thick hands caught him and roughly stood him back up. "What do you want Grandfather?" His low voice grumbled.

"Is that any way to address your senior? I came to invite you to work with me today so we can have some time together, but now I have a mind to just give you a good beating. What are you up to anyway?" His gray brows raised as he peeked inside. He couldn't help noticing the fully-packed rucksack sitting against the wall and the walking staff in

Ham's hand.

For a moment, the young man's dark eyes swung back and forth nervously, as though he was looking for a way out of the situation, but when he finally responded, his words were cold. "I'm leaving. There is nothing for me here, so I'm going to go get what I need."

Lamech looked hard at him, gray eyebrows quivering with outrage, and he held up his arms against the doorway, blocking his grandson's escape. "You ungrateful little child. Do you realize what our God has done for you? What I have done for you? And you are going to just leave us all in the moment we need one another most so you can go on some foolish search for satisfaction? I don't think so, son! You will have to go through me -"

At that moment, Ham did just that. He panicked, realizing he would never make it out of there if he kept listening to his grandfather, and rushed the old man. Pushing him aside, he unknowingly knocked Lamech off-balance, sending him tumbling to the floor where he hit his head - hard. Ham didn't look back, and so he didn't notice his grandfather get injured. As he ran away into the forest, however, he heard a bloodcurdling cry in the distance. "Lamech is dead!" His heart stopped and his breathing grew so labored that he sat down to recover. What had he done? Thoughts raced through his mind like flames through dry brush, but he couldn't imagine a way he could go home without admitting that his grandfather's death was his fault. So, he kept moving. He didn't belong there anymore.

For the first hour Ham ran as hard and fast as he could, feeling as if the very hounds of hell were on his heels. In a way, they were. All through Kadish, he was followed by Wormwood's cohorts. They just watched, pleased that their master plan, though foiled in part by the angels, was yet bearing some fruit. There was no need to interfere with Ham at this point, however. He was going to ruin his own life just fine.

Ham had taken several of the family's tools with him so that he could trade them for a horse, which he did the moment he made it far enough into town. He had to pawn the tools and use the cash to get the beast, because anything else would look suspicious. Most in the town knew his family, but he'd heard that the new pawnbroker didn't care who he got his loot from, so long as he could sell it, and these were tools of the finest craftsmanship.

After acquiring a mount, the young man immediately made his way out of town, heading north along the river as quickly as his brown steed could carry him. He wanted to make as much headway as possible before dark - and afterwards if need be - so that he could put some distance between himself and Kadish. He hoped that if he went far enough he could put his troubles behind him. He had enough food for several days and planned to make his way towards Eshcol, as he'd heard there was work and women aplenty in places like that.

After hours of nonstop riding, his horse began to flag from weariness, and he made the decision to camp for the night. He had heard enough about bandits to know that he didn't want to be caught napping out in the open, so he scanned the area in the dim twilight to see if there was a safer place to bed down. Seeing a small gully with a rocky overhang down by the river, he made his way there. No one would find him under that. He tied the horse up next to him and covered the opening with some branches, confident that he had made an expert hideout. It wasn't long before he fell fast asleep from exhaustion, despite the thousand guilty thoughts scurrying through his mind.

The next day, he woke groggy and irritated that the sun was up. Surely he could sleep as long as he liked now that there was no one to work for at the crack of dawn. The sun needed to show some respect! Hadn't he made certain that his hideaway was covered, anyway? He looked around sleepily, eyes struggling to focus in the light, then realized that there was no covering over his hideout. In fact, he sat entirely exposed to a mob of men who were staring at him with mischief in their eyes. Bandits.

One weaselly looking fellow nudged what appeared to be his leader, sniveling, " 'Ey look here, sleeping beauty is awake!" The fellow was promptly walloped on the back of the head. "You don't say?" growled the larger man from atop a fearsome looking dragon. His eyes never left Ham's for a moment.

Ham was itching to move, but knew that he had no control over the situation and wasn't about to get himself killed, so he did the only think he could think to do - he lied. "I'm so glad you all found me," he said as convincingly as he could, "I'd heard there was a band of the fiercest warriors in the land around these parts, and I was hoping to find you so I could join up. I'm young and ready for plunder! What do you say?" He was sweating profusely, aware that the chances of his bluff working were slim to none.

The leader snorted derisively, a gesture that was met with loud guffaws by his cohorts. He stopped suddenly, glaring at Ham. "That's the most foolish thing I've ever heard, but you've got guts. I like it." Ham's heart skipped a beat. That had gone extraordinarily well.

"But I'm still debating whether I want to kill you and take your horse, or take you up on that promise of yours to join us." He looked around, smirking at his men, several of whom began calling for his death. Then, he raised a hand to shut them up. "Tell you what, I can always kill you later. For now, saddle up." He patted Ham's horse that sat next to him. "We have a caravan to pillage, and we always need good bait."

CHAPTER 19

Betrayal

HAVILAH BELONGED TO THE TWELVE KINGDOMS NOW, and its leaders were practically rolling in gold. Countless crates of the stuff lined the coffers of the late queen Arissa's underground kingdom, and that was just the beginning. Already, scouts had ridden deep into the mines to find cave after cave glittering with precious potential. Once Tubal-cain brought his men to retrieve it, there would be no stopping the coalition of leaders. They could take over the world and build each of their kingdoms many times over. The question was, who would lead the pack?

Already, Iram's ambitious instincts had picked up on the grumblings of the other rulers, and he knew that he had to do something decisive if he wanted to remain in a position of any real leverage. The only thing that had kept them at bay for so long was the fact that they needed his father's mining capabilities to dig into the heart of the black mountains, but, while that was valuable enough, they had all lost respect for the wishy-washy warlord when he chose deliberately to distance himself from the war. Now, it was up to Iram and Oshik to fix that issue before their father's cowardice ruined their own fortunes, and his younger brother, unfortunately, was too much of a dolt to do much to help. No, Oshik was a follower at best, and so Iram needed to develop a plan that would ensure their survival and advancement in the near future. Lucifer had similar ideas, so he coached the young man well in these crucial moments.

"You know, you really are the greatest man in your family." Lucifer said slyly, buttering him up. No one doubted their own thoughts when it felt good. "You've always pushed harder than your brother. You really *want* it, and you'll go get it, whereas he just hopes the world will come to him. As for your father, he has always been respectable in his own right, but he, like all great men, has declined with age. He isn't worthy to wear a crown and rule over the earth at the head of the greatest army the world has ever seen. He didn't even have the courage to come out and ride at the rear of the pack to witness the victories, like any king could, much less lead the charge. But you, *you* did it all. You led the men. You cut down whoever stood in your way. You won the respect of men more than twice your age with ten times the experience. *You* can rule it all. The future belongs to the young." Iram liked where this was going, and he did feel as though he had earned his place in the world...Maybe it was time his father stepped down and gave way to the new generation. Or, if it was necessary, they could make him step down.

As all stood gloating over their treasure, Iram pulled his pigheaded brother aside as if to congratulate him. Oshik was lifting his meaty hands to his lips, kissing newly minted gold coinage, and his brother slapped them out of his grip, irritated. "You fool, don't act like you haven't seen gold before. These are *powerful* men, and they already don't give us enough respect. Don't give them more reason to doubt us." Oshik was staring daggers at his brother, but he knew the words had truth in them. They still yet needed to guard themselves among such traitorous company. He couldn't resist a pompous quip, though. "You know they need our father's mining operation to get the rest of this gold. Surely they wouldn't bother us and risk harming their chances."

Iram smiled, as though his brother had made a point, then ripped the rug out from under him. "You do realize that at this point, their army is so powerful that they could literally take *everything* our father owns by force if necessary?" Oshik's dark eyebrows lowered, annoyed, but there was stunned realization dawning in his eyes. "All it takes is for them to decide that our father is expendable, and that is happening rather quickly already since the fool wouldn't join us on the battlefront. So, we must win their respect and their loyalty, and we must offer them something to secure it."

He glanced about furtively and lowered his voice, careful not to be overheard. "You remember what father was talking about on the day the leaders first convened?" Oshik nodded, eyes bright with greed. "The tree," he whispered.

"Yes, yes my brother. If we were to eat of that tree...we would live forever. We wouldn't need to worry about these fools' respect then. We would be invincible," Iram replied. Lucifer watched with sick satisfaction, thrilled to see his pupil taking such bold steps. "In order to lead the campaign for the tree, however, we need to be in a position of authority. We have to make a bold move, one that will regain the respect our father has lost, and we can't let anything or anyone stand in our way." Oshik was on board. What the younger brother didn't know, however, was that Iram had no intentions of sharing leadership; he had other plans entirely.

That night, the brothers announced plans to travel back to Tubal-cain's lands to alert him of the victory and prepare the mining operation to be dispatched to Havilah straightaway. The other leaders agreed with the plan, eager to see their pockets lined that much sooner, and sent them off in the morning. When the young men were gone, several of them discussed plots to murder the lads upon their return, once the mining had been done. There was no need for them after that point. Had not Satan and his forces been behind the scenes, the coalition would have made certain the boys didn't live long, but the devious mastermind had other plans for the former ironworkers.

When Iram and Oshik arrived at their father's encampment a few days later, they were stunned at what they found. There was no fanfare, no public welcome of any sort. The duo had expected a triumphal entry where both their father and the people heaped them with praise for their mighty deeds. Instead, the people hid in their homes out of fear or scurried quickly by them in the street, and their arrival at their own doorstep was no less disappointing. The only greetings they received there were the nervous mutterings of the servants who informed them that their father was not well. Astonished at the news, they hastily made their way to his bedchamber, wondering what illness had befallen him.

Iram was first inside, and he was immediately stricken with a wave of hopelessness, as though all the life had fled from the room. Oshik followed close behind. Scanning the empty room for their father, they did not see him at first, but then a groan sounded from the bed. They hurried over to find Tubal-cain lying there, rail-thin and pale. He had lost so much weight that his clothes pooled around him in the bed, and his breathing seemed labored. This was not the larger-than-life figure who had raised them and taught them to wield a hammer with strength and skill. This was a shell of a man.

Grunting, the sick ruler's eyes fluttered open. He'd realized there was someone there. Looking about bleary-eyed, his eyes fell on Iram, and he gasped in surprise. "Oh, my son, you have returned. And Oshik?"

"Here father," Oshik said, slightly irritated that he hadn't been noticed first.

"I am glad you two have made it back. I have had such fears about you going to battle and meeting your death on the front. It's a balm to my soul to know you are safe and finished fighting." Tubal-cain rattled.

Iram's brows lowered in consternation. "We are *not* finished fighting, father. *We* are committed to seeing this through to the end. Oshik and I have led men into battle for victory after victory, and we will not stop until we have what we seek, until the mission is done. I wish I could say the same for you. Look at you," He snorted. "You're a pitiful sight. What happened to the man you used to be?"

His father's eyes dimmed at this, heavy with shame, but then he revived somewhat, as though a crucial thought had occurred to him. He spoke, "My sons, I know I created this...empire. I sought it with all my heart, because I wanted to build something for you that would last, something you could be proud of - "

"We *are* proud of it, father. But you have forsaken it and laid down to die!" Iram was fuming. He was conflicted, however, because he was also secretly pleased; his father's passing meant that he as the oldest son would be the sole leader.

His father waved his hand; he had more to say. "I did not tell you that because I want you to be proud of what I've built. I am not proud of it. I have allowed you both to get off of the path of honor. You kill without mercy, and the people fear you; they do not respect you. This is my doing, because I did not guide you. I want you to abandon this fool's errand and get back to what we know, the honest work of your hands. I wish we would all die with a hammer in our fists, making the finest tools the world had ever seen. You both have the gift! You can do so well. That is enough to be remembered by."

This was not what the young men had yearned to hear. They were intoxicated by the alluring power of conquest and riches, and had thrown their whole souls into that quest with abandon. They could not turn back, or it would mean that every evil act they had committed was for naught, that the ends did not justify the means. They could not make such a choice.

During the conversation, Ashtoreth had been lounging languidly on the couch in the corner, invisible, watching the spat unfold with devilish delight. Lucifer had updated him on the situation, and this looked like the perfect time to jump in and lend a hand. He swept across the room in one flood motion, pausing a mere breath away from Iram, and whispered to him, "It's too late. It's true, you can't turn back now. Remember, too, your father still has power as long as he lives, however little, and he would use it to oppose you. You must silence him. It's time for the old to die and the new to reign. What's a little more blood to shed for the sake of the future - an eternal future?"

Wickedness stole across Iram's visage like a dark cowl, and he was captive. His own ambition would rule him. He turned to his brother and pulled him aside. "Oshik, our father would ruin what little chances we have for a kingdom of our own and eternal life. He would die soon, anyway, but we cannot risk him foiling our plans before that happens. We should...help him along a little bit. What do you say?"

He was suggesting murder, so Oshik was noticeably shaken, but he, too, realized that they had already dug themselves into quite a hole. There was no way out but through. He nodded, resolved. Iram held his eyes for a moment, then motioned to the pillow next to their father's head. It had to look as though he had passed from sickness. They did not want the servants to spread any other story. Oshik, the stronger of the two, moved to the pillow, seeing his father slipping in and out of consciousness. Taking it in his strong hands, he gulped, then thrust it over his father's face, smothering him until his frail body shook for the last time. It was done. The emptiness of soul that the young man felt at that moment was totally unexpected. It was as though a part of himself had died as well. He immediately regretted the deed, though he did not tell his brother.

Though he felt a brief twinge of feeling which he quickly squelched, Iram watched all of this with a detached air. It didn't matter. The fool would have died within days. Besides, the blood was on his brother's hands. Now, he could concern himself with the real business of ruling a nation, and, more importantly, achieving immortality. Before he could take a step, however, Ashtoreth hissed one more word of advice into his ears, one that he could not ignore.

Iram turned to his brother and grabbed his shoulder, a gesture that Oshik thought must have been a moment of solidarity between them, an agreement that this course of action was right. Then, without the slightest warning, the older brother thrust a dagger into his heart. Oshik's eyes glazed over with pain as his life faded, and he couldn't help but wonder how they'd gone so very, very far.

Turning to face the door, Iram mustered up his best pained expression, then cried for the servants. "Murder! The king has been murdered!" As they rushed in one after another, he fed them a tragic tale of how he had caught his brother in the act of murdering his father, and had only just managed to stop him, but it was too late. His father had faded too fast from weakness, and there was nothing to be done. The people had better get ready for a new king.

The day Ham joined the bandits was the first time he could remember deliberately staining his soul. Before, he'd made mistakes aplenty, but always in the passion of the moment when tempted by his desires. This decision, however, marked a new season of calculated self-serving, and it had not stopped with that first choice. In the days following his conversion to piracy he had stooped to ever-increasing depths.

First, the leader Ziklag had merely had him pose as a struggling vagrant asking for alms, using him to lure unsuspecting travelers to their doom. However, it was not long before the cruel captain had prompted him to join in the occasional bloodshed - or be killed himself. Ham already detested the idea of being a part of robbing the innocent, and the new request pushed him entirely too far. Yet, when the time came and he imagined being served as fodder to the dragons, something primal rose up in him, pushing him to protect his own life at any cost. And so, he had taken a life - that of a grown man who doubtless had innumerable sins to account for, of course.

The next time, though, it had been easier. Ham had begun to feel a sense of power over others, and he liked it. He felt like he could control his own destiny, a feat which had for so long evaded him in early life. Plus, the more willing he was to do Ziklag's dirty work, the more all the men respected him - or, at least, that's how it seemed. He had the sense that he was becoming part of something, and he began to tell himself that it was worth whatever price he had to pay for it.

Now, the caravan was headed north, farther even than Eshcol where

Ham had intended to head on his own quest. One of Ziklag's men had heard tell that there were vast areas of the north decimated by war, which at first glance did not seem overly exciting to the leader. That was until another fellow made the remark that he'd once passed through a place stricken by war, and there hadn't been a man in sight. That had perked Ziklag's interest; no men meant no defenses. They could pillage at will. So, the course had been set, all the way to Havilah itself. No self-respecting pirate could resist a chance at limitless gold.

Sure enough, as they crossed the border between Eshcol and the far northern lands leading to Havilah, they found evidence of conflict. Village after village was populated with women and children only, or with no one at all: ghost towns, ravaged by violence. The marauding band had a field day! They made their way unopposed into abandoned homes, ransacking them at will, gleaning hordes of valuables of every kind. Unfortunately, they didn't stop with the empty houses. Their greed knew no bounds, and stoked as it was by the prospect of endless gain, they took from even the homes whose women or elderly yet remained. If any put up a fight, they were dispatched.

On one such occasion, they entered a town whose inhabitants were struggling to rebuild. They were a hardy people, not willing to give up without a fight. That's why so many of their men had gone to war. And now that it was past them, they weren't about to lie down and die. In fact, that's exactly what the young woman said, standing fast in the doorway of her home shielding her children from the bandit force. Ziklag's reply was firm. "Ham, teach her a lesson." By that, everyone knew what he meant, a lesson she couldn't forget.

Despite all of the filth that had entered the young carpenter's soul, however, and all of the despicable choices he had made, there was a line in his soul that he was not willing to cross, and striking a woman to do her harm was a leap beyond that line. Knowing what would come, his reply was firm, though his voice wavered slightly. "I will not." At first, Ziklag acted as though he hadn't heard, waiting for another answer. When it was not forthcoming, he turned his loathsome gaze upon Ham. "You will if you value your life," came the deadly return.

Ham twisted in his stirrups, uncomfortable but unwilling to grovel this time. "Listen, we have already taken more than enough from this town, and there are still yet more homes without occupant that you can rob as you please. Let's just leave her be. There are children." By now, the other men had taken an interest in the exchange, and were watching eagerly to see what their leader would do. He did not disappoint.

"Chain him up." He snapped his fingers, motioning to his men to move in on Ham. "I know just what to do with you."

Before he could think to react, Ham felt a sharp pain in the back of his head and lost consciousness. When he awoke, feeling around groggily, he could tell that he was chained as the leader had said. However, the surface underneath him was foreign, like the bottom of a wooden crate, and he couldn't see much of anything. As his vision cleared, he did notice that there was light peeking through what appeared to be a tarp cast over an enclosure. He was in a wooden cage.

The cage rocked steadily beneath him, so he knew that the caravan was moving, but what he couldn't figure out was where they had gotten such a thing: perhaps they'd stolen it? They usually traveled as light as possible, carrying minimal supplies and empty baggage to fill with loot. What's more, Ziklag was not one to waste resources; if he wanted to kill Ham, he'd have done that, but he wouldn't keep him around without purpose either, especially in a slow contraption like this. What was going on?

After a while, whatever was hauling the cage ground to a halt, nearly throwing Ham into the bars. They had arrived somewhere. He heard voices calling to one another, but couldn't make out what they were saying. Then, the tarp was yanked away, revealing the blinding presence of the late morning sun, and through the sunspots he could see that he was not with the pirates anymore. This was a slave caravan.

So, Ziklag had sold him, choosing to turn a profit rather than leave him for dead. Ham supposed that was better...maybe. It depended on what the slave traders would do with him. He had heard tell of huge ships manned by hordes of slaves who never saw the light of the sun and subsisted on meager rations of water and occasional crumbs of bread. Compared to that, death didn't seem so bad. But then, he reminded himself, he deserved the worst. That realization came upon him like a raging flood. He had abandoned his family in their hour of greatest need to become a murderer and a thief, and he wasn't even there to help mourn the passing of his grandfather. Yes, he supposed, whatever God would throw at him was nothing more than justice.

That thought caught, sticking in his mind like a thorn in a glove. God. He was the judge, his father had always said. He would give to every man according to his deeds. What did that mean for Ham? He was suddenly reminded of what Methuselah had once told him. "God waits for us to come home." It was a simple thought, and he had never seen the point of it before, but now...it enlivened him; it gave him hope. Would God forgive, if he turned back? Could he turn back, having gone this far? He was willing to do it if God would give him the chance.

The experience with the wounded at Ophir had changed Boaz for life. He now knew what it was to love, to have compassion and feel *with* others. Life was most decidedly *not* about him. Since that day, he, of his own accord, had pushed with Methuselah to spread the love of God to all that they could. Seeing the wounded had reminded them that the time was short for so many, and so they had continued on to other villages to find those in need. Some of the men had passed before they left, but they were mourned in a new way, in the light of the promise of resurrection, and that comforted the weary souls who tended to them.

Every excursion brought them closer and closer to Havilah, where they had heard from the locals that the armies were converging. Today, they were heading out on yet another journey further afield, leaving behind a beautiful but suffering community who had struggled dearly to receive anything they had to offer. They just had too much pride. It hurt to realize it, but Boaz had to understand that knowledge did not save a man. It took a submission of the will, a choice to hope outside oneself.

Amaris ranged ahead of the two old men. Her stallion was never content to mosey along at the careful pace of the other mounts, so she often scoped out the path before them and reported back what she found. Near noon, she caught sight of something on the horizon that looked somewhat like a settlement from that distance, but it appeared to be moving, so she trotted back to tell the others.

"Up ahead I see what is probably some sort of caravan. What do you say?" Amaris asked, deferring to Methuselah as usual to decide the course of action.

He scratched his beard, looking at the sun to see the time, and replied cheerfully. "Let's pay it a visit. Perhaps we might be a blessing to whomever it is, and they to us. It's been a whole half day since we had company, anyway, and that's intolerable!" He laughed, winking at his son.

The trio overtook the caravan rather quickly, implying that it was not on the move for the time being, but when they came within earshot of it, they could see a long row of cages. Coming even closer, they soon realized that this was no innocent merchant's train or anything of the sort. The faces peering out of those cages were human.

Boaz and Amaris's first instincts were to turn back, but then they thought of the suffering they had witnessed already on their adventure, and they wondered if God had brought them here for a reason as well. The last village had loaded them down with provisions and had hidden a little gold in the bottoms which they later found when digging for a bite. Perhaps they could purchase one of the slaves, but only one. There was no way to free them all. Methuselah, however, always the bold one, was already waving gaily on his way over to meet the slave traders.

Coming up to a man whose unwashed stench assaulted their nostrils, Methuselah smiled as best he could, praying in his heart that they did not have weaponry. He greeted the man. "Hello! We saw you at a distance and thought we might do a little business. I see you have many good-looking subjects there. Perhaps we can make a deal?"

The fellow's watery eyes had been devoid of emotion until he heard the word "business," and then they lit up like a torch. "A deal, you say? Do you have money?" Boaz nodded, patting his baggage with confidence. He had decided to play along. It was their best chance at seeing the prisoners.

They followed the slave trader over to the cages as his cohorts lifted the tarps from one after another. It was like buying cattle. Methuselah scanned the faces of the captives, many of them emaciated from lack of care or bruised, trying his best to remain composed while he asked God how on earth they could pick one to free when it was needed for all. A gasp from Amaris interrupted his thoughts. Had she found one? He looked at her and followed her eyes to a cage about six down from the front. His jaw dropped.

It was Ham. His great grandson was chained up like an animal. How on earth had this happened? And so far from Kadish! Amaris, on her part, did not know Ham from Adam, but she felt drawn to him, seeing in him what felt like a mirror of her own self, her own soul. She felt a connection to him, and knew that this was the one they had come to save.

The slave trader was waiting expectantly, having babbled on about each slave's particular merits until he was blue in the face. Now, he saw what had taken their attention and ran over to that cage to continue the spiel. "Oh, yes, this is a good one! He is fresh, just caught today. Fresh, fat, and strong. Good for work. Do you want him?"

Did they want him? What a question! "Yes!" Methuselah said far too excitedly, then, catching himself, continued, "We will take that one. He seems satisfactory." Ham had not moved since they had showed up, and they wondered if he recognized them from that distance. Surely, he also had not expected them to meet in this way. Then, when the trader let him loose and Methuselah saw him face to face, he realized that the young man was ashamed. He would not look at them. What sins had brought him to such a state? Boaz realized that this did not need to look like a family reunion or the trader would charge triple the price, and they did not have it, so he nudged Methuselah and paid the man, taking Ham away as quickly as possible.

The dark lad trudged along beside them, not saying a word, but when they were out of sight, Methuselah turned and yanked him up into a tight embrace, exclaiming, "My son! My dear grandson! How did you come to be enslaved, and so far from home?"

Ham had not reciprocated the embrace, leaving his arms hanging limply by his sides, as if his touch would contaminate them. He responded quietly. "I have sinned. I am not worthy to be called your son. I have done...terrible things." His eyes swam.

His grandfather could see that the young man truly was in the throes of a deep anguish, and he believed there was real repentance in his face. He put his grizzled hands to Ham's cheeks and lifted his head, looking him full in the eyes. "You never had to earn a place as my son. And you can't lose it. I see my boy that I love, and God sees a son that He loves. You can't lose who you are. Turn and receive His embrace, and He will forgive you. I already have."

Overcome with emotion, the young man sank to his knees, weeping.

CHAPTER 20

Lord of Hosts

NATHAN WAS ONCE AGAIN ON THE MOVE. After leaving Ophir the Lord had overwhelmed his spirit with the sense that there was a great conflict waging that could change the course of history, and it was time to intervene. While there, he had so looked forward to the chance to see how his old friend Agatha had been doing. She was one of the people he had met when he had lived in Ophir on assignment: just an old woman who had fallen on hard times that he had often felt led to bless. Several times he had rescued her home from the stony barrage of some of the same misguided lads that he fed on other occasions. Unfortunately, the angel found out that Agatha had long since passed when he made his way to her abode and found it occupied by squatters. As for the young lads, they had either deserted the town or fallen alongside the town's other men.

Now, Nathan was speeding towards Havilah to see what had become of the great conflict the Lord had impressed upon him. All he knew was that it was massively important and that he needed to head that direction. Mid-route, however, he was stopped in his tracks. Below, there was a column of men in battle array as far as the eye could see, stretching beyond his field of vision towards the very place he himself intended to go. This *was* a great and terrible army, and it was rising up to meet him, headed towards - no, could it be? He had just flown over the fabled garden of Eden, and they were aimed right at it.

The angel was reeling. No one had ever dared try to conquer that holy place. There were cherubim guarding its entrance with a flaming sword covered in holy fire whirling about to bar entry to all. It didn't seem possible that any human army would attempt such a feat. But, then, perhaps this was no mere *human* army. The Lord had called him to see this, so there was no doubt that it was a real threat. He decided he had better go down and take a better look.

Nathan soared over and made his descent quickly and quietly by the right flank, aware that there might very well be a sizeable demonic presence among the army, but betting that they'd be near the front. They were ever a pretentious lot after all, always seeking to be first. There, the angel alighted by a soldier whose fellow had stopped briefly to tie his sandal, and he appeared as one of them. The man he'd replaced was considerably confused when he looked up, attempting to return to a position that was clearly occupied, so he fell in with the next row.

From this vantage point midway behind the front lines, Nathan was able to use his superior angelic sight to scope out the leaders from behind. He could see a young man he did not know with dark hair and darker eyes sporting the beginnings of a beard, thin but athletic in build. Next to him were several well-known world leaders of the day, armed to the teeth and looking rather smug and self-satisfied. They thought this plan was actually going to work. What the angel didn't understand was why these men would keep company with such a green recruit, treating him as an equal. That smacked of Satan for certain.

The presence of real devils, however, eluded Nathan. The chances that not one of them was involved in an attack on Eden was slim to none, so he suspected that they, like he, had taken human form to avoid suspicion. Perhaps the boy himself *was* Satan? Or one of his cohorts? Regardless, their sure march on a forbidden area with such a gargantuan force meant that Nathan was going to need reinforcements. It was time to go see the King.

Without notice, the angel disappeared into the spirit realm, winging away towards heaven with holy purpose. The soldier he'd displaced had been eyeing his counterpart suspiciously, and at this point he nearly fainted when Nathan's body winked out of existence. However, the soldier's eyes were not the only pair that caught sight of Nathan fleeing the scene. Moloch was in the ranks as well, and he recognized the angel instantly from their conflict in Tubal-cain's encampment. He did not forget a face, particularly when he had been wronged. The list of those who had crossed him and thereby deserved death on sight was a long one indeed.

Silently, he leapt into spirit flight and raced after Nathan, burning with hot anger. He would take the puny angel captive, inflicting his revenge and earning Lucifer's praise for having blocked the Enemy's reconnaissance. They could even use the angel as leverage if the Enemy came against them in Eden. Black, leathery wings heaved with mighty effort, cutting the distance between the demon and his prey short in seconds. He was going to catch the fool without even being noticed. It was almost too easy.

Nathan's spirit twinged, overtaken by foreboding, and he knew that an evil presence had come after him. He turned his head mid-flight, not stopping because he was sure there was someone just behind him, and saw Moloch's beastly visage glaring up at him with a hungry look in his eyes. The demon was nearly within reach, ponderous horns stretching so far that they nearly touched him. Nathan's fighting instincts kicked in and he whipped around, hands yanking a bow from his back as he fired a light arrow straight into the fiend's face, striking him in the eye and stopping him cold. He shot off two others in swift succession and made a rapid retreat. He'd been right. The devils had been in disguise.

If Moloch was involved, that meant that there were high level demonic forces at work, and the Devil himself was sure to have his hand in the mix. They had been aching for an age to get their hands on the tree of life, because it had been created by God to give everlasting life to humankind before they had fallen. If the enemy could get the fruit of that tree into the hands of any human, it would spell disaster for the entire earth; a corrupt man would reign without end. The Almighty God would certainly not let that happen, and his angel armies would rise to defend the tree at His call.

Tearing away at lightning speed, Nathan made his way through the veil between worlds into the courts of the Lord. He needed to assemble an army, and there was only one individual that God would put in charge of such a task. Michael the archangel. He went in search of the angel, ignoring the thousands of shining souls streaming past him in flight on their various missions, and found him already waiting. "The Lord sent you to speak with me?" Michael asked. This angel, the chief prince of all his brethren and guardian of God's people, was acting commander of the armies of the Lord.

"Yes," Nathan responded anxiously. "We have an urgent objective! Twelve kingdoms of men and their armies are swarming united across the north towards Eden, intent, I am sure, on conquering that land and taking the Tree of Life. They are led by demonic powers, but I do not know how many. Moloch alone appeared to me, but they had disguised themselves as men, so their number is incalculable."

Michael took all of this in steadily, his stoic countenance unchanged except for a slight lowering of the brows in consternation at the gall of the unrighteous invaders. He was a veteran of many battles, and had faced Lucifer himself before. His reply was sure. "A move as bold as this could have no author but Satan. We must expect that he and possibly his entire force are with the armies of men. But we need not fear! Our God is a consuming fire, and He could lay them low with a blast of breath from his nostrils! We will assemble the brethren and launch an attack to meet them at the border of Eden. They must think that they have gained the garden before we descend upon them."

With that, he turned and sent another angel with a booming voice to call up the troops, thundering across the heavens, "Assemble, army of the Lord! The enemy marches on Eden and we are called to action!" Everywhere, angels in the thousands dropped what they were doing and flew to muster. War was imminent.

Meanwhile, the leaders of the twelve kingdoms had arrived at the entrance to Eden. Men who had never seen an angel in their lives - or even believed they existed - were confronted with the mind boggling reality of mighty flying beings many times their size who shimmered with otherworldly light. What's more, a colossal fiery sword was roaming about of its own accord, menacing the intruders with certain death. How does one defeat a disembodied sword? The coalition was understandably shaken to their core. If not for the ready encouragement from their invisible allies, the whole force may quite possibly have sounded a retreat.

But Lucifer had expected this. He knew the weakness and cowardice of men, and he also knew their pride. He knew that they could be coaxed into anything if their reputation was at stake. So, he gave young Iram a touch of vitality and moved him to address the army. Riding out in front of them, Iram cried out, "We are the greatest army the world has ever seen! There is nothing, *nothing* that can stop us. Any man who fears for his life may leave now, and forever lose the opportunity at ultimate victory and eternal life. Whoever flees will have their life, but let it be known that they are considered a coward and a traitor, and they have no place in the twelve kingdoms from this day forward." He raised his sword in defiance, turned to face Eden, and led the charge, pounding towards the cherubim at breakneck pace.

Lucifer rode with the young ruler, protecting his investment. So, when the flaming sword came swinging at the young man's head, it was thrust powerfully aside by some unseen force, and Iram was convinced the gods were with him. The men behind him, too, were emboldened and barreled headlong into the fray - but they were not so lucky. The holy blade swept through dozens of men with each fell stroke, slicing armor and sinew like butter. Hundreds had fallen within moments, but the force was so large that a sizeable number made it past the sword to the cherubim just behind Iram.

The young leader was sure to be decapitated when the mighty creatures came at him, as Lucifer was only one against two, but he was intoxicated with battle lust and felt no fear. Just as he passed between the two cherubim, their swords flashing in the sun, two demons streaked past him and slammed into his foes, occupying them long enough for he and Satan to make it into the garden with a few others. On to the tree of life!

In that moment, the skies broke. A tremendous rift opened between heaven and earth, and from it poured the most fearsome, awe-inspiring sight: wave after wave of gleaming warriors wreathed in flame astride horses and chariots of fire, descending on the invading armies like the plague. There was no escape. Angelic fighters tore through the enemy forces with all the fury of a raging inferno eating up wood, and the humans stood no chance.

Demon soldiers arose in droves, however, meeting the angels in airborne battle. They fought with all the ferocity of caged animals wildly throwing off chains to attack their captors. There was a longtime feud between the light and the dark, and all the pent up rage of battles lost burst forth in the hearts of the evil spirits. It was *their* time, and they would not lose the opportunity without a fight.

However, the onslaught did not cease, and yet more blazing troops flooded from heaven until the enemy was overtaken and the remaining humans fled the scene. Lucifer watched the battle angrily, infuriated beyond belief at the foiling of his plans. Ever the strategist, he hung back from the fray as he saw Michael the archangel cutting through his cohorts with ease, and though he longed to thrust his blade through the angel's self-righteous innards, he stayed his hand. Vengeance plays the long game, he told himself. He would have to improvise.

Seeing that there was no hope of victory, the enemy turned to his wild-eyed young protege. Iram had not yet been noticed by the angels, cut off as he was from the main force, and Lucifer could see the young man's gaze beginning to fill with fear as he witnessed the utter destruction of his army, so the Devil quickly prodded Iram's survival instincts. He would escape into the depths of the garden. All was not yet lost.

The day that Methuselah and Boaz found Ham felt like his new birthday. It was as though he had started over, fresh as a newborn babe. When he'd heard those words from his grandfather's lips... He'd never felt so much relief, like an ocean wave smashing into him, cool and cleansing. What he had done could not change who he was. He was a *son*, and he was *loved*. Forgiveness was available... He couldn't believe all of the times he had turned God away, spitting on his offers for forgiveness, for closeness and help. Now, it was all he could do not to double over and weep at the mercy that had been poured out on him.

All the horrible things he had done did still plague him at times, especially the first several days. Yet, as he tramped along next to his rosy-cheeked grandfather and newly hopeful uncle, he began to ride on the wave of their joyfulness. Boaz truly was much changed since last they'd met; his uncle had never been one to smile often - while *walking* at that. He hated having to travel, and had always maintained that it was a great waste of time. Now, he moved along at a deliberate but unhurried pace, glancing about with a look of gleeful expectation as he provided the rest of the party with rousing conversation (for his standards). Then there was the girl.

Amaris was a gem, a sparkling jasper with the radiance of a thousand suns in an otherwise dull world. Or, at least, that's what Ham thought in his more poetic moments. Seeing her with them had been a shock, to say the least. Never had he expected to find such a vision keeping company with these old coots, but there she was, and he couldn't keep his eyes off of her. If she turned towards him, however, he would look away without fail. There was too much shame in his heart. He couldn't face someone so pure as that without tainting her, he was sure.

But she was so easy to love! Each day, she would greet him and the others with a sweet good morning, addressing Ham by name, though she did not know him. Then, she'd ride alongside him, keeping an eye on him lest he fall. "Head injuries are the worst of things. You could lose your balance!" she'd say. If he didn't love the attention so much, his pride would have bristled at the idea that he couldn't stay on a horse, but from her, it was music to his ears. She cared about *him*. When they stopped, she would tend to his wounds; he had several from the beating the bandits had inflicted upon him before he was sold. There was no use denying it: he had fallen head over heels for her.

Now, they were traveling together to the midlands of the north, away from Havilah and towards Assyria, looking for another village where they might find families affected by the war that could use their help and prayer. Before the trio had picked up Ham, the occupants of the last town had told them that there were rumors the great army was on the move again, having conquered the land of gold already. That news was astounding on its own, as no one in living memory had ever heard of that stronghold even being breached, let alone conquered, but it also had bearing on their mission. They did not want to march straight into the army by traveling towards Havilah as they had originally intended.

It had already been a number of days since they had set the present course, and they still had not found a sign of life. At this point, they were passing beyond the reach of even Amaris's considerable knowledge of the region, so they were, in a sense, flying blind. Today, Boaz finally said as much, "Abba, I don't know if we are wise to continue this direction; the land is barren as far as the eye can see. Perhaps we should turn back? If not towards Havilah then perhaps towards home?" His voice wavered with the last words.

Methuselah's expression did not change in the slightest. His eyes were fixed, firmly ahead, as though he could see something that none of them could see. "We have to keep going." He said confidently.

Boaz wasn't going to let up that easily, however. "Listen, I know that you believe we set this course for a purpose, but sometimes we're just wrong. You've told *me* that enough times. Home doesn't seem like such a bad idea, either, considering we have found Ham. His father is going to want to see him and know that he is alright. There is no telling *what* they are thinking by this time."

A pained look flashed across the older man's face at that remark. He did know what his son must be feeling, but he could not ignore the burden God had placed upon him. There was someone out there...someone who needed them, and they only had so much time to get to there.

"I can't shake the sense that if we don't keep going, we are going to miss something that we are meant to do. It draws me Boaz. We must continue on." Looking at him in that moment, Ham could see that underneath that aged, rickety exterior there was an inner vitality that knew no limits, a spirit striving to be set free. He had always been a jovial fellow, but this was new. It was powerful. Ham trusted Methuselah. The young man, on his part, was not eager to go home anyway. It meant yet more challenges, and he was thankful to be here, now, with those that he was sure would not judge him. He wasn't at all certain what awaited him back at the scene of his first crime.

Boaz was still yet uncertain as to the wisdom of his father's course of action, but he submitted to it. Methuselah had been right most of the time since their journey began. He had an ear for the word of the Lord.

"So, Ham..." Amaris began, trotting her mount up to ride beside his. "I keep hearing about your family. Could you tell me more about them? I'd love to know." They were mostly out of earshot from the other two men, so Ham knew he could be honest, but did he want to? He fidgeted nervously as he thought it through. There were so many things about the family that were not yet reconciled for him, and though he earnestly wanted to share everything he had with this woman, he feared what it would do to their new but fragile relationship.

Seeing his reluctance, the young woman just waited, sure that he would come around. Ham plucked up some courage and spoke. He had to at least answer her question. "Family life is...complicated for me right now. I can tell you that I have a wonderful mother and father, still living, and two brothers. We lived and farmed together before I left...What else do you want to know?" He glanced at her, and he saw no judgment in her eyes, but the already saw the answer to his question there as well: she wanted to know why he left.

Amaris patted his arm lightly. "It can be hard to share things with people, because you don't know what they will do with what you give them, or what it will do *to* them, but I can assure you of this: nothing you say will surprise me. My life, too, has not been all that I hoped it would be." She took a deep breath, then continued, "But these two have helped me to see that God can meet us where we are, and still love us." She glanced back fondly at the old men.

She was right. He felt it so clearly when she spoke. There was just an honesty about her, a purity of spirit that he had not met elsewhere in the world. He felt moved to reveal his secrets to her. Maybe she *could* handle it. The idea that she had done things she regretted though seemed so foreign to him. He decided to take a chance.

"Okay, here it goes." He gulped. "I...accidentally caused the death of my own uncle, and fled the scene without even telling my family. Since then, I have lived for myself, and myself alone. You already know I joined the bandits who sold me to the slave traders. That was *my* choice. I did that, and it is I who must pay the price for it and bear the judgment that is due. It weighs on me." He looked at her woefully, eyes misty. "I understand if that is too much for you."

Her dark eyes told an entirely different story as her cheeks rose in a slight, mournful grin that said she was there for him but knew his pain. "As I said, nothing surprises me. I have done many, many wicked things in service to the false god I served before they found me...all selfish, all without thought to my fellow man and the true God. But now, I know I can be clean, and I know I am made in God's image and worthy of love, despite what I have done." She turned to look him full in the face. "So, I challenge you to turn to God and receive that same truth, to believe that His love for you is not unwarranted, that you are valuable despite your misdeeds. It will lift the weight from you, and free you to love and be loved." There was a wistful quality to her voice as she spoke the last words.

He yearned to do exactly as she said, and find that freedom to love...her. He wanted to love her, and be hers. His spirit felt knit to hers.

Perhaps they did somehow belong together, in spite of everything. Would God do so much good for a sinner such as he?

Their thoughts were interrupted until a later time, as just then Methuselah's eyes found the sight they had all been longing to see for days: civilization. "There!" He shouted gleefully. "There it is, the place we have been searching for. That is where we must go! Onwards everyone!" He shook the reins and took off towards what was still yet a dark speck on the horizon. The others had no choice but to follow.

As the party neared the village, they noticed that it had a small wooden sign out front, ornately crafted, that read "Debir". It was an interesting name; it meant "most holy place". Methuselah wondered what could have happened there in that place to warrant such an honored title. The sign's quality bore witness that there were some of his own carpenter folk there, and skilled ones at that.

Upon entry, they found that the town was, unfortunately, much like Ophir: largely lacking in manpower. They looked up and down the street for a carpenter's shop, because Boaz had the idea that they might start there looking for a person of peace to receive them into the village. Eventually, they saw a building with a saw emblazoned on the door frame, and assumed they had found the place. However, upon knocking, the building proved empty, and they walked away perplexed.

Nearby, they found a pub and made their way inside, tying up the horses before entering. Perhaps someone there knew where the carpenter had gone off to. The place was not overfull, but there were at least a few locals to talk to, some of them men. Boaz waved the bartender over. "Hello there, we're new to these parts, and we were hoping to make contact with a fellow tradesman. Do you know where the carpenter has gone to?"

The bartender was a swarthy fellow with a rather large gut that bespoke of what he enjoyed most in life, and his previously cheerful expression fell slightly as they asked the question. That didn't seem good. "Oh, he hasn't been around since those devilish soldiers passed through here, demanding he fix their chariots. They told him he had two days to repair a hundred wheels. *Two days!* And when he couldn't do but about twenty, they ran him through." He sighed, then poured himself a drink. "It's a terrible thing. So, you fellows carpenters yourselves? You know we could use some of that sorta work around here. I don't know how much we could pay, though, but if you need supplies for travel we may could work out a trade of some sort. With Izhak being gone, everyone else in town might need your help too."

That was just the sort of opportunity the group needed to gain a foothold in the town and build relationships with the people. Methuselah didn't hesitate. "We're your men! Lead on, my fine fellow. What's to be done?" His three companions had no choice but to just smile and follow suit. May the Lord help them all.

CHAPTER 21

What Greater Love?

THE ANIMALS WERE COMING. The first sign had been a pair of ravens congregating next to a pair of pigeons on the rooftop when Noah's family awoke in the morning, which, although abnormal, did not raise any suspicions. Then, when the next day brought garish toucans and warbling skylarks in company with the others, they began to wonder. It wasn't long before their homes were covered in fowl of every conceivable variety under heaven, cawing and crowing and squawking away as the family went about their daily duties. So, it had begun.

This revelation yielded mixed reactions from the family. It was exciting in one way, because it meant that God had kept His promise! They weren't a bunch of lunatics: there was a miracle happening before them to testify that God was true to His word. For Noah, the flood of animals gave him hope that all of this hadn't been for naught. In the wake of his father Lamech's passing, it was a much needed consolation.

Lamech had been so very dear to them all, and such a help for the work on the ark as well, that it had felt like certain doom when they found him dead. What would they do without him? Could God have known this was coming? Though Noah believed God day to day - enough to spend all of his time building an ark - it was still difficult from time to time to trust in what he could not see, and so a sign from heaven had been just what he needed. However, this preemptive herald of things to come was not entirely encouraging. In the face of recent tragedy, it was also a cause for much worry.

Ham had been away for quite some time, and it was beginning to look as though he wasn't coming back. Noah feared for him, and Leah worried twice as much. What's more, Lamech's passing seemed inextricably linked to Ham's departure, and though they all wanted to believe Ham would never *murder* someone, the evidence stood strongly against him. Noah worried that his brothers had already condemned him in their hearts, and he didn't even want to imagine what it would be like if they all had to face the flood without Ham on board, knowing he was out there being destroyed, without reconciliation. That was the tough part. The presence of animals meant that the flood was coming soon, that all the world about them would be lost in a deluge of water, and everyone who was not on that ark would perish. It brought with it an inescapable tension of spirit, as they all desired to be saved, but detested the notion that it would be them alone.

Their minds were occupied though, thankfully, by the now imminent need to finish the ark and fill it with food. Several days into the immigration of the beasts, they had begun to divert almost all of their attention to that task. God had mentioned that they would need to store up food of every kind for themselves and for the animals that would come, but they had not felt pressed to pursue that goal early on, and so it had been a minor thing all along the way, some fruit here, a vegetable there. Now, though, they went after it in earnest: the ladies cramming crates full of fruits, vegetables, nuts, and seeds while the young men loaded them onto the lower decks of the ark. It wasn't hard to feel motivated, because by this time the ark was surrounded by beasts of every sort: hedgehogs, rhinoceros, dogs, felines, crocodiles and more.

The population had increased without ceasing every day since the birds had come. Moles had popped from the ground, pink noses sniffing the air. Foxes, weasels, and stoats were caught playing tag in the garden. Lions, giraffe, and baboons turned their forest into a jungle. Their several-acre lawn was trimmed practically overnight by pairs of goats, cows, and horses champing away in earnest. Even dragons of every sort began to make their way onto the property, and most of those were very young - thank God. It was the most unique sight, because only two of any kind ever appeared, and many of them were mere babes without any parents to be seen. It was a good thing that the ark was nearly done when all this began to happen, because not much construction went on afterwards. Even as the ladies collected produce, llamas and alpacas would nose their way into the crates, stealing a bite when no one was looking. They had to learn to be on their guard at all times! It wasn't all bad though. Several of the creatures were incredibly helpful at procuring fruit from the tops of the trees: most notably the stripe-tailed lemurs.

Shem had quite a time with those.

Today, after the animals had long since made their home on Noah's land, it was time to put the finishing touches on the ark. Everything was done except the door, which had been built slowly and carefully over the past several weeks by Shem and Japheth between supply loads. All that was left to do was install it. To mark the occasion, the family was gathering together to pray over the ark and celebrate its completion.

Leah, Tabitha, and Naamah left their supply-duties and congregated by the ark while Noah accompanied the young men to transport the door. It was hefty, and would take all three of them just to lift it - if not an angel as well. Once it was moved, the whole bunch huddled around it and Noah put his hand on the smooth surface, letting it symbolize the ark itself which was far too gargantuan to encircle. Then, with everyone quiet in expectation, filled with every imaginable emotion, he prayed,

"Almighty God, Ruler of the earth, we come to you as our only hope in time of trouble. The world grows ever more evil, as we have experienced firsthand, and we know that we would be the same if not for your grace on us. Already, some of us have strayed..." He paused, choking back tears. Everyone was thinking of Ham. "But we choose to trust you to keep your promise and ensure all of us are together on the day the flood comes. Already, you have proven to us, Lord, that you keep your word, as you have brought the creatures of the earth to us to care for them, and have so blessed the work of this ark that it has come this far. Already, you have sent us angels to confirm your truth and protect us from harm. Already, you have even taken Lamech home to be with you as we knew must happen...though I wish it had not happened as it did. Above all, we choose, now, at this moment, to put our trust in you yet again. We commit this ark to you that you have helped us build, asking that you carry it with your own right hand and keep us from drowning. Bless every part of it and the journey ahead so that we come through safe and with faith still in you. Do not let us doubt you, as we are so easily driven to do. Instead, lead us to step forward with you into the great unknown, believing that you will build a future as assuredly as you have built our lives thus far. We offer ourselves to you as a sacrifice, holy and pleasing to you. We pray in your name, Yahweh. Amen!"

The whole assembly was overcome with emotion, and so silence reigned for several moments after the prayer as everyone did their best to receive the weight of what was coming to pass. Tabitha was the first to speak afterwards, "What about Boaz and Methuselah? They haven't returned either." Noah had feared to speak or pray of this, because he knew in his heart that it was probable they would not return. Whatever fate had befallen them, they were not destined to make it on the ark with the rest. But how could he say that to this young woman? He settled on the only hope he could give. "We will see them again, one day."

In that moment, a blinding light burst into their vision, and Micah and Gurion appeared, hovering over the gaping entrance to the ark and illuminating it like a blazing beacon. The lead angel looked down at Noah, and spoke with authority, "Greetings yet again, my friends. The Lord has heard your prayers and answered. He blesses this occasion and this vessel of salvation with His own mighty power that holds all things together, assuring that it will not fail you in the time of greatest need.

He also sends word that the flood will come in seven days, and that you must prepare to board the ark. Your salvation is near."

Amaris and the boys were hard at work. The bartender had meant business. His pub had been damaged by more than a few brawls the last time the soldiers came through town, and his first order of business was to have them restore whatever they could - which, for Methuselah and Boaz, was a lot. In return, he would furnish them with whatever supplies they needed to get back home when the job was complete. So, they'd gone straight to work, or very nearly so. Since they hadn't brought tools with them on this journey, they had been required to elicit the help of a local locksmith to reopen the carpenter's shop where they found nearly everything they could possibly need.. The locksmith had been only too happy to oblige, requesting that they simply help him with a few projects while they were there. He wasn't the only one, either. Someone had come along nearly every day since with a need for a repair or construction of some kind, as though the group had just started up business in town.

Now, having already fixed about four oak tables and a dozen stools for the pub in addition to building an extension to the bar, the little band of carpenters was getting a bit overwhelmed with orders, and they'd only been at it for several days! This was mainly due to the fact that Methuselah was so eager to bless the town after what it had been through that he wouldn't say no to *anyone*. Boaz realized this, but his voice of reason was easily squelched, as his father would just mention how the specific set of skills God had given them was exactly what these people needed right now, and he honestly couldn't argue with that. However, they all realized that it was too much work for just the two older men to do, so Ham had risen to the task and then began to teach Amaris how to do some simple things as well.

On this day, she was enjoying herself immensely. A mother had come in who had lost her husband, and she had requested that they make a seesaw for her children. She had a pair of twin ten-year old boys who just really needed distracting at this moment in their life. She had been hesitant, saying, "I know you have many, many more important things to do, but if you can find any time at all, I will wait. It would give them such joy." And that was enough. Ham couldn't say no; he didn't even want to. So they'd started it that same day to surprise the family. Meanwhile, Boaz and Methuselah were taking care of deliveries, as that was their past-time. The pair of them were finally alone.

Amaris watched Ham taking such care with the seesaw, planing the plank by hand for hours so there wouldn't be the slightest possibility of a splinter or sharp edge, and she knew - this man had it in him to be a good father. He would run his hand over the wood each time he finished a spot so that if there was anything out of place, it would harm him instead of the children. She wondered if he thought about children at all. Considering he had been on the run for the last weeks or months, it seemed likely that he didn't.

"Come here," he said softly, interrupting her reverie. He held out a calloused hand. She took it, expecting a rough embrace, but he was gentle with her, as though handling fine china. He brought her over to stand by the center round that was meant to be placed underneath the seesaw plank, and handed her a sanding cloth, pointing at one last spot that was not yet as smooth as silk. "I want you to finish it. The feeling of a complete work of art is unlike any other," He said wistfully.

He took her hand in his and she felt its warmth seep into her skin as he began to slowly move back and forth over the workpiece. "Just like that. See, you're doing a great job." He stepped to the side, watching her finish, and she could see that he really did get a tremendous amount of satisfaction from seeing her take part in the process. She, too, enjoyed every shared experience with him. This was not the only time he had allowed her to help. All day she had been given a task here or there, and he had showed her what to do then patiently waited while she took her first wobbling steps towards success, often failing entirely, but he was never irritable with her. On the contrary, it seemed as if he took advantage of the moments that she made mistakes, rushing to her aid excitedly because it meant she needed him.

"You think you've got it?" He asked eagerly, looking her in the eyes to see if she was satisfied. Amaris blushed, then stammered, "Y-yes, I think it's about ready." He waved her over excitedly, wanting her to come stand next to him. "Come, come look at it with me." She hurried over to where he was standing in the center of the room, and, to her surprise, he put an arm around her shoulder as he gazed on their hard work. "It is rather beautiful, isn't it?" she said, impressed and thankful to have been a part of it. He turned, looking her full in the face, and replied huskily, "Yes, I've never seen anything more beautiful in my life."

Their tender moment did not last long, as Boaz burst through the door just then railing about the inadequacy of the food in town. "What do they mean, serving garbage like that? I've half a mind not to do anymore work for that pub owner until he improves the quality of our grub. What's the point of getting paid in food if the stuff isn't worth a sack of rocks?" He was clearly perturbed, his beard wagging to and fro, but Methuselah just looked at him with an expression that appeared to be something between pity and disgust and denied him the pleasure of a reply.

When the old man saw Amaris and Ham, though, he spoke up. "What's this? Have you finished the whole thing already?" He giggled. "That's mighty impressive in one day! It's not even dark yet. We may even yet have time to get it to the boys before they go to bed." Even Boaz brightened up by that point, as he had a soft spot for children. "Let's give it a shot. The children will be so excited! You two make a *very* good team!" he said, giving Ham a wink.

With that, they packed up the huge toy onto the cart they'd borrowed from a local farmer and prepared to set off. While they were loading the seesaw, though, Methuselah and Boaz took Ham aside to have a man-to-man talk. "You see that young woman in there?" Boaz asked, pointing through the window at Amaris. Ham nodded, not sure where this was going. "She is *special*. God picked her out of all the people we came across to belong to Him and to come with us. We weren't looking for her, but He *sent* her to us. That was no accident."

Methuselah joined in. "She just might be for you, Ham." He could see the young man squirming slightly, so he held up a hand to calm him down. "Listen, I know you've done some things you aren't proud of, but I don't even need to know the half of it to tell you that our God has enough mercy to cover you. He can still give you good things, and it can be *right*, if it is what he chooses." Ham couldn't keep quiet, feeling as though they still didn't quite understand. "But how will I *know* if God has chosen that for me?" The two old men exchanged wry glances. "Ask Him, and you'll know. Just don't pass it up when good comes knocking because you think you don't deserve it. God's gifts aren't ever deserved," Methuselah told him. "See you soon." Without further ado, they headed off down the road again, racing against the clock to bless the little ones before nightfall.

The cart rattled up to the young mother's house on the edge of town just a half hour before dark. They'd made it! The two carpenters hurried to unload the seesaw, then Boaz went to the door to let the family know they had arrived. He was looking forward to surprising them. As he drew close, however, he saw that the door was cracked, and he couldn't hear the sounds of children - or of anything else, for that matter. An uncomfortable sense of foreboding fell over him. He hoped everyone was alright.

He knocked slightly anyway, in case there really was nothing amiss. He didn't want to burst in on the boys' mother without warning. When no response came, he decided it was worth going inside. Easing the door fully open, Boaz tiptoed through a small hallway towards the main living area, feeling as though stealth was important for whatever reason. All he

could hear was some slight scuffling coming from inside now, so there
was definitely someone present, but he wasn't sure who he might find.
What he saw when he entered the room, however, was like something
out of a nightmare. The woman who owned the home was seated on the
floor with her hands tied up and a rag stuffed in her mouth, and her two
sons had been given the same treatment.

A large armored soldier - probably a deserter - was busily ransacking
the place, stuffing small valuables into a sack. He was muttering to
himself, "Gonna need someone to carry all of this stuff when I get out of
here." Then, as if he had an epiphany, he looked gleefully at the two
boys and said, "How about you two? You'd make fine armor bearers, at
least once you've been toughened up a bit." The man was going to steal
her boys! Boaz had to do something.

He attempted to steal up behind the man quietly, and the boys'
mother saw him and gave him a pleading glance, eyes wide.
Emboldened, he took a few steps, nearly upon the intruder, then leapt to
grab the man's blade. Just then, the man turned, battle-hardened reflexes
kicking into gear, and he swung his sword up underneath Boaz's ribs,
running him through. Boaz had just enough energy to whisper, "Run!",
before he threw himself against the man to knock him over and buy
them some time. The pain of that movement had to have been
excruciating, the young mother knew, but she did not waste his sacrifice.
She ran behind the boys, struggling to help them up while bound, and
they tore off towards the door stumbling as they went. Heart pounding
wildly with fear, she and the boys made it through the door and nearly

ran smack into Methuselah.

He was there, just about to knock, when they burst through the opening and shocked him near to death. The old carpenter reacted quickly though, realizing that they must be in danger; he threw a hand towards the cart to show them where to go and then blocked the door with his body, prepared to sacrifice himself, too, for them if necessary. It was a good thing he did, too, because the soldier came stampeding into the doorway berserk with rage, moving so quickly he would surely have caught the family. Instead, he slammed right into Methuselah, sending both of them flying into the dirt. Meanwhile, the fleeing family had gained just enough time to make it into the cart and took off to get help from the village.

Ham and Amaris were sitting and eating dinner together when the pub owner came by with the news: Methuselah and Boaz had been attacked protecting the twins. The couple exchanged worried glances and leapt up from the table, nearly knocking it over in their rush to be out the door. A small party went with them, including the bartender and a couple of other men, but not everyone was eager to help. They valued their own lives more than the lives of strangers.

What they found when they made it to the woman's home broke Ham's heart. Both Methuselah and the soldier were on the ground, surrounded by a pool of blood - whose, they didn't know. The young man ran to his grandfather and knelt by his side, cradling his white, matted head in his arms. He felt so cold. What had happened? Looking around, he noticed that the soldier's blade was protruding from his own chest. He must have fallen on it when he'd run into Methuselah. So why was Methuselah unconscious?

Amaris was by Ham's side, fidgeting and shifting her feet nervously. She was worried for him. After all that he'd been through...how would he take a loss like this? Ham was just thankful for her presence. He needed someone to be close to him right then.

He tried to wake his grandfather, but no matter how much he shook him, nothing changed. Methuselah had finally left the world to be with his father.

The other men had gone inside to check on Boaz, and they came out shaking their heads. He was gone, too. "I don't understand...." Ham groaned, eyes brimming with tears. "Finally, I appreciate these two, and they are taken from me." Amaris touched his shoulder, feeling it shake with emotion.

"Yes, I am sorry, Ham." She waited a few moments, just letting him grieve, then encouraged him. "You know they had hope, a beautiful hope beyond words. They are with their Lord now, the one who has taken care of them all of their lives, making them into the men that you knew. And they lived such long, *good* lives! It's because of them that I know God at all," she said, lifting his chin to look at him. "And it's because of them that we have each other."

She was right, and it was amazing that they had done so much good. They had even died heroes! That woman and her sons were alive and well because Methuselah and Boaz had given their lives to secure their safety. What more could someone ask for? But it didn't fix the pain. They were gone. He voiced what he was feeling. "I'll never see them again."

Amaris took his hand in hers and smiled, her own eyes swimming now. "Yes, yes you will. In the resurrection, you will be together again." He heard her, and he looked up to the sky, now filled with stars. Yes, he would see them again. What a God they served!

CHAPTER 22

Taste and See

AFTER BOAZ AND METHUSELAH PASSED AWAY, it was left to Ham to bring their bodies home for burial. The family would need to know what had happened, yes, but also seeing the bodies would help them grieve, and Ham believed that he owed them that at least; the way he had left would leave them forever doubtful about whether his word could be trusted. What's more, the family all shared a future hope of resurrection, and so burial was somewhat of a sacred rite. It was a difficult thing to face, the idea that he would go home to face his family as not only a thief and runaway, but as the herald of tragedy and death. He half-heartedly sought God for a way out, but there was nothing for it: he wanted to be a new man, and there was no way out but through the valley he'd dug for himself.

Amaris was beyond supportive through it all. As he wept the night away in Debir, ashamed in so many ways but unable to stop the flood of tears, she was sitting by his side, her hand on his shoulder reminding him he was not so terribly alone. Then, when he broke the news to her the next morning that they had to prepare the bodies for burial now so that they could make the long trip home, she was, once again, willing and eager to help him, unafraid of the discomfort that such a task would surely involve. They did it together, wrapping his dear uncle and great-grandfather in burial cloths soaked in frankincense and myrrh oils. Ham had never done anything so difficult in his life, and her support meant more than he could say. He loved this woman.

The townspeople also did their part, graciously providing the couple with a covered wagon to carry the bodies back to Kadish. So, they set off on the homeward journey, brokenhearted but finally together. Never since they'd met had they been completely and utterly alone together as they were now. It was just them and God, and that, at least, was solace to their souls.

The two spent several days travelling nonstop southward without a hitch, getting to know each other more each day, and when the tip of Kadish's twin peaks loomed high in the distance, it hit Ham that he was about to bring Amaris to her new home. She had forsaken her life in Eshcol to join Methuselah and Boaz on their journey, not knowing that she and Ham would meet, but now, there was nowhere else for her to go. His grandfather's words struck him just then, as they rode along together in the early twilight. *God's gifts aren't ever deserved.* Could it be true? Could he really have a woman so beautiful in body and soul? He had asked when he'd know if it was right...but wasn't it right *now*? He loved her, and he could both see and feel how deeply she cared for him.

Could she love him?

The young man stopped the wagon. He had to try. Taking her hand in his, a bold move on its own, he stepped down and helped her to disembark, watching her curious, smiling expression with a mix of adrenaline-driven excitement and anxiety. She had no idea what he was about to do. Keeping hold of her hand for perhaps the very first time in their relationship, he knelt down before the carriage, looked deep into her dark eyes, and spoke,

"I know you haven't known me for a long time, but I want you to know that I've never met anyone so wonderful, and I've been sure of it since the first time you spoke to me. Each day, each moment that I spend with you only makes my heart more sure that you are God's gift to the world. You have loved me through action from the very first day, when you had no idea who I was, because that is who you are, and I love that about you. In fact, the more I get to know you, I can't imagine a life without you by my side. I love you... When I realized it, my first thought was: I don't deserve this woman. I am like so much filth beneath her feet, unworthy to be loved by her, much less to love her. But then, I realized that there is no chance on earth that anyone could ever deserve you, so I began to hope that you might be willing to at least receive my love. So, that is what I bring before you, my heart on a platter, beating for no purpose other than to love you, and only you, for the rest of my days. Will you be my wife?" He finished breathlessly, aching to know her answer but dreading it at the same time.

She had sat through this with such poise and grace, watching him in abject wonder as he bared his soul. Never had she seen a man show such emotion, especially not to her. If he hadn't looked away so much out of fear, he would have seen that she couldn't contain her joy as she listened to his heartfelt proposal. Now, he dared a glance for the first time, and she returned his gaze with a look of complete devotion, adoration even. She wanted him to know just how much she had waited for this moment. "Yes," she whispered, giddy. "I'd love nothing more! I've loved you since the day we met, and you'd be a fool to think that you don't deserve me." Ham was overwhelmed, sweeping her up in a passionate embrace. She was all his. God did give grace to the worst of sinners.

The next day they trundled up to the farm with mixed emotions. They had the best of news and the worst of news. What they saw as they came into view of the house, however, left them breathless. The ark was complete! It soared as high as nearly ten men standing atop one another, and it was ten times as long, but that wasn't all. Every animal under heaven had congregated on their lawn, spilling through the garden, carpeting the house and outbuildings in living color. Ham was amazed, but there were no words to describe how Amaris felt. It was like being in a dream-world, and her faith in the God who had pursued her was at least tripled in that moment. He was a mighty King, the King of all things, truly.

The view was so obscured by furry creatures that Ham wondered if they would be able to even move the wagon, let alone find his family in the chaos, but they only struggled for a few minutes when they heard a voice call out to them through the din. "*Ham! My Son!*" came the desperate cry. In that moment, his father appeared, thrusting aside the beasts that stood between them and running headlong towards him. Even from a distance, Ham could see that he was crying. His father, the strong carpenter and leader of them all was weeping. Was it sadness? Disappointment?

Ham stepped down from the wagon to meet him, asking Amaris to give him just a moment, and Noah came rushing into him, sweeping him up in a huge hug that forced the breath from his lungs. "Oh my son, you are home." He gasped. "We have missed you."

The young man was struggling to understand this wave of emotion. He had expected quite a different reception. He gathered up all of his courage and replied. "Father, I have sinned against heaven and against you, and I am no longer worthy to be called your son. Would you forgive me?"

Noah pulled back, cupping his son's face in his worn hands, and looked him full in the eyes. There was no questioning what Ham saw there. "My son was dead but is alive; he was lost but is found! I have no greater joy. All is forgiven. Come, let us feast in your honor! We have much to discuss." His son was overwhelmed, nearly driven to his knees by thankfulness that God had prepared such love for him when he had expected condemnation. He could only croak, "I love you, father."

Then, remembering Amaris behind him, Ham's face split into a wide grin. "Father, I have someone I want you to meet." He went and took her hand to help her down, handing her to his father gingerly. "Amaris, my betrothed." Noah's face lit up like sunrise and he burst into a joyful, laughing fit. "God has smiled upon me this day! My son is home and he

has a beautiful woman to love him! My God, can this day be any better?"
Then, he turned, remembering just how much everyone else would need
to hear this as well, and said, "Let's go and tell your mother and
brothers. They will be so excited!"

Before he could walk away, though, Ham grabbed his father's arm,
stopping him. "I have other news, too." He said solemnly, gesturing
towards the covered wagon. "Boaz and Methuselah...are with the Lord. I
have brought their bodies home." It was difficult to describe how his
father looked upon hearing those words. First, pain flashed across his
face, as though he'd received a heavy blow to the gut, but then, it slowly
faded, leaving behind a steady, resolved expression. He responded
calmly, putting a hand on Ham's shoulder. "Son, this is a tragedy, but I
think I knew that they were gone...after all, our Lord did not include
them in the prophecy. I believe their work on the earth is done, and it
was time to go home. We must try to see it that way, but I know this
must be hard for you, coming back after all that has happened. I will
break the news to the others." Relief flooded Ham's soul, washing over
him like a tidal wave. He did so love his father.

Within minutes, they had found his mother and brothers and begun
a most spectacular reunion that lasted long into the night. There was
feasting and laughter and more than a few tears, but the overwhelming
sentiment was joy. God clothed the gathering in it, making them
thankful that they at least had one another, and that those who had
passed before them had found their final rest. No one condemned
Ham, as much as he had dreaded it, though he choked up so much
during the beginning as he spoke of Lamech's death that he nearly

didn't make it through it. Even his brothers were just glad to see that he, too, was safe and had a woman by his side. The women all felt immediately at home with one another, sisters in spirit, because God had brought them all together through the most special of circumstances. This was it, the family that would survive the death of the world, and every one of them was glad they had each other.

The next day was a day of transition and ceremony. A full four of the merry gathering were to be wed, but this time, rather than gathering under the tree where Japheth and Tabitha had said their vows, the two happy couples commemorated their union on the bow of the ark, high in the air, overlooking the beautiful scene below. From that vantage point, the world below looked like a verdant garden ripe for harvest, and the notion that it was instead ripe for judgment - that it was all about to be swept away - felt unreal. As the family prayed over the couples though, ending the ceremony, the reality hit home. Their unions marked the beginning of a new age, and their children would fill an earth that had been washed clean. A fresh start.

When the wedding finished, there was still yet one more ceremony, the memorial of Methuselah and Boaz. The family gathered together and said their goodbyes as Noah prayed, asking God to bring them all together again in the resurrection. Each person came up and spoke, telling tales of the great, loving deeds of the two men and the good times they had shared together. Everyone had been encouraged by their wisdom and changed by their charm and attitude. They died heroes, really and truly. The two were buried on a high point overlooking the countryside, a spot that always stayed in the full light of the sun and was never darkened by shadow or shade, a choice that symbolized the constant, unrelenting presence of God their light that now shined in their presence eternally.

After a lovely wedding night for the young romantics, the next day brought a cloak of solemnity upon the camp. It was time to board the ark. The week God had given them was nearing its end, and they needed to prepare. So, everyone did their part, rushing to and fro to usher animals on board and pack the ark tight with the last of the food. They each packed their bags for the very last time, knowing they would not see this place or its people ever again. It was an occasion for mourning, as they had to grieve the loss of all that they once knew, so there were some sniffles and hard moments all throughout the day. At its end, however, the family took all that they had and entered the ark, shutting its mighty door against the world and forever closing that chapter of their lives. It was time to wait. The flood was coming.

Iram was close - so close. He alone had braved the Cherubim and had been rewarded for his courage with entry into the most sacred of places on the earth: the Garden of Eden. It hadn't taken long, however, for him to realize that no one had managed to follow him. He could only hear the dreadful din of battle raging behind him as he rode. Stopping, he had turned and watched as the greatest military unit the world had ever seen was decimated within minutes by the manifold wrath of heaven's armies.

Satan was keeping a close watch on Iram's thoughts, staying always in conversation with him when they were together so that the young man would remain on a tight leash. So, the devil had moved him along, prodding him towards the prize waiting in the center of the garden. There was too much riding on him, especially now. Now that the Enemy and His forces had gotten wind of this attack on Eden, it would doubtless be impossible to ever get anyone else inside. This was their only shot.

As Iram rode along, armor clanking unceremoniously in the still quiet of the garden, he worried whether he might be yet discovered. The silence felt ominous, oppressive. He could not get the vision of angelic warriors streaming through a torn sky to leave his mind. What God was there that could summon such a force? Was this God watching him now as he made his way towards a tree that was forbidden for man to touch? Would he be stricken down the moment he did so?

Satan could see the nervous sweat beginning to bead on the young ruler's forehead, so he intervened, whispering slyly, "You have nothing to fear. You alone of all the men on the earth has made it to this sacred place. You are special, a warrior beyond compare. What man so young as you has accomplished so much in so short a time? You have led great armies and held world leaders in the palm of your hand. Thousands have sought after what you are about to find, but only you will achieve it. You deserve this prize. Eternal life is your due for what you have accomplished." Puff the man up with pride. That was always the best play in moments like these. Lucifer had learned that well.

Iram listened, nodding to himself as though having his own personal conversation. That was right. He *was* special. No one had ever done what he was about to do! He would be a legend! His fear left him to some degree as his pride swelled, crowding out every other emotion to leave a single, unquenchable desire: greed. He wanted that fruit, and he wanted it all for himself. Nothing would stop him from getting it.

As he meandered through what was really more of an overgrown forest than a garden, whacking away at the underbrush that choked his path, he couldn't help but notice that this was a place unlike anything he had ever seen. There was so much color: bright cyan and pink and emerald green, yellow flowers that could outshine the sun, red roses with such dark hues they reminded him of blood. It seemed as if every conceivable plant under heaven had found its dwelling place right here. Surely it had once been a place of unparalleled beauty.

Endless trees stretched high above him, nearly blotting out the sun, making it difficult for him to discern which way he needed to go or how much time was passing. He began to wonder what he would do once he found the fruit. When eternal life filled his veins and he was invincible, what would be the first order of business? Much of his army was gone, or had fled at least, and no doubt the remnant was now firmly under the command of one or more of the surviving kings. Yet, that would be easy enough to remedy. He could waltz right into their midst and take his army back, dispatching anyone who stood in his way if necessary. Furthermore, there were mercenaries aplenty and his people were already digging deep into the mines of Havilah, extracting its hidden rewards. He could just buy an army as Queen Arissa had once done, if it came to that. Oh, the possibilities!

Lucifer liked the path the young man's mind was taking now, and he stoked the flames of ambition with glee. "You will be a king like no other, the only man on earth whose reign will never end, who can rule with an iron fist through the ages. Whatever you wish will be yours in a moment, and who will there be to stop you? The future of the earth belongs to Iram the Great." What Lucifer didn't tell the naive fool was that he would be the demon's own personal slave, and that the things he was seeking would tear apart his soul, leaving him bereft of any true meaning in life and consigning him to an eternal living hell of condemnation and self-loathing. That was the part Satan most looked forward to: the pain that Iram would bring upon himself and others. He so enjoyed seeing the humans suffer, because every jab that landed firmly in the heart of man also wounded the spirit of the Almighty God who made them and loved them.

After probably two hours of slogging through the heavy undergrowth, Iram was drenched in sweat from sheer exertion. This really was *not* much of a garden. A few moments later, though, he was sure he caught a glimpse of light through a break in the trees. He pressed harder, hacking away with abandon as his eyes searched hungrily for a better view - and there it was: the most precious sight his eyes had ever beheld in his life. There was no better way to describe it than majesty: pure, unbridled natural grandeur. He saw a broad, hilly meadow immersed in the soft glow of the late afternoon sun, the light of which was made all the more vibrant as it reflected off of the crystal clear waters of a river that flowed right through the center of the clearing. That river...it was like a living carpet of stars, so much so that Iram felt that if he could only jump into it, he would find himself floating in the heavens.

He stopped looking long enough to bend down and touch the grass, which brushed against his hand as softly as so much velvet. He longed to just lie there on the ground and sleep forever in bliss. That was how the whole place made one feel. He looked up, though, and next to the river bank, right at the heart of the scene, he saw his prize. The tree of life. It was magnificent: the bark appeared to be a living garment, more like his own skin than a brittle covering, and its branches stretched up towards the sun, their source of life, wrapped in near-transparent leaves. Then he saw the fruit, the real reward. He couldn't put a finger on what to call its color. It seemed as if each time he looked at it the color changed, but it shone with an inner vitality, as though life itself really was dwelling inside it. He had to have that fruit!

Throwing off his armor in his excitement, he sprinted out of the woods towards the tree. Satan just sat at the edge of the clearing and watched, eager to see his work come to fruition. There was no stopping them now.

As Iram ran, he began to feel the ground about him lose some of its luster, and, looking over, he saw the river turn dark, its stars winking out. It was not time for night yet, though, was it? He paused a few strides from the tree long enough to look up and study the sky. Sure enough, it was menacing. The clouds had turned a deep, threatening gray, and it was beginning to broil with activity. What was this? He knew, just then, somewhere in his soul, that this was God's judgment on him, and it scared him to death. What was there to do now, though? He had to try. Iram turned and shot towards the tree, legs pumping with everything that he had. He was nearly there....He jumped, grappling for purchase on a branch with all his might, and felt his hand close around the delicate, warm flesh of a fruit.

Then the earth shook, rocking beneath him and throwing him to the ground. The fruit, seemingly by miracle, was not smashed, but it had rolled a few spans away from his grasp. He leapt up, expecting to just walk over and pick it up, but the ground swayed beneath his feet, making him lose his balance, and he was immediately knocked back down as the earth gave another mighty heave. He was so close! Eternal life was within his grasp! Lucifer watched in mystified horror as his puppet was tossed about, knowing in his spirit that this was the Lord's doing. His Enemy had intervened yet again! Would the young ruler make it?

Iram was not giving up, however, and he began to crawl, clawing his way across the quaking grass that was beginning to split in places. To make matters worse, it was beginning to rain. His fingers grew slick and slipped as he pulled himself along, struggling. Eventually, his arm was within reach of the fallen fruit. He could just nearly touch it...almost...and the ground erupted underneath him, sending a shower of scalding hot water and rock high into the sky and ending his life. The house of Tubal-cain was no more. The Devil looked on in abject agony.

He had been thwarted again.

Huddled together on the ark, the four chosen couples waited with bated breath, eyes looking up in fearful expectation for the bottom to fall out of the sky. After boarding at noon, they had sealed the door and settled in. At first, they'd all expected the flood to begin at any moment, but as a few hours passed, a slight whisper of doubt begin to set in as their eyes tired from straining at the sun. It stubbornly refused to be obscured, and its bright, cheery visage mocked them like the many sneering villagers who had scoffed as the family built the ark.

Was God going to do what he had promised? Though none of them had ever *wanted* the flood to come in the first place, by this point they had all invested so much hope and so much of their very lives into preparing for its event that they now yearned for it to come, practically begging God to send it. They needed it now, to validate countless hundreds of hours of work and fear and suffering, all endured out of obedience to God. Surely, he would not fail them now.

Even that thought, though, the idea that they wanted this judgment to come, left them incredibly conflicted inside, and part of them began to fervently wish that God had changed His mind. Could the world have somehow repented and God relented of his wrath? No one spoke, at least not for the first hour, and only after that in hushed whispers to their partners. All were lost in contemplation, adrift in a sea of innumerable hopes and fears. Wasn't it odd that their very salvation was also a sea, ominous and deep, waiting above the heavens to descend and drown the world?

Then the boat moved. It happened so suddenly and slightly that the family nearly dismissed the event as a figment of their imagination, but only a moment or two passed before it happened again. This time the boat shook with enough force that they had to grab onto the ship for support. Something was happening, but what on earth did this have to do with rain?

The next second, streaking down from the sky like a shooting star without a sound, a single stray drop of rain fell. It landed right on the upturned tip of Noah's nose, and he blinked. The rain was coming. "Everyone get inside!" He bellowed, adrenaline coursing through his body. They needed to get off of the deck. It was rocking back and forth as though already surging over the ocean waves, and he didn't even want to think about what would happen once the rain really came down. They could easily be washed over the bow! "My sons! Get your wives inside! Leah, go!" He was hastily ushering them indoors as he scrambled about the deck, stumbling every other step as quakes jolted the ark. Thanks be to God, they listened. Before long the carpenter was the only one left standing on the deck, drenched from head to toe in rain as he looked out, awestruck, at the spectacular scene playing out before him.

Geysers of muddy water were shooting into the sky all about them - upwards from the ground. He'd never seen anything like it. The fountains of the deep were bursting forth! That would explain the earthquakes. As it happened, bits of rock and dirt started peppering the deck in front of him, some of the missiles nearly as big as his torso, signaling that it really was time to get inside. The last thing he saw was the appearance of a near impenetrable sheet of rain between the ark and Kadish, like some great wall that barred his vision of the town that he once called home as the world was deluged with watery judgment. They had their answer. God was faithful, and the world was judged.

Once inside, soaked to the bone, Noah's family met him with hugs and tears. Already they had feared the worst. "Well, it happened, just as the Lord said," Ham said, his voice dripping with melancholy, "Yes," Japheth answered, barely audible over the now deafening roar of the rain, "As it's been said, 'May God be true and every man a liar.'" With nothing else to be said, the gathering settled down to wait as the rain pounded incessantly on the ark.

The first hours and days were pregnant with apprehension. They had felt it when the ark lifted free of the ground, buoyed up by the sheer volume of water covering the land. The scary part was that - if the ark was floating - everything they once knew had been covered with water. Their home, their life, even the people who had not believed them, were all gone. It was then that everything began to feel truly, incontrovertibly final. The rain was washing the world clean, and it didn't stop for forty days and forty nights.

For more than a month, the family grew used to going about their daily lives accompanied by the perpetual pattering of endless torrents of rain, so when the last drop fell, it was as though their entire world was plunged into silence. Life stopped. Then, as the raucous clamor of thousands of animals started up again in earnest, they realized that it was done. The rain was gone! The young men rushed upwards towards the top deck, nearly tripping over one another in their excitement, but when they opened the door, they were thrown off of their feet back into the cabin by the mighty heave of an enormous wave, the top of which washed in through the open portal, drenching them in salty water.

At Noah's behest, they hurried to close the door before another one came crashing in, and then the boat jerked viciously like it had been doing all month. So it wasn't finished. "But I saw the sun! I saw the sky, and it was clear, beautiful blue, and there was a fresh wind blowing from the north," Shem cried, exasperated and elated at the same time. It had been forty days! Surely God was finished. "Let us pray then," His father said, coming alongside them and clapping him on the shoulder. "If God made a promise, He keeps it. Does He not?"

Even as they prayed, they could hear all about them a mighty rushing of wind, and it was not long before the boat ceased to shake. With their hearts in their throat, the men opened the door together, and were met with the glorious sight of a vast, unsearchable ocean with no horizon. The waves were still, and the sun shone upon them. It was done!

They brought the whole family out to enjoy the view and celebrate together their deliverance from the downpour, and Noah sent out a raven to see if it could find land. When it returned rather quickly, they realized it was going to take a while for the water to subside. At the Lord's behest, they had packed enough food for months on end, after all. Perhaps it was going to be a long wait. So, they began to live as though their new lives were starting right then, on the boat with the animals, but they did so now with hope. God would never leave them or forsake them.

It took a full five months for the waters to subside significantly, and even then, the doves that Noah sent out weekly afterwards did not return until a fateful day around month ten, when one surprised him with an olive leaf in its beak. It was that day that they first saw the tops of mountains. Joy flooded their souls! A week later, the next dove never came back. Soon, very soon, they would be able to set foot on land again.

Then, the day came. Nearly a full year after the flood had begun, on the heels of Noah's six hundred and first birthday, they opened the door of the ark, and it thumped onto dry ground. They were saved! There, atop Mount Ararat, they were setting foot on the soil of a new world. A new life could begin!

Together, Noah and Leah, Shem and Naamah, Japheth and Tabitha, and Ham and Amaris stepped down from the ark, raising their hands to the sky and shouting to their God, "Praise be to God on High, who has delivered us from the waves!" They were so thankful it hurt, and tears of joy flowed unrestrained down their cheeks as the young men kissed the ground with glee and their wives danced about like children.

Before long, Noah gathered them all together to offer up a sacrifice to God, and, as they began, Micah appeared before them, gleaming in stark, sparkling white. He was smiling. "My friends! You have made it! Your faith has been rewarded!" He exclaimed. The family was speechless. Next to him appeared Nathan and Gurion, they too glimmering like fallen stars. Nathan chimed in, "Though I fear you may have thought so, we never left you. Your God was with you every step of the way, and He had us watching over you through the days and months of waiting." Gurion followed up, booming his assurances, "Never, ever, do you walk alone on the earth. We are your guards, a ready aid in times of trouble." When he said it, they believed it.

Micah continued, "Our God sends a message, yet again. He accepts the sacrifice of your faith, and blesses you as you begin your new lives. He gives you the world. It is yours! God says: Go, be fruitful and multiply and fill it! Everything that lives on the earth is yours. God makes His covenant with you, his firm, unbreakable agreement that He will never destroy all flesh through a flood again. He sets his bow in the clouds, to appear after a rain and remind you and Him of the eternal promise He has made to you."

With that, he and the angelic duo ascended into the heavens before them, disappearing into the stunning brilliance of the sun. Behind them, a shimmering, multicolored arc appeared in the sky, a herald of a bright future.

A Word from the Author

If you have finished this book, then you have seen something of what the God of ancient earth was like. He loved Noah and his family, and they were under His protection and received His help and guidance. Yet, as we saw through Methuselah and Boaz, God also loved the world, though it had turned far from Him. Noah's family was unique only in that he trusted God, expecting to find his reward in God alone. For this, Noah was *counted* righteous. God *considered* him righteous because of his faith, not his deeds. As the word of God says, "Whoever wishes to draw near to God must believe that He exists and that He rewards those who seek Him."(Hebrews 11:6 ESV) Even so, God also is a God of justice, and as we all seek to see evildoers pay the price for their crimes today, so God would not allow the people of the world in that day to escape the price of rejecting their Maker and destroying each other, corrupting His world. We will not escape either, unless we let Him make us righteous through faith.

This same God is the God of the world today. He always is, always has been, and always will be. He knows you just as He knows me. He promises that, "He determined the times and places where people should live, so that they would seek God and perhaps feel their way towards Him and find Him. Yet He is not far from each one of us..."(Acts 17:26-27 ESV). God draws us and desires us to know Him, because in Him we are fulfilled. We need only believe Jesus, the Son of God who was made flesh so that God could live among us. He became our sin so that we could become the righteousness of God in Him - so that we could be called good sons and daughters in His place. He died to face our judgment, and He rose from death by the Father's power to defeat it for us once and for all! Though we face a world where pain and sin is rampant, Jesus promises that He will return to make all things new, and there will be no more mourning or crying or pain anymore. He only waits, He says, because He is not willing for anyone to perish, but for all to reach repentance (2 Peter 3:9-10 ESV). He waits for you and for me, for our neighbors and friends. He waits for all to turn to Him so they can have life, and life to the full! Jesus is the way, the truth, and the life, and there is no way to God except through Him.

ABOUT THE AUTHOR

Thank you for making this journey with me! I took a trip in my own soul this year in writing this book as I grappled with questions of how to walk in faith through trials into the vast unknowns of life. It does my soul well to know that you too have committed your time and your heart to plumbing the depths of this work. I plan to write many, many more: several in *The Hidden Kingdom* series and countless more after that. If you would do me the honor of walking the path of truth with me, I do believe it will be a choice you won't regret, and I will try my best, by God's guidance, to continue to produce beautiful stories that will bless your heart.

CONNECT WITH ME

I hope you enjoyed the book! Please support the series by leaving a review at amazon.com. If you have any thoughts or questions please feel free to contact me via my facebook page "Fiction Reborn".

Visit my blog at www.fictionreborn.com to gain access to book samples and even advanced book copies. You'll be able to see regular updates on upcoming books as well as articles on literature and truth.

You can also email me at fictionreborn1@gmail.com, particularly if you would like to receive free books before they come out!

Keep reading! It would give me great pleasure to have you continue to join me on this fascinating journey into the hidden kingdom!